Short Stories

Volume Two

Neal James

PNEUMA SPRINGS PUBLISHING UK

First Published in 2018 by:
Pneuma Springs Publishing

Short Stories - Volume Two
Copyright © 2018 Neal James
ISBN13: 9781782284673

Neal James has asserted his right under the Copyright, Designs and Patents Act, 1988, to be identified as Author of this Work

British Library Cataloguing in Publication Data. A catalogue record for this book is available from the British Library.

Artwork and Cover Design by Lewis Bates

Pneuma Springs Publishing
A Subsidiary of Pneuma Springs Ltd.
7 Groveherst Road, Dartford Kent, DA1 5JD.
E: admin@pneumasprings.co.uk
W: www.pneumasprings.co.uk

Dedication

For James

Acknowledgements

In bringing this collection of short stories to publication, my thanks must go to a number of individuals who have made a significant contribution to its development.

To Robert Eldridge I am, once again, deeply indebted for his editing skills. Rob is an essential collaborator which any author needs – someone skilled in the art of the English language and its structure, and with a keen eye for detail. He also understands how my mind works – sometimes I do not envy him.

Laura and Phillip Holland, beta readers of the first draft, gave me the comfort of knowing that the early manuscript was running in the right direction. They also prompted me to question some of the story lines which, I must confess, go back to my early days of fiction writing.

In Lewis Bates, I was fortunate to have access to the services of an accomplished graphic designer. His outstanding artwork and cover concepts provide the perfect illustrations of the essence of the book.

As in earlier books, there are a growing number of my readers who expressed a wish to be written into the text. My thanks go to the following individuals for putting themselves at my mercy: Nikki & David Spencer (*Blind Faith*), Allan Greagsbey (*A Friend in Need*), John Haywood (*Clock*), Heather McBain (*Coles to Newcastle*), Haydn Wright & Chantel Rogers (*Ebony Eyes*), Linda & Steve Bennett (*Grapes and Wrath*), Julie & Ben Brown (*Last Christmas*), Molly Green (*Layers of Innocence*), Joyce & Dean Gallagher and Alison Whatmore (*Mirror Mirror*), Amie Napolis (*Needle in a Haystack*), Keith Goodrum (*Rose Cottage*), Steve Hackett (*Sorry*), Victoria Lewis (*The Damocles Legacy*), Jessie Masoner (*A Dish Served Cold*), Gerald & Joyce Richmond (*Jumping to Conclusions*), Sandra & John Devine (*Behind Closed Doors*), Charlotte Swinscoe (*The Sins of Charlotte Swinscoe*), John Gurnhill and Stephanie Hughes (*Wishful Thinking*), Chris Meade (*A Cut above the Rest*).

Finally, my wife, Lynn, who has lived and breathed all of these stories down the years as she has with all the other nine books which have made it beyond the confines of my imagination.

Contents

Blind Faith

Nikki and David Spencer were just an ordinary couple. Ordinary, that is, until the night that fate plunged them into a murky, violent world where the gun and the knife ruled supreme.

A Friend in Need

You don't always realise it at the time, but the actions you took many years ago have a habit of coming back to bite you. Allan Greagsbey found that out to his cost when the tables turned on him in his hour of need.

Clock

John Haywood knew that something was amiss. He should have walked away the minute he stepped out of his Dodge into the empty, eerie, main street of Stanfield. Lazlo Domarski saw him, and from that moment his fate was sealed.

Coles to Newcastle

Trust, once broken, was not something that Harold Coles would willingly give again. Heather McBain, however, was something else, and he broke his golden rule for her. The intervention of fate was to be his undoing, and the loss of his one true love a tragic result.

Cutting the Cloth

Would you know the truth from fiction? Could an outrageously improbable set of occurrences really be historical fact? Stranger things have happened, and sometimes you just never know, do you?

Ebony Eyes

A chance meeting, a beautiful girl, a melting heart. Haydn Wright was staring at a vision and Chantel Rogers smiled back just for him. So, what was it with the spooky song which seemed to follow him around everywhere?

Grapes and Wrath

As unhappy marriages went, Linda Bennett's was certainly up there in the top ten. Getting rid of her idle husband, Steve, was going to be a problem unless something unexpected cropped up. The 'crop' of grapes was to be her lifeline to a fresh start.

Engine Trouble

Reading between the lines had never been one of University Grant's strong points, but you'll have to do more than your fair share with this one to see the funny side of the matter.

I Am

Silence, stealth, and senses on high alert. Patience, and just waiting for the perfect opportunity, all came as second nature. Now was the time to strike.

In the Nick of Time

Finding the job at the boatyard was a real godsend for Nick, and the guy there certainly needed someone to show him the error of his ways. Shame he couldn't stick around to see the final outcome, though.

Last Christmas

Christmas is never a good time to be moving home, but when the whole family is involved the disruption isn't so bad. Julie and Ben Brown's leaving present came from an unexpected source, and in the most dramatic fashion.

Layers of Innocence

The stalker had Molly Green running around in circles as she struggled to come to terms with the sudden death of her husband, Mark. The tragic circumstances surrounding the evening with her friend, Wendy, sent her reeling into uncertainty once more.

Mirror, Mirror

The face in the mirror was not her own, and Joyce Gallagher stood transfixed. Those eyes - they just stared out at her, and the mouth moved with a silent plea from another dimension.

Needle in a Haystack

It's bad enough looking for a needle in haystack, but when it turns up unexpectedly, that's a bonus. The man standing before Amie Napolis was the image of her husband who vanished six months earlier. Had fate returned him to her and their children?

Rose Cottage

One last look at the little place, and that would be it. No sense in hanging around any more. So why was the figure in the centre of the room making Keith Goodrum feel as if he'd seen her before?

Sorry

Steve Hackett was about to wipe the slate clean of all his errant behaviour and go cap in hand to his long-suffering wife. Getting the bullet was not what he had anticipated.

The Damocles Legacy

The invaders have come. They're up there just waiting. Waiting for the first move of a belligerent race which could see the destruction of them all. Tensions run into overdrive, and suddenly they're gone; but will they return?

The Smell of Fear

Mickey was a peaceful kind of individual, and never had much time for bullies. That was before George turned up and started taking a more than passing interest in Millie. This was the catalyst for action, and something which Mickey needed to get his teeth into.

The Spiders and Johnny Bailes

"The only thing preventing these buggers from being our size is their respiratory system. This bloody thing has lungs!" Mick Parlour's eyes were out on stalks as the first of Johnny's 'friends' to be caught lay on the lab table.

A Dish Served Cold

A sudden and unprovoked attack, witnesses nowhere to be seen, and a police force seemingly powerless to act. Ben's murder could not go unpunished, and Jessie Masoner had all the tools he needed to effect revenge.

The News at 1066

In our age of high-speed satellite communication, news gathering is almost instantaneous, but for those reporting events in earlier times, weeks or even months may have passed before any details emerged. The circumstances surrounding the Norman invasion of England, if related using modern technology, may have sounded something like this.

Jumping to Conclusions

One last cigarette and it would all be over. It had been over for a while already, but the conclusion that Gerald Richmond had jumped to was not the correct one for him.

Behind Closed Doors

What was the significance of the doors in Sandra Devine's dream? She had forgotten all about them until the New York holiday brought the memory flooding back.

The Sins of Charlotte Swinscoe

She had never considered herself to be a bad person, so what was it that was drawing Charlotte Swinscoe to Daniel Thorpe when she had been so content with Raymond Martin?

Wishful Thinking

John Gurnhill had always been one for a good fancy dress party, but his encounter with the beautiful fairy, Stephanie Hughes, was one which brought unexpected consequences, and thrust him under the spotlight of the Metropolitan Police and DCI Dennis Marks.

A Cut Above the Rest

An idyllic, peaceful setting in a Derbyshire country park is torn asunder when the bodies begin to appear. Time for the local police, and DS Chris Meade, to get their teeth into the matter.

Neal James

Blind Faith

The noise of the life support equipment was the only sound in the room. The steady 'beep-bip, beep-bip' of the ECG monitor was the only assurance David Spencer had that his wife, Nikki, was hanging on in there, albeit kept alive by the myriad of tubes festooning her body. She lay in the Intensive Care Unit, where she had been for the past month or so, as still as death. There was nothing more that the medical staff could do, and it was now only a question of time before he would be faced with the emotionally catastrophic decision of when to turn off the machine. As he sat at her side, where he had been continually for the entire period, he scanned Nikki's face for some small sign that she was coming back to him. The flicker of an eyelid, a twitch at the corner of her mouth, anything... just something that would take away the responsibility for what he knew he was going to have to face.

The staff had been very good. He had a bed made up in the private room where she lay, and they'd looked in on both of them at regular intervals. It seemed that he himself had become more of a focus of attention than his wife – they appeared to have given up on her. David couldn't remember the last time he'd eaten anything, and water was the only thing he felt able to keep down. His face had become quite haggard for a twenty-something young professional, and the growth of beard which had accumulated in the intervening time served only to accentuate the almost derelict appearance of his crumpled clothing. It seemed a lifetime ago that they were leaving the football match on that Tuesday night, both a little down after their team's defeat. His head dropped into his hands and, not for the first time, sobs racked his body. Tears fell like rain onto the tiled floor as he fought to regain control of his rapidly deteriorating senses.

Yes, that Tuesday night was one which David would dearly have loved to live all over again. The roar of 28,000 voices as the winning goal went in at the Trent End of Nottingham's City Ground was only surpassed five minutes later as the referee signalled the end of the game. They had waited inside the stadium with the rest of the visiting supporters as the bulk of the crowd made its way past the riverside bottleneck and over Trent Bridge – perhaps they should have braved the crush after all. Perhaps... what? Perhaps they shouldn't have gone to the game at all. Perhaps the meal at the Trent Bridge Inn was the mistake which delayed their return to the tram stop at the Phoenix Centre. Perhaps then they would not have witnessed the violent confrontation in the Meadows area of the city. Then there would have been no involvement with the police drug enforcement programme. Then Nikki might still be laughing and smiling the way she used to. Too many variables, and much too late for all that now.

They had both been in witness protection after walking in on some kind of punishment killing in what had become the gun capital of Great Britain. Nottingham's Meadows and St Ann's areas were run by rival gangs constantly involved in turf wars. Narcotics had served only to increase the intensity of the conflicts as each sought to muscle the other out of the more profitable territories. Guns and knives were freely available to those wishing to use them, and the incident in question had been one of sickening brutality.

The old area of Arkwright Street had been demolished in the late 1960s and early 1970s, to be replaced by a patchwork of maisonettes. Old slums had been replaced by modern ones, littered with little back alleys and cul-de-sacs ideal for drug dealers to peddle their wares. It was within this maze that, as strangers to the city, they had become lost, and noises around a corner stopped them in their tracks. The unmistakeable sound of a hard object meeting flesh, and the agonised cries of the recipient, echoed around the immediate area. Curtains twitched as they were pulled tight shut by residents too scared to take a look outside.

David and Nikki saw what was happening from the shadows cast by a low streetlight. Their dark clothing made them all but invisible, and with bated breath they awaited the end of the beating and the disappearance of its perpetrator. Then they would be able to move on once more, possibly pausing to summon the help of an emergency vehicle. What neither of them was prepared for was the stomach-churning finale to what had been a truly ferocious attack. The young man stood back from his now kneeling victim and removed the knuckle dusters from his hands. The sight of a battered face loomed out of the night, half lit by the very same streetlight which was acting as David and Nikki's own protector. From deep within the folds of his coat, the assailant produced a gun, cocked the hammer, and pointed it directly into the other's face. A laugh of demonic quality bounced around the neighbouring buildings as the kneeling figure held hands out in supplication, begging for his life. David had never heard real gunfire before, and both he and Nikki recoiled into a wall as a single bullet destroyed the face of the victim. There was blood and brain matter everywhere and, as the gunman turned to leave, his features came out of the darkness in sharp relief – it was a face which neither of them would ever forget.

Frozen with fear, and ears ringing with the gunfire, they cowered in the shadows which were their saviour on that night. Neither had the wish to investigate any further, assuming, quite rightly, that the victim was dead. After what seemed an age, they made their way quickly and quietly through the maze of alleyways to the top of Crocus Street, within clear sight of the city's railway station. Back in the relative safety of well-lit streets, David made a brief 999 call from his mobile phone, giving details of the body's location, before they boarded the last tram back to the Phoenix Centre and the escape route which their parked car would provide.

Until now, neither had spoken about the incident which they had witnessed, but locked in the metal cocoon which the BMW provided Nikki broke the silence.

"What now? I mean, that man was murdered, and we saw it happen. We have to do something."

"We did, Nikki. The police will be there now. It's up to them to sort it out. We don't know what was going on and I don't fancy sticking my neck out."

"But that was, what…? An execution, David? We can't leave it at that. We witnessed an execution."

"Leave it, love, please. You know what these places are like – it's on our local news at home regularly. People like that don't take prisoners. We'll be in danger if anyone finds out what we saw tonight."

Nikki saw the futility of arguing with him right now. He was scared - *she* was scared. Back at home later that night, and with several whiskies inside him, David was even more determined not to become involved in what was clearly a gang-related shooting, and they locked up and went to bed. The next morning, he had almost convinced himself that it had all been a horrific nightmare when the BBC News 24 channel carried a report on the incident. What made him recoil in horror was the fact that information had been released relating to his call to the emergency services. The killer would now know that there had been at least one witness to the murder.

It was three days later, and David's initial fears for their safety had reduced somewhat, when a knock at the door brought the entire incident back to life. He was faced with two men in suits and carrying warrant cards identifying them as officers of the Nottinghamshire Constabulary.

"David Spencer?"

"That's me; what's this about?"

"I'm Detective Chief Inspector Barker, and this is Detective Sergeant Palmer. We'd like to talk to you about an incident in Nottingham last week. May we come in please, sir?"

David ushered the two of them into the lounge and out of the way of nosey neighbours, a number of whom had conveniently found some urgent gardening to do. It was then that he noticed the blue and red lights atop the squad car had which accompanied the detectives.

"How can I help you?" David's pulse had started to race.

"Information has come to our attention that you made an emergency call on Tuesday evening after a football match on our patch. We traced it to your mobile phone, sir."

David sat down, clearly unsettled by the whole matter, and now aware that any denial would be pointless. His contract phone was traceable; a pay-as-you-go would not have been. Another variable – perhaps he should never have bothered; the man was dead anyway and was probably as much of a criminal as the one who had killed him.

"Did you witness the killing, sir?" Barker pressed home the point, seeing the uncertainty in David's eyes. "Sir?"

"What? Oh, it was dark, and we were lost. I'm not even sure how many were involved."

"Yes, you are!" Nikki had chosen that moment to make her entrance, having heard the rest of the conversation. "We saw him quite clearly; he was right under that streetlight. You said you'd never forget that face for the rest of your life."

"Sir?" Barker raised one eyebrow and stared into David's face. Spencer capitulated.

The statement given to the two officers over the course of the next hour was detailed and clear. It was only when David realised that they would both have to stand up in a court of law and repeat what had been said that a sense of foreboding permeated his entire being.

"That'll mean we'll both be known to the killers. I don't know if I like the sound of that."

"Mr Spencer," said Palmer, "without your testimony these thugs will walk free. Free to carry on with a reign of terror in an area of our city already crumbling under the burden of organised crime."

"We'll also need you to come to Nottingham with us in order to identify those responsible," Barker interjected. "It won't take too long, and then you can return home until we need you further. You will, of course, be under police protection at all times."

"You mean a witness protection programme?" Now it was Nikki's turn. "We've heard of people in those schemes before and they don't seem too safe to me."

"Mrs Spencer," the DCI said, smiling, "you mustn't believe too much of what you see on television police dramas. There's really nothing to worry about, and we can move both of you to one of our safe houses if that makes you feel any better."

Barker had a disarming smile and he knew it. Sometimes he wished that it would also work on members of the criminal fraternity, but life was never that simple. Nikki melted under its influence, and the two of them agreed to make the short trip from Birmingham. An hour and a half later they were seated in an interview room at the city's Radford Road police station. Palmer entered the room carrying a stack of what looked like family photograph albums. Barker, already in the room, pushed them across the table.

"I know this might take a while, but we'd like you to take a look at some of our favourite local lads. See if anyone looks familiar and please take your time. This could be a very important break for us."

"That's him!" David and Nikki had turned only the first few pages, each in separate books, when David jabbed at an image on the third page with his index finger.

"Are you absolutely sure?" Barker's voice had changed from the genial policeman to the battle-hardened cop.

"Yes, I'll never forget. I was about twenty feet away and in the shadows with a streetlight shining right into his face. That's him all right; I'm absolutely certain."

Palmer looked at his boss and nodded.

"On my way, and I'll take an armed response unit with me."

"Who is this man?" Nikki pointed at the picture, confirming the statement which David had made.

"Billy Steel." Barker spat out the words as if the very sounds were distasteful to him. "Nineteen years old and the youngest member of Colin Carrington's militia. He's the son of Carrington's sister and on his way to becoming a psychopath."

"And Colin Carrington is...?" Now David stepped in, all the uneasy feelings beginning to return.

Barker went on to explain Carrington's background. Having come to the city as a youngster with his family from Manchester in the 1960s, he earned himself a reputation as a hard, but apparently fair, businessman. With interests in the motor trade, hotels, betting shops and transport, he had quickly built up a network of associates in similar trades. Having laid the foundations for what were, on the face of it, legitimate dealings, his interests evolved into the more dubious areas of loan sharking and escort agencies. These in turn led his organisation into the dark and criminal world of prostitution, drugs, and robbery. Nothing could ever be tied back to him of course, and there were always a number of his minions prepared to take the fall for an appropriate monetary reward. He had come to regard himself as above the law, and there were whispers that he even had a mole within the police itself. Every attempt to bring him to justice had failed. Now, though, it looked as though someone very close to him may have overstepped the mark.

"So, what happens now?" David asked nervously.

"We bring young Billy in for questioning and an identification parade. Hopefully, following on from that, we charge him with the murder of Mark Travis. He's the man you saw killed. Carrington's solicitor will try to get the lad released on bail, but we'll oppose it and keep him on remand. Don't worry, no-one will know who you are, so you're both quite safe."

As Barker expected, it didn't take long for both David and Nikki to independently pick Steel out of a line-up; the youngster was charged and scheduled for the following morning's magistrates' court sessions. Despite all of Colin Carrington's attempts to get the youngster out on bail, Billy was held at Lincoln Prison pending his trial five weeks hence. The Spencers returned to Birmingham, now convinced that their involvement was almost at an end. Had they knowledge of a meeting on the far side of Nottingham, those feelings might have been altogether different. Colin Carrington had called a council of war, and senior figures from within his organisation were seated around a table in an upstairs room of a Hockley pub.

"I don't care what it takes, Billy's not going to trial! All right, George, before you start, I know he's a stupid young punk. Anyone else and I'd leave him to rot, but he's our Karen's lad and blood's thicker than water. I'll deal with him myself when this is all over and he'll wish he'd never been born!"

Loyalty within the Carrington clan ran deep, and even extended towards those trusted lieutenants now seated with Colin. Nobody crossed him and lived to tell the tale, and several bodies had been pulled from the River Trent in recent years to bear testimony to the man's determination and ruthlessness.

"Mickey!" A balding man in his forties jumped at his name being called out, "Find out from our friend on the inside who this witness is. Maybe a little gentle persuasion can be applied to make our point of view appear to be the one which should prevail. Try bribery first; it's always a good place to start. We'll leave the rough stuff until later if it's needed."

The smile returned to the face of Michael Benson. He'd never known Colin's softly-softly approach to work before, and it always gave him pleasure when it failed. There really was nothing like a bit of what you might call 'constructive discussion' to turn the mind of a witness to your way of thinking. He'd take the baseball bat along just in case.

The Spencers' house in Solihull was in a quiet cul-de-sac and was fronted by a well-kept garden with a gravel path leading up to a stone porch. Michael Benson looked up and down the street before raising the brass door knocker. Not a soul was about – perfect for the conversation which was about to take place. Letting the hammer fall onto its plate, he stood back from the oak front door and turned to admire the car which adorned the driveway. BMW 5 series - very nice, and a 525i SE as well; had to be worth £35,000 of anyone's money. The sound of the door opening dragged his attention back to the job in hand.

"Yes?" David Spencer rubbed the sleep from his eyes and checked his watch; eight fifteen on a Saturday morning was not the time he expected visitors.

"Mr Spencer? Mr David Spencer?"

"Yes," he said. Who are you? And what do you want?" A little testy when faced with unanticipated and official-sounding requests.

"My name's not important, but the man I represent would like to make you a small refund of your expenses. It must have been extremely inconvenient travelling all that way to Nottingham for nothing, and we'd really be grateful if you'd accept this gesture of appreciation."

He produced a plain white envelope from his inside pocket and handed it to the still drowsy David. One look at the contents was enough to consign the last vestiges of sleep to memory. Thumbing across the wad of twenty-pound notes, David estimated the value to be in the region of £10,000 and stood in complete silence as the significance of what was happening finally dawned upon him. He frowned at the now smiling Benson.

"What is this? A bribe? A veiled threat? Here, take your blood money and tell your boss what he can do with it."

He threw the envelope back at Benson and turned to go back into the house. Carrington's enforcer made no attempt to stop him and continued to smile. Anyone passing the property would not have given a second thought to the scenario which was being played out. His words however, were delivered with chilling menace as he picked up the envelope and retrieved the baseball bat from the outside corner of the porch where it had been stowed.

"Well, yes, okay. I will do that for you, Mr Spencer. Oh, there's just one thing before I go – did you know that your front light cluster appears to be broken?" He nodded towards the BMW, David's pride and joy.

"What do you mean? There's absolutely nothing wrong with it."

David moved forwards off the porch step and looked around Benson at the car. Mickey turned and produced the bat which had been concealed behind his back. One more glance up and down the street, and a sharp blow to the nearside array had the entire thing in pieces, glass scattering across the drive.

"Oh yes, I think you'll find it's totally useless. Be a shame if anything else went wrong with such a beautiful motor, now wouldn't it?"

"You bastard! I'll have the police here in no time."

"Yes, I daresay you will, but with no witnesses..." he waved up and down the road, "… and several colleagues who will swear to being in the same Nottingham pub with me at precisely this time, I really don't see what good that will do. I'll be well on my way before the plods arrive anyway."

He smiled and walked back down the driveway to a waiting car. Pausing at the passenger side he looked back towards the house and pointed a finger.

"Take care; we'll be in touch."

David was shaking with rage at the threat and the damage to his car. Back inside the house he picked up the telephone and dialled the Nottingham number given to him by DCI Barker. The detectives' arrival just after lunch had curtains twitching once more at neighbouring windows, and David glared in distaste at the ghoulish nature of people whom he had considered to be above that sort of thing. He explained the morning's events following the arrival of Mickey Benson, and his description of the man left Barker and Palmer in no doubt about the nature of the threat which faced their star witnesses. Nevertheless, Benson's assurance of his alibi would doubtless hold true, leaving the two detectives powerless to help with the damage to the car. It was, however, time to consider moving the Spencers to a more secure location, and after a hurried packing session they were whisked away in the back of the unmarked vehicle.

The fact that David and Nikki Spencer had been removed from their home to a safer refuge was of no concern to Colin Carrington. A single telephone call to an untraceable mobile in the possession of his mole had information relating to their current whereabouts in his hands within twenty-four hours. Plans were now advancing apace to the next stage in his campaign to convince them of the error of their ways. With a round-the-clock guard in place, Barker had considered the danger to the Spencers minimised sufficiently to enable him to approach the now less than self-assured personage of Billy Steel.

Banged up, and within the imposing walls of Lincoln prison's maximum-security wing, the young man's demeanour had softened considerably during the time he had been there. Deprived of all contact save for that of prison guards and the family solicitor, his will had weakened enough for Barker and Palmer to pay him a call. What they found was something far removed from the truculent, confrontational, and self-confident young thug whom they had arrested shortly after the murder of Mark Travis. He was now a nervous, pitiful wreck, and his eyes flitted frantically around the room as the two officers took their seats before him.

"Billy..." Barker murmured in an almost father-like tone "... what *are* we going to do with you?"

"Mr Barker, you gotta help me. Colin'll kill me when I get out."

'Mr Barker', thought the DCI. My, that *was* a change from the 'filthy copper' which had been spat out during the arrest. "What makes you think he'll still be around by the time that happens?" Barker frowned in mock concern. "You won't be spending much of the next twenty or so years outside the confines of a prison cell."

Clearly the consequences of the events leading up to, and surrounding, the killing of Mark Travis were completely lost on Steel. When Palmer explained the likely course of events which were due to unfold at his trial, and the maximum penalty which he was almost certain to incur, he broke down in tears. Of course, Palmer continued, should Billy find it convenient to reveal some of the finer details of the Carrington operations, the trial judge might be persuaded to err on the side of a much bigger picture – he might be out in, oh... ten years with good behaviour.

Offered this last straw to save his wretched neck, Billy Steel had no hesitation in agreeing to anything that the two detectives might want to know. They would, they said, be back later with all the equipment necessary to record a full account of the activities, legal and otherwise, of the Carrington organisation. This was going to be the biggest breakthrough in Nottingham's fight against organised crime for many a year.

Notwithstanding this latest coup brought about by Barker and Palmer, an early morning attack was currently at the advanced operational stage in an area of Mansfield hitherto considered outside the scope of the criminal fraternity. True to his word, the mole had provided Carrington with the details of the safe house in the Woodhouse district of the town and, under cover of darkness, six black-clad figures approached a semi-detached house at the end of Burton Street. Each carried a bottle of petrol the neck of which had been stopped with a rag soaked with its contents. At a given silent signal, each of these Molotov Cocktails was lit and thrown through separate windows in the property. Within minutes the whole house was ablaze - the perpetrators had made their getaway in a stolen Ford Sierra.

Colin Carrington had been unconcerned as to whether or not the Spencers had managed to effect an escape from the inferno. His intention had been rather to terrify the two witnesses into retracting their eyewitness testimony than to kill them. That the net was, irrespective of this, closing quickly around him as a result of the events at HMP Lincoln completely failed to register. Billy Steel had delivered what amounted to a death blow to his empire.

The occupants of the Mansfield house had escaped with nothing more than mild effects of smoke inhalation due to the prompt and professional action of the uniformed police in attendance. Now under armed guard at Nottingham's Queens Medical Centre where they were undergoing check-ups, the Spencers received a visit from Barker and Palmer where they were appraised of developments in the pursuit of the Carrington clan. A series of arrests had been made across the city during the night of the firebombing in the neighbouring town, and all but one of the senior staff in the organisation were now under lock and key. The only member of Colin's inner cabal to escape the purge had been Mickey Benson – he had been out of town at the time and was now lying very low.

Six months later, and after one of the most publicised trials since that of the Kray twins in the 1960s, Colin Carrington and all those arrested along with him were convicted on a variety of counts at the Central Criminal Court in London. Carrington himself received a minimum sentence of thirty years with no prospect of early release, whilst his lieutenants were sent down for terms varying between ten and twenty. Billy Steel was given a new identity by the Home Office and sentenced to serve out a term of eight years at an undisclosed location within the British Isles.

David and Nikki Spencer read all this with an enormous feeling of relief after the events of the past year. Their lives had been turned upside down by a single act of chance in a city where they had become lost. It was with this sense of returning normality that they ventured out alone once more, free from the possible attentions of Colin Carrington's henchmen. With the damage to the BMW now repaired, David had suggested a trip to the east coast, and he and Nikki set off one Saturday morning. They had been travelling for something approaching two hours, and were making their way along the Lincoln bypass, when a vehicle in the rear-view mirror caught David's attention. There was something disturbingly familiar about the figure at the wheel of the dark green Ford Mondeo which had been following them for the last five or six miles. It had made no attempt to overtake, but had remained close behind at all times. David started in his seat, and Nikki picked up on the sudden stiffening in his driving position.

"What? What is it, David? What's wrong?"

"There's a car following us. It's been there for a while now... Nikki! It's Benson. Take a look; it is, isn't it?"

"I don't know, it could be. You were close to him that day. I can't be sure, I only saw photographs that the police showed to us."

"It's him, I'm certain. This'll be Carrington's revenge on us for what we did!"

David was becoming increasingly agitated, almost oversteering on a couple of occasions. Other motorists passing by sounded their horns in annoyance at his erratic driving, but he remained oblivious to all their insults as his attention focussed on the car still tailing them. He never saw the on-coming articulated lorry which crossed the central reservation after a blowout on one of its front tyres. Had he been in full control, evasive manoeuvres would have taken the BMW out of the path of the juggernaut. As it was, the unstable load of steel girders whipped the trailer around and caught their vehicle a glancing blow. The force of the impact was enough to send the car into a violent spin which only ended when it collided with the support pillars of the next flyover. It ended up on its roof, and David blacked out.

His injuries were relatively minor and, apart from stiffness in his neck where the seat belt had anchored him in place, he had only a few cuts and bruises to show for his part in the accident. Nikki, however, had not been as fortunate. Facing the rear of the car at the point of impact, and with her seat belt pulled aside to enable her to look at the pursuing car, she had suffered multiple injuries to her neck, legs, and arms. As the emergency vehicles approached, David had been able to struggle free of the now crumpled BMW but it took almost an hour for Fire and Rescue crews to cut Nikki free. From that day to this she had remained unresponsive in ICU at Lincoln General Hospital, and David had been told by medical staff to prepare himself for the almost certain result that she would not recover. The driver of the car following them was not Michael Benson at all, but some other poor unfortunate individual caught up as a fatality in the carnage.

So, here he was, sitting where he had been ever since the accident, and staring at the equipment keeping alive the only person he had ever loved. Faced with the decision to turn off the life support which had kept her warm and life-like, his heart sank not for the first time at the prospect of carrying on his life without her. The 'beep-bip, beep-bip' of the ECG mocked him in harsh tones as his hand wavered over the switch. The Resident at his side had been an almost ever-present during the traumatic time he had been at Nikki's bed. He had listened kindly to the one-sided conversations which David had used in an attempt to reach her. Now that was all behind him; all his attempts had apparently failed, and it seemed like Colin Carrington would have his revenge after all.

"Mr Spencer?"

The voice of the doctor shook David out of his reverie, and he blinked away his tears.

"Yes. Yes, I know, it's time. There's nothing left to do; you've all been very kind. Just one more moment... please."

The white clad figure nodded, smiled a weak and hopeless smile, and closed the door behind him. He had seen it all before, and a few moments longer would not matter. David turned back to the bed, taking his finger off the switch.

"Nikki, darling, it's time. I've got to go now. I'm so sorry, this is all my fault. I should have just pulled over. Now it's too late... goodbye, my love."

With one last huge sigh, and a sob which could have brought down the Philistine Temple without Samson's help, he flicked the switch powering the life support equipment. The ECG monitor banished the last flicker of Nikki's life from its right-hand side, and the cruel flat lines of death marched across its screen from the left. David planted one last kiss on the warm, pink, cheek of his beloved wife, and turned to the door. There he paused one final time and looked back.

There was a flicker on the ECG screen.

He shook his head, convinced that it was no more than an illusion.

There it was again... and again... and another - stronger this time. Standing transfixed he yelled for attention and a herd of medical staff barged him out of the way as they crowded around the bed.

One hour later, and with all the paraphernalia of the ICU now removed, David smiled down into the deep brown eyes of his wife. Still swathed in the bandages which adorned her head, he could not remember when she had looked more beautiful. He wouldn't be needing the Temazepam prescribed by Doctor Lodge now, and the bottle of Scotch could be saved for happier times.

"David?"

"Yes, my love?"

"Did I die?"

"Of course not, silly, you've just been away for a while. Time you got up out of that bed, my girl. We've things to do."

The blind faith that they had both placed in the hands of Barker and Palmer very nearly cost them dear. It was not something he would ever consider doing again.

A Friend in Need

'A friend in need is a friend indeed' is a statement that the ones who stand by you in times of trouble are those whom you can truly regard as friends. I failed a good friend completely through self-interest when I was needed, and the real shame of the matter was that a quiet word from me in the appropriate ears would probably have stopped the whole thing before it really had the chance to get going. I bottled the opportunity out of fear. Fear that I myself may well have become a target for the sort of abuse and ridicule which was heaped upon someone who had befriended me as a stranger to the area when I was nine years old. By that time, the bullying, for that is what it had become, had spread throughout the entire school, and I could well have stopped it from even germinating – I didn't.

Dad's job was relocated when I was half way through junior school, and we had to move with it. This took me away from family and all the friends with whom I had grown up. It is a time of major upheaval when you are nine years old going on ten, and I looked forward with trepidation to my first day at a new school where all the other pupils knew each other and I, as a newcomer, would be the focus of interest for some two hundred and fifty minds. Mum and Dad took me in that first morning, and the headmaster was a welcoming, friendly, face. My parents were assured that I would be well looked after, and one of the boys in what was now 'my year' was summoned to take me to class. Mr Hardy, the headmaster, had the kind of comically stern manner which he carefully cultivated towards the children, and they obviously loved him for it.

"Ah, Greagsbey. Come here, boy!"

Allan Greagsbey was two weeks older than me, about my height, bespectacled and with light brown hair. He stood to attention in mock response to the sergeant major command.

"Yes, sir."

"Take Peter Nelson to Mrs Graham's class, lad, and don't lose this one. It took us ages to find the last unfortunate we trusted to your care."

Allan smiled at this clear attempt to ease me into the comfortable routine of Seddon Street School, and my worried expression at Mr Hardy's words. One look back at the head told me that this was to be the standard of all humour within the establishment when he was around. It was the start of two wonderful years, and the beginning of a friendship which was to last for seven more before I managed to completely ruin it by abandoning a friend in his time of need.

We moved from our rented accommodation after finding a suitable property less than half a mile from Allan's house, and that was when our camaraderie really cemented itself. I was quickly absorbed into his circle and accepted readily by all his local friends – my being a more than useful footballer may have helped. At secondary school, we shared an interest in chess and joined the after-hours club, whilst outside of all that, the ruling passion of the time was Subbuteo table football. The school ran a league and we spent much of our weekends playing games either 'home' or 'away'. There was no hint at that time of the problems lurking just around the corner, and when we both moved to the local grammar school I assumed that the lives of the two of us, and all our classmates, would continue much as they had done over the previous three and a half years.

There may have been a combination of factors which conspired to marginalise Allan at the new school. His dad had been injured in an accident at work which affected the family income and I know that, for quite a while, things were financially tight for all of them. His grandmother died shortly after the move and I noticed that he developed a marked nervous twitch. Things like that tend to get picked up by new class mates, particularly those from a competing secondary school in the area. It became noticed by new faces. Their comments reverberated quickly around the school and were adopted by older pupils who started following us around at break times and lunch. To his credit Allan ignored it all at first, but when something happens every day from the start of lessons until you go home, I suppose it can be wearing.

Nowadays, bullying in school is much more in the spotlight than it was when we were there, and our teachers rarely got to find out about it. This was the first instance where maybe, along with the rest of our small group, I should have stood up for him against the name-calling and we could have prevented the escalation. Matters came to a head one Thursday afternoon during the double games period. It was always football, and usually all differences were forgotten during the one and a half hours we spent kicking the ball about on the playing field under the watchful eye of the games master. Unfortunately, that watchful eye only extended to the pitch, and not to the horseplay which went on in the changing rooms later.

Allan played in goal, mainly because he loved it, but also because no-one else wanted to; he even represented the school on a couple of occasions when injury to the first-choice keeper demanded it. On this day he had a blinder, and even his wearing of spectacles didn't prevent him going in head first at the feet of onrushing forwards. He saved a number of point-blank shots from the school's best player, and the guy started to take the whole thing very personally – by the end of the session it was clearly daggers drawn, but Allan had no idea that there was any problem.

Whilst he was in the shower, three of them tied his clothes in knots after taking a knife to the trousers, and locked the whole lot inside his games case. I saw it all and could have identified the three of them to the games master. Instead, coward that I was, I chose to look away. By the time he emerged dripping wet from the shower room, he had no means of drying off and getting dressed. His appeal to the teacher in charge was treated with some disdain until someone eventually found a way of releasing the lock on the bag. I still remember the look on his face when he saw what had been done to his school uniform, and can only imagine the effect it had on his cash-strapped parents. Still I said and did nothing, and when he looked around at me all I could do was shrug, shake my head, and stare at the floor.

I knew, then and there, that I had lost the trust of my closest friend; it was to be a further three weeks before he even spoke to me again. Normal practice was that I called for him on the way to school, and we would catch the bus together, but suddenly he was not ready when I knocked at the door, and I would leave alone. He then went to a different stop and took to sitting in the upper area of the bus. He avoided me at school and started spending time alone in the library at breaks and lunch – this of course went down very well with the teaching staff. However, it only served to exacerbate the situation; he became known as a swot and that gave rise to more bullying. Even at this stage I could probably have done something about it.

Allan's parents could not afford a telephone, so the only means of getting in touch was for me to actually walk to their house. I tried this on several occasions, and although his mum and dad were aware of our falling out and what had caused it, they took great pains not to become involved. I let the matter ride for a couple of weeks, but in the end my dad told me that if I valued the friendship I should meet the problem head on. Allan's weekends were taken up with football on the local recreation ground - a place where I had always been welcomed. Taking Dad's advice, I walked down there one Saturday to find a game in progress. Normally, latecomers were just told to join one particular team and the match carried on. This time it was different. They spotted me early and everything stopped as I walked on to the field. It was clear that I was no longer welcome, and Allan came running up from the other end of the pitch as Big John approached me.

"Leave it, Johnnie," he shouted. "It's my problem."

He was too far away, and I never saw the punch coming. The next thing I recall was looking up into a blue sky with many very angry faces staring down at me.

"Think you're clever, don't you? Mates are supposed to stick together. That's what *we* do around here. What's up with you?"

A sharp kick in the ribs reinforced the point, followed up by several handfuls of dirt scraped up off the pitch. Allan arrived too late to prevent the assault, breaking past all attempts to hold him back.

"I'm really sorry about that, but you shouldn't have come. It's lucky for you that they don't know all of what's happened."

I got up, dusted myself down, and wiped the blood from my lip where the punch had landed. I tried to explain that we still needed to talk, and that I wasn't prepared to let our friendship die without a fight, but his reply shut the door firmly in my face.

"You should have thought of that weeks ago. I gave you enough opportunities to say what happened, but you bottled it. I would have stood by *you* without a second thought, and if you were as much of a friend as you imagined, you would have done the same for me."

He walked slowly away and went back to the game, leaving me standing alone and friendless. Suddenly, I knew exactly how he had been feeling all that time. It was the last time we played football together. I had to smile, though, when he got his revenge on the lot of them in one go, and it must have given him endless pleasure even through a considerable amount of pain.

The school team had been selected to play a trial match against the newly formed county under fifteens, and the regular goalkeeper was on holiday. Those who had perpetrated the dressing room slashing of Allan's uniform were all in the side that day and must have thought that he had been put firmly in his place. His reliability between the sticks had never been in question, but when a clash with the county centre forward resulted in a dislocated finger, Allan was clearly in some pain. An appeal to the games master went unanswered and, as the finger swelled up, his willingness to handle the ball diminished and the opposition quickly cottoned on. A 15-0 drubbing ensued, and he was the only school player to leave the pitch smiling. A hairline fracture was the result of the accidental clash, and the games master was reprimanded for his lack of attention. Allan never played for the team again.

So, now I sit here, years later, waiting for my interview appointment, an unemployed English teacher with a family, a mortgage, and enough credit card debt to choke a pig. The screening panel consists of the school headmaster, the head of English, the chairman of the board of governors and the finance manager - one Allan Greagsbey. I want the job, and if ever there was a time for a friend in need, it is now – ironic, isn't it?

Clock

The craft hovered silently in the night sky over the small mid-western town, lights dancing in a strobe-like rhythm around its circumference. There was, to any observer who may have been present, a sudden faint but clearly discernible hum before it disappeared towards the North, leaving only a band of bright, but rapidly fading, light to betray its presence. The deliveries had been made, and it was now merely a question of time before the new home would be ready.

There had never been a clockmaker's shop in Stanfield before. Indeed, the township boasted only five thousand souls and, as a sales catchment area, was far too small for any retail establishment other than the local grocery/grain store. Nevertheless, a clockmaker had set up in business in one of the vacant premises long abandoned by a bankrupt business which had singularly failed to generate an income for its unfortunate proprietor. Stanfield itself had no industry, forming merely a staging post along Route 63 between Waterloo and Rochester for the cornfields that were the mainstay of the state of Iowa.

There had been much discussion amongst the residents as a series of vehicles, delivering quantities of shop fitting equipment, came and went over a period of three to four weeks. The premises were transformed during that period from a ramshackle façade concealing a series of small and dingy rooms into a bright and welcoming emporium opening out into a single showroom. Lighting was diffused and easy on the eye, and there played in the background a gentle, almost hypnotic, strain of music which no-one could quite recognise but which, within a few days, all had committed to memory and were now whistling and humming as they went about their daily lives.

Lazlo Domarski was the owner of the town's newest enterprise, and no-one thought to question his wisdom in setting up such a curious trade in an otherwise stagnant backwater. If you were to ask him, he would tell you that he came from 'somewhere near Krakow' but that was all, and his engaging smile would automatically dismiss all thoughts of further enquiry from the mind. Clocks came from nowhere, appearing in quantities inconsistent with such a miniscule market, and at strange times in the daily cycle. They were of every design imaginable and suitable for all tastes. Within weeks virtually every household in the little township had acquired one, at $100 each, discarding existing, and sometimes long-serving, timepieces without so much as a single thought. The till at Lazlo's shop rang sweetly, and very soon he had cashed in to the tune of around $50,000. It was time to implement the plan.

John Haywood stumbled upon Stanfield having taken a wrong turn off Route 27 whilst heading for Charles City on 218. He cursed his navigation skills and wished now that he had brought his wife along. Parking the Dodge outside the grocery store, he headed inside. There was an eerie silence, even allowing for the size of the town, and the only sound was the steady *tick, tock* of the wall clock which hung behind the sales counter. There was no bell and, after a brief look around the place, he decided on a more direct approach.

"Hello! Anybody home?"

Complete silence greeted his loud hail and, scratching the back of his neck, he peered through the open doorway just behind the counter into what appeared to be family quarters. Normally, such a door would be closed and bearing a curt notice that entry was for 'Staff Only', or alternatively marked, quite bluntly, 'Private'. John was not a man for taking liberties, but when his second request for assistance went unanswered, curiosity got the better of him and, lifting the counter flap, he stepped through into unfamiliar territory.

Passing through the central alleyway of what was clearly a stock room with rows of shelves to either side, he came upon a closed door which did, in fact, bear the aforementioned curt reminder that beyond lay private quarters. He knocked and waited. He knocked again, and a third time. Frowning, John looked back the way he had come, and a cold sensation began to run its fingers down the centre of his neck. He shrugged it off and tried the door handle; it turned, and the opening revealed a comfortable sitting room containing all the usual trappings of Middle American life. The smell of cooking assailed his senses and led him further into the premises to a kitchen/dining area where a light shone. He could now hear the faint sounds of a radio in the background, but none of the normal chatter which accompanied a mealtime.

He had seen *Psycho* as a kid, and had instinctively known what was going to happen to the private investigator who mounted the stairs at the Bates Motel. He had hidden behind a cushion as his dad smiled, but that feeling had remained with him ever since. It was here now, screaming at him to turn around and walk away, begging and pleading that he didn't really need to take the next steps into the room before him. Too late; curiosity was the overriding sensation as it had been throughout his formative years. It had got him into scrapes in the past, but somehow he'd always come up smelling of roses and it lent him a feeling of invulnerability. Without even thinking about it, he was entering the back room of the premises.

The sight which greeted his intrusion was odd to say the least. John was standing at the threshold of the family's cooking and eating area. The room was what you would expect in a town of the size of Stanfield, with all equipment functionally sited along the appropriate wall in an ergonomically efficient manner. There were four places set, and four meals served up on a pine table – quite clearly a dinner had just been laid out prior to the shop closing temporarily at midday. A man, his wife, and their two children were sitting there... just sitting, staring out into space, unmoving and wide awake.

It was a while - John was not sure how long - before he decided to make a move of any kind, but a slow and measured walk around the table revealed nothing more than he already knew. They were alive, he was certain of that from the slow rise and fall of their chests, but all four displayed not the slightest inclination to move despite a snapping of fingers before each of their faces.

Shaking off a feeling of unease, he retraced his steps back into the shop, making for the front door with the intention of seeking help of some kind. Turning back as he closed the door, John's attention was caught by the clock he noticed as he entered some time before.

The steady *tick, tock* was still the only audible sound in the shop, but this time he noticed that there was no movement from the second hand. Checking his own watch, John noticed that it too had stopped. The exact time on both was the same. That *Psycho* feeling was now running up and down his spine like some demented millipede, and the hairs on the back of his neck were standing to attention like a group of parade ground recruits. He knew that getting into his car and just driving away was the sensible thing to do... he knew that... he did. A cold sweat was now running down his chest, but he was drawn by the irresistible urge to find out what was going on. The only way that was likely to be achieved was in finding someone else in this town and, turning to the right, he walked off the sidewalk and headed for the first available house.

Behind the large glazed window of the clock emporium, Lazlo Domarski had seen Haywood's arrival and had watched every move that he made, both inside the front of the shop and outside on its porch. He frowned; the last thing he needed was some busybody poking his nose in just at the wrong time. He picked up the telephone.

"Grainger?"

"Yeah."

"Domarski. You'd better get down here; company's arrived. We may have a problem; use the rear entrance. We don't want him spooked."

Cole Grainger was the county sheriff and had been one of the first to purchase a timepiece from the new retailer. A long-standing officer of the law, he was well respected both inside and outside the district. This rendered him invaluable to Domarski and the plans which he had been charged to carry out; no-one would question the actions of the local cop. His arrival from the rear of the premises coincided with Haywood's exit from the property adjacent to the grocery store.

"He been in there long?"

"No," Domarski replied, "but long enough to work out that something isn't right. Look at him. If we don't take him out right away he'll spread the alarm. We can't allow that to happen."

"He's comin' over."

"Get in the back and stay out of sight. I may need you if things turn awkward."

John had reached the middle of the street as Grainger made himself scarce, and never saw the lawman's hasty exit. He stood briefly outside the shop before pushing the door and stepping inside. Although modern-looking, it had one of those spring-loaded door bells to announce the visitor; it seemed oddly out of place. The figure behind the counter stood with his back to the room and was very still, almost as if frozen in mid act just like the others.

"What's going on here!?" His gaze swept the room, temporarily leaving Domarski. The unexpected reply startled him.

"Sorry, I was engrossed in something. Can I help you?" The shopkeeper's benign face was a picture of hospitality, and John was taken aback.

"What? Oh, well, I didn't expect... you know." He cleared his throat, embarrassed at his own surprise.

"Is there something you wish to purchase?"

"No, thank you. I just wondered... look, is everything okay around here? I just came from the store across the way and there's people in there just staring into space. The folks in the next house are the same."

"You mean Dawson's shop? Well, I don't know about that, but Mrs Dawson just came out of the door. Look." He pointed across the street.

A middle-aged woman was polishing the shop window as they spoke, and two children came running out of the premises and down the street. From the property next door, a man in a suit and carrying a briefcase walked to a Buick, got in, and drove away. John shook his head in disbelief.

"No, you don't understand. I've just been in both places and they were as good as dead... except they were still breathing."

He was now aware that he'd started to gabble, and that what he was saying made no apparent sense. Nevertheless, he had seen what he had seen, and this odd-looking man was practically telling him that he was crazy. Domarski was staring at him in a manner which could only be described as condescendingly polite. Any moment now John would be patted on the head, told not to be such a silly boy, and to go along on his way. That riled him.

"Mr...?"

"Haywood, John Haywood," he snapped.

"Well, Mr Haywood. You can see for yourself that all appears to be well. I really don't know what else to say. Are you certain that you are feeling all right?" That smile again.

"Yes, I am! Don't patronise me. There's something wrong here. I'm going now, but I'll be back with someone who'll listen..."

The words faded suddenly, and John dropped slowly to the floor as the hypodermic administered by Cole Grainger took effect. The Sheriff had worked his way unseen around the back of the visitor, and now broke the fall; the last thing they needed was any unexplained injuries, particularly to a stranger. Working together, he and Domarski carried the now sleeping figure into the back room where John Haywood was gagged and tied securely to a chair.

"Now what?" Grainger's voice had an uneasy edge to it.

"Stay calm. It'll all be over very soon and he'll not be bothering us for four or five hours. By the time he wakes up there'll be nothing to corroborate anything that he's likely to tell an outsider."

"I hope you're right. Everything depends upon you."

"Go back to your office and wait. I'll get in touch when it's over; then you can tidy up. Just don't answer any phones for now."

With Grainger now gone, Lazlo Domarski returned to the work he had been doing on the remainder of the clocks. It was vital that all the rest of the consignment were fitted with the devices without delay in order to transmit the instruction to the last batch of townsfolk. Those already treated would not be discernible from the remainder to an outsider, but Haywood had stumbled upon the Dawsons and their neighbours in the middle of one of the processes. That had been unfortunate, and completely unforeseen.

He would need only a couple of hours to make the last alterations to the dozen or so timepieces which were yet to be delivered; then the job would be finished. Perhaps then he could get rid of this ridiculous disguise and go back to his proper job. Two hours later, and with John still out of it, he made his way to the far end of the small settlement armed with the last of the clocks. They had really not anticipated such an easy victory over such a sentient species. Not a drop of blood had been spilled, and as far as anyone was aware no lasting damage had been caused to those targeted. One final adjustment to the frequency back at the shop, and a catatonic trance would be induced in those now in receipt of the last of the timepieces. Less than one hour later they would awaken none the worse for the experience, and the job would be finally complete.

John Haywood shook his head and tried to focus his eyes through the mist which was slowly clearing. The town of Stanfield lay before him just as he remembered it. Or did he? Checking his watch, he saw that he had lost a few hours. It was now late afternoon, and he had arrived at this place around noon, of that he was sure. The pain in his head was beginning to subside and he drove the Dodge carefully into the main street, parking up outside the store. *Dawson's Groceries* it said above the door, and a creepy feeling of déja-vu ran through him like ice.

Now he remembered, and the longer he sat there the more came back to him. Gunning the engine, a squeal of tyres and a black cloud of burning rubber had him speeding back down the main street in the direction of Waterloo. There had to be someone who would take his story seriously.

In the clock shop, Domarski and Grainger watched the departure with misgivings. This was not how it was supposed to end. The treatment should have erased Haywood's short-term memory and have obliterated all recollection of the past few hours. The sheriff radioed ahead for his deputies to intercept the speeding stranger who, they were told, had just tried to rob Domarski's Emporium. That would be enough to hold him until help could be summoned from outside. This time they would have no choice in their method of dealing with the intruder.

Haywood stared out of the bars criss-crossing the small window in his padded cell. He had been in the sanatorium now for over three months. That they had railroaded him was beyond doubt in his own mind, but with no independent corroboration of his story and a violent confrontation as he had tried to evade capture, he must have appeared like some psychotic on the loose. They had even managed to convince his wife and family of his mental instability and he had to admit that, with a track record of unpredictable behaviour, things did not look too good for him.

Lazlo Domarski, or Robert Barringer as he was properly known, was, at that moment, sitting in a meeting room deep within NSA headquarters at Fort George G. Meade, Maryland. With his disguise now a welcome thing of the past, and the debriefing completed, he could afford to relax. Now that the last of the inhabitants of Stanfield had been restored to their former selves, the alien invasion threat had finally been removed. There had been several isolated incursions across the world, reminiscent of the 1960s film *Village of the Damned*, and, in an unprecedented show of co-operation, international action had been swift and decisive.

They had been expecting something of this nature since Roswell in 1947. The remains of the alien craft had revealed a sophisticated set of instruments, one of which had turned out to be a form of mind control device. Subsequent experiments had shown that the equipment was capable of transplanting brainwaves from one 'volunteer' to another. Clearly this was a part of some plan to invade the Earth and take over its population. That the weapon had, in fact, required a period of time before the host mind became totally subservient had given the security forces the opportunity to counter its effects.

It had taken over fifty years to devise a counter weapon, and now that field trials had been completed on what was assumed to have been a proposed landing site, the world was ready. John Haywood's unwitting intrusion into the US counter-offensive had almost compromised the entire campaign. It would be a long and lonely wait until he was deemed safe to rejoin the rest of a society which he had, unknowingly, almost destroyed.

Coles to Newcastle

The warm days of summer were gone now, and with the changing colours of the foliage in the grounds of the Westfield Retirement Home, Harold Coles felt the autumn of his years take a firm grip upon his constitution. He had been a resident for the past five years and, with the passing of each one, time had seemed to increase its relentless march with an ever-quickening pace. The place was comfortable, clean, and welcoming, with efficient and caring staff; at the age of seventy-five he took the decision that living alone in his large four-bedroom house was no longer a sensible option for him. With no living relatives of his own generation for company, the choice of selling up and moving here had not been a difficult one, for he had always been a man in favour of taking the sensible line in life. At 81, and with a successful business life behind him, he could have no real complaints at what fate had served up to him. His one regret had been the lack of a companion in his later years, and thoughts inevitably returned, again and again, to the one opportunity which presented itself to him, and which he rejected out of hand – Heather. Suddenly the memories came flooding back once more, and as he sat in the lounge they took him on a journey back in time.

He was born in 1920 to a Newcastle dock worker, Jack Coles, and his wife, Beryl. One of eight children, he left school and was apprenticed to a joiner in Wallsend where, over the next five years, he excelled. The outbreak of war in 1939 prevented him taking up the trade, and he joined the army. He survived Dunkerque, was involved in the push through Italy during 1943, and witnessed some of the most horrifying examples of man's inhumanity before being demobbed in 1945. After a brief return home to the North

East, he travelled south to London to take up his vocation as a carpenter, thriving amid the post-war rebuilding of the capital. By the time he met Heather McBain in 1955, he was a successful and well-respected local tradesman living in Tottenham. She was twenty-four, from Manchester, and their meeting was one of pure chance at the F.A. Cup final of that year between Newcastle United and Manchester City at Wembley Stadium. They seemed to hit it off straight away, and after several visits to both sets of prospective in-laws, they became engaged to be married at the end of that summer.

It was whilst they were apart during the run-up to Christmas that Heather met Steve, an American airman who had stayed in Britain after the war. Like many of his fellow countrymen at the time, he exuded a charm and sophistication with which few of his British counterparts could compete. He was twenty-six, nine years younger than Harold, and appeared like a Monet painting, full of life and colour in comparison with his dull and drab everyday rival. He dazzled her with stories of life across the Atlantic with its promise of riches and opportunities, and within a matter of a fortnight she had returned her engagement ring to her fiancé with a brief note of apology. They departed for the USA to Steve's home in Michigan and the promise of a job in a Detroit automobile plant. Harold was devastated, and wrote via Heather's parents begging her to return to him but she never replied. That day at the Cup Final, with all of its promise, now seemed like a distant and fading dream.

The following five years saw Harold Coles move to the Midlands and set up in business as a joinery manufacturer in the Staffordshire town of Newcastle-under-Lyme. His skill as a craftsman soon earned him a good reputation, and by 1960 he was the owner of a thriving business making a variety of household goods, and employing thirty men in a converted warehouse. He had almost forgotten about Heather and Steve when a note arrived from his mother containing a letter bearing a Detroit postmark. It had been forwarded to Tyneside from his address in London and was four weeks old.

"Someone to see you, Mr Coles." said Annie, one of the care assistants.

Harold was jolted firmly back to the present by the appearance of his niece, Julia, on one of her periodic, but unpredictable, visits. He always enjoyed their brief sessions together and she was one of a few of his younger relatives who took the time and trouble to make him feel that he had not been forgotten. She stayed for tea and told of all the family news since the last visit, before walking around the grounds with him prior to departure with a promise of coming back soon. Smiling as she waved goodbye, he sat down in the conservatory overlooking the extensive and well-kept lawn. His thoughts returned once more to Heather and the letter, and he took it out of his pocket, beginning to read its crumpled, age-worn, page for what seemed the thousandth time.

14th September 1960

Dear Harold

I hardly know where to begin to tell you of the events of the past five years, and I am not sure that you will understand how I feel after the way I treated you.

Steve and I separated three years ago, and we are now divorced. I tried for a while to support myself and our son, Steve Junior, but things were just too difficult, and I will be returning to Manchester to live with my mum and dad for a while.

If you can forgive me for what happened, perhaps we could meet and maybe work out some sort of future together. I made a terrible mistake and would like to put things right.

Heather

Harold stared out once again into the late afternoon sunshine, and his mind drifted back over the years to the events of the weeks subsequent to the letter. He did indeed write several times to Heather at her mother's, but was reticent about agreeing to meet her until he was more certain of her intentions. Finally, with all his old feelings for her returning, and against all the logic which had stood him in such good stead over the previous five years, he gave in. He told her to let him know of the time of arrival of her train in Newcastle, and he would be at the station to meet her. A brief note arrived by return of post giving details of a date and time some two weeks hence, and he found the excitement of a reconciliation taking first place before all other personal and business considerations.

When the day arrived, and with no other communication from Heather to the contrary, he made his excuses at work, dressed in his best suit and tie, and set off for the station. The postman arrived with the morning mail fifteen minutes after his departure. The drive to the station, normally a matter of twenty minutes, seemed to take forever, and despite constant checking of his watch to ensure that he would not be late, he couldn't settle until he had parked and was making his way to the platform. It was like being on a first date all over again, and the only thing missing was the bunch of flowers - perhaps he should have bought some. He made enquiries about the arrival from Manchester and was directed to Platform 2 where, despite available seats, he was unable to relax, and paced up and down until the tell-tale cloud of smoke in the distance heralded the arrival of the train.

It ground to a halt amid a cloud of steam, and doors opened along its entire length as busy travellers were disgorged onto the platform. He waited with bated breath for a lone female bearing some resemblance to the Heather he knew in 1955, but as a crowd of commuters passed him without comment he was left standing alone. The train pulled away, and yet he still half expected a late passenger getting out of a moving carriage. She was not there. He said it out loud to convince himself that it was true. *She was not there.* He hurried out, off the platform, in case she had been carried past in the rush, but there were only incoming pedestrians for the next train. *She was not there.* Confused, he returned home to find the morning mail on the door mat. Amongst it was a letter bearing a Manchester postmark. He tore it open – it was from Heather's mother informing him of Steve's arrival in the UK in search of his ex-wife and son.

So that was it. For the second time she had betrayed him. Against all his better judgement he had allowed her to play with his feelings again, and she had let him down. He felt such a fool, and now wondered at his pride and conceit in thinking that she could settle for a humdrum existence with him after the excitement of America. His sadness turned to anger, and then a determination that this time he would never forgive her, even if she came to him on her knees. He tore the letter into shreds, threw it into the fire and watched as it turned to ash.

At that very moment, a woman was standing on Platform 4 of the station in Newcastle-upon-Tyne, wondering what had delayed the man who was supposedly meeting her off the train which had left the town fifteen minutes earlier. It had never occurred to Heather that, like Fanny Robin rushing to her wedding with Sergeant Troy in Hardy's *Far from The Madding Crowd*, she had gone to the wrong place. In her haste to read Harold's letters, she had failed to notice the post marks on the envelopes. Coincidence had dictated that there were two trains leaving Manchester for Newcastle that afternoon, one bound for the North East, and the other for the Midlands. To Heather, however, this seemed like a supreme act of revenge by a man whom she had so badly wronged, but of whom she had thought better. Returning to Manchester by the evening train, she was back at her mother's before midnight. Within a month she had returned to America with Steve once more, apparently reconciled.

"Another cup of tea, Mr Coles?" Annie again, bless her. Always on the look out for an empty cup in need of a refill.

"No, thank you, Annie. I think I'll go to my room."

He settled down in front of his television but couldn't concentrate on the programme, and switched off the set. Picking up a book he started to read, but the afternoon sun had made him feel drowsy and he dozed off. It was rare for him to dream, being of habit a sound sleeper, but the day's reminiscing must have stimulated his mind into this unusual state. Before him stood the image of his long-lost Heather and he couldn't resist a smile, even after all this time.

"Hello, Harold." A voice with a strange but somehow familiar accent awoke him with a start.

There she stood, for all the world as if she had never been away. She must have been seventy, but didn't look a day older than fifty. He was completely awake now and moved to stand up.

"No honey, I'll sit down. We have a lot to catch up on, and I have some fences to mend."

They talked late into the evening, both finally realising the trick which fate had played on them forty years before. She told him of Steve's death and their son's graduation, subsequent success at Harvard and his marriage to the daughter of a wealthy industrialist. An air of sadness pervaded the room when Heather rose to leave, promising to return the following day. Harold Coles was destined not to make that meeting, as fate took another cruel twist in the final chapter of their relationship. The stroke which took him from her in the middle of the night was massive, and as she stood at the graveside a week later, the tears ran down her face onto the dedication card amongst the twelve red roses which she placed against the headstone. There was nothing left in this country for her any more, and with a heavy heart she turned and left the cemetery.

Cutting the Cloth

The year is 1901. Queen Victoria reigns supreme over the far-flung British Empire, and the Lancashire textile industry is at the peak of its industrial might. Products from the mills of Manchester, Bolton, Blackburn, and a host of other crowded towns and cities travel the world, satisfying an increasing demand from Britain's dominions. In the small town of Rochdale, a place amidst the centre of the Oldham-Blackburn-Halifax triangle, a small acorn of a merchanting enterprise was extending its roots into the fertile textile soil of the north west of England.

George Napkin had shunned the spinning, doubling, and weaving industries in favour of a trade wherein he saw the potential for greater, more rapid, growth in an already crowded market place. The large producers already had the market tied up in cottons (both American and Egyptian), lace, silks, and wool. His passion, and that of his father before him, was linen. Alexander Napkin had started the family business in the early 1850s, and a relatively modest but sustainable trade had provided an adequate living for him, his wife Caroline, and their brood of four daughters and one son.

When Alexander died in 1896, George, as the only son, took over the company. His years of tutelage under the watchful gaze of his father had given the young man a keen eye for business. This, together with a detailed knowledge of the trade, was to stand him in good stead as the sharks of the industry circled following the funeral. He was to surprise them all with his commercial acumen and the speed of his reactions to changing market conditions. Many had fallen victim to his sharpness in the trade, and the Manchester Cotton Exchange was full of the stories of the man's ingenuity.

By the age of thirty he had expanded the family concern beyond all recognition, and from his humble beginnings in a relatively small town house, he and his family had replaced their abode with an almost palatial residence on the outskirts of Rochdale. He had married Beatrice Armitage, daughter of a well-to-do mining family in neighbouring Ramsbottom, and *their* three daughters and two sons had the finest that money could buy. All were educated at the best local schools, and no opportunity for their further advancement was neglected.

In the cut-and-thrust world of business, George Napkin was without a local equal. Those of envious disposition were inclined to judge him as an out-and-out opportunist with no business ethics. Others of more equable temperament saw the altruistic nature which lurked very close beneath the otherwise hard-nosed surface. To his employees, Napkin was intensely and fiercely loyal. He paid well and, consequently, was never short of feet to fill the shoes of those misguided souls who sought greener pastures elsewhere.

Never one to look a gift horse in the mouth, an opportunity presented itself to George in the form of a large quantity of top quality linen cloth bales for immediate shipment from New York. The supplier was one of a number of regular and trustworthy trade contacts, and he had no hesitation in accepting the offer. The value of the shipment would tie up all his available liquid capital until the goods arrived and could be distributed throughout his chain of customers. Nevertheless, Napkin weighed all the risks and decided that the gamble was worth taking.

Documentary credits allowed for payment within sixty days of delivery at the port of Liverpool. With everything now in place, George sat back and waited for his ship to come in; when it did, it was with completely unexpected results.

An urgent telegram from his Liverpool agent was the bearer of potentially disastrous news. The vessel bearing his cargo, along with a multitude of other goods, had run into a violent storm in the middle of the Atlantic. The tempest was so fierce that part of the main rigging and mizzen mast had been brought crashing down onto the decks below, causing several fatalities amongst the crew. All efforts had therefore been concentrated on securing the safety of the vessel and its remaining men, with tarpaulins being thrown across whatever cargo had been stored on deck to protect it from the worst of the weather.

George Napkin's bales of linen cloth had been amongst the items left exposed to the violent elements, and had sustained considerable damage as a result of the wind and rain in addition to the sea water washing across the decks at the height of the storm. When the ship docked on the banks of the River Mersey, the full extent of the Rochdale merchant's problems became apparent. Only those bales at the very centre of the stack had been spared the ravages of the weather, with the remainder sustaining varying levels of spoilage.

He journeyed to the North West port, along with his wife, to assess the impact of the disaster. It was at this point that he discovered to his horror that the shipment had been travelling uninsured. A clerical error, made when the bills of lading had been prepared by one of his clerks, had resulted in the goods being classified 'Free on Board' instead of 'Cost, Insurance & Freight' – there would be no compensation for the losses sustained. There was no doubt in George's mind that he was facing financial ruin. Sitting with his head in his hands in a corner of the bonded warehouse, there appeared to be little chance of salvation.

However, he had reckoned without his quick-thinking wife, Beatrice. Looking over the still damp and discoloured bales of once creamy cloth, she saw beyond the current difficulties and had the warehouse staff unroll one of the water damaged bales. Over the course of the next couple of hours, she busied herself in a series of measurements and scribbled notes until she was satisfied that an answer was there for the taking. Shaking her husband out of his near suicidal frame of mind, she outlined a plan to rescue them, and the company, from bankruptcy. His eyes widened in amazement at the simplicity of the scheme, and he quietly cursed for not thinking of it himself.

An astounded dock manager was given the instruction to prepare the whole consignment for delivery to the firm's Rochdale warehouse at all speed in order to mitigate any further degradation of the cloth. He shook his head sadly at Napkin's apparent madness, but complied with his customer's wishes.

Within the hour, the whole shipment had been loaded onto transport and was on its way into deepest Lancashire.

The next two weeks were busy ones for the Napkin family. George's credit for the linen bales was determined by a 60-day draft due for settlement in around forty-five days' time, and to avoid default he would have to sell whatever he could of the produce from his wife's scheme within that period. The supreme salesman, he toured the towns and cities of Lancashire, promoting his wife's new idea. Small pieces of linen cloth to be used at only the best restaurants and other eating houses, and bound with a metal ring, would provide the finishing touch to any place-setting where the great and good of industrial and corporate Britain chose to take their repast.

To his great delight, the scheme was an immediate success, and orders flooded in for the new product. So heavy was demand, that extra labour needed to be drafted in to meet the new schedules. With five days to spare, all the available cloth had been re-cut, edged and sewn to meet Beatrice Napkin's design. They were out of material, but the funds generated from the project had more than made up the amount falling due on the bill of exchange. The family and the company were saved.

Quick to take out a patent on the product in order to protect his investment in its development, Napkin reaped the benefit, over the next ten years, of his wife's foresight and ingenuity. They prospered as they had never done before, expanding production into a new warehouse, and also licensing the new tableware at highly beneficial rates of commission to other willing manufacturers, whilst driving down the price of the cloth using new-found commercial muscle. He became a legend in his own lifetime, founding a dynasty of linen-dealing offspring. The re-equipment during the inter war years saw further expansion, this time into Europe with its innumerable fashionable watering places. The napkin became a household name, and soon adorned the table of all but the poorest families in the country.

So, the next time you sit down to a meal with friends, spare a thought for the Lancashire entrepreneur who almost went out of business to provide that small piece of seemingly insignificant linen cloth, bound in a metal ring, which you use to brush against your lips at the end of an evening's dining. The napkin had been born out of adversity, but would forever bear the name of the fortunate man who saw an opportunity amidst disaster, and had the strength of character and self-belief to take it.

Ebony Eyes

Her name was Chantel - Chantel Rogers - and Haydn had never seen anyone so beautiful in his life. At five feet seven, she had dark red hair, and eyes of such a deepest brown that they were almost black. She wore a smile that could charm the birds out of the trees, and she was everything that he imagined a woman could possibly be. Those eyes were like pools, and he would willingly have drowned in them. She was eighteen to his twenty-two and it had seemed as though they were destined for each other. She hailed from Springfield, a smallish town just outside of Nashville, and Haydn had used that as the ice-breaker, asking her how Homer and Marge were doing. It made her laugh, although he imagined she'd heard it all before.

Haydn Wright was a Chicago boy born and bred – he lived and died with the White Sox in summer and the Bears in winter. He loved his job at Mullins Motor Mechanic in Lincoln Park, and could strip down and rebuild the engine of most cars you'd care to name. He'd been there since high school, and although the older guys sometimes gave him a hard time, he took it all on the chin. Had to keep the new kid on the block under control, didn't they? He'd been there almost six years, but to the rest of them he was still a baby.

He'd been out with his buddies one Saturday when Joey, his best friend, had suggested the trip to Orlando. Why they hadn't thought of it before was a mystery, but by the end of the following week all the arrangements were in place, and they were on Stateside Airlines Flight 714 out of O'Hare for a week at Disney World. It was a place he'd wanted to go since he was in short pants, but his mom and dad never had the money. Now he was earning for himself things were different, and it wasn't like he had a family to support.

They'd spent the first few days messing around on the rides, eating too much, drinking way too much, and generally acting like some stupid bunch of kids, when they bumped into a group of girls out on a similar vacation. The numbers were equal and a pairing off was almost inevitable. Joey had smiled at Chantel, but her eyes had been fixed only on Haydn. There was an immediate chemistry between them, and Joey slapped him on the back, winked, and strolled off arm-in-arm with one of the others. Moving around the theme park during the daytime, the group split up after dinner to go off in pairs. Haydn and Chantel ended up just walking around, holding hands, and staring into each others' eyes. Strange – all alone with a girl and all he could do was gaze into her eyes, her beautiful eyes, so beautiful that he'd never noticed their colour until right now. They were brown, dark brown. No... not dark brown, almost black.

The holiday was over too soon and on the day they all packed up to go home, Haydn and Chantel exchanged addresses and telephone numbers, promising to keep in touch. Despondently, he told himself *that* never happened. She would go back to her boyfriend, and their meeting would be nothing but a dim and distant, albeit pleasant, memory. He smiled as he and his buddies got off the plane back at an overcast and rainy O'Hare, shook the thoughts from his head, and resigned himself to the daily grind back at the workshop.

The phone was ringing when he got to his apartment at the end of that first day back at work, and usually it was his mom *'just checking that you've gotten back alright'*. Sometimes he wondered if she wanted to know that he'd changed his shorts each day.

"Hi, Mom. How're you doin'?" he sighed, ready for the usual interrogation.

There was a silence at the other end before the voice he hadn't expected cut in and sent his mind reeling back to Florida.

"Mom?" She laughed, and he could feel his face starting to burn with embarrassment. "Haydn, it's Chantel. Don't have to check in, do you?"

"No, no..." He stalled while his brain caught up with his mouth. "She does this all the time. Hey, it's you."

"It's me... I missed you."

"Me too." He could feel the treacle in his throat with the way the conversation was going. "You got back ok, then?" Ugh; what a bummer of a thing to say.

They talked forever about everything and nothing as he sat on the floor with his back up to the wall. The coat he had taken off was still in the hallway where it had fallen from the rack, and the rest of his daily kit was just inside the door. Her voice was like a summer breeze, and blew away all the disappointment which comes with the first week back at work. She did take him by surprise however by suggesting a trip to The Windy City.

"Haydn..." It came out of the blue, "... I'm coming to Chicago."

Haydn was not sure that he had heard her correctly.

"You what?" There was a silence at the other end before she came back at him.

"I'm coming up there."

She had some time due, and her aunt in Rockford had been asking after her for a while; she could kill two birds with one stone. Haydn agreed without thinking, now sensing that something special was on the horizon; maybe there *was* no boyfriend after all. A rainy day just got a whole lot brighter.

It would, she'd said, be another two days before she could make the trip, and each hour seemed to drag like someone had tied a concrete block to his feet. Back in the workshop, he'd been working on an old Chevrolet when he had to pull out from underneath and go get a wrench from the tool rack. *Whitesnake* had been blasting out of the radio at top volume; heavy metal was the order of the day at Mullins, and you either listened or ignored it. He kind of liked the beat, and 'drummed' his way across the shop as Chris Frazier went into one of his solos. The crackle that greeted Haydn's arrival at the rack where the Hitachi hung had heads turning all around the work room, and from out of nowhere the sound of two voices in close harmony oozed across the airwaves. It was just two lines of a song that Haydn had never heard before

"Wright!" The raucous holler of Steve Kelly, the foreman, split the air like a thunderclap. "What in tarnation is that?!"

Haydn turned, hands spread out at shoulder height in a gesture of innocence, and shook his head in bemusement.

"I didn't do nothin', Steve."

"You put that back onto rock right now, or I'll have your ass on a plate!"

Haydn's turn was rendered irrelevant, as the radio crackled once more before returning to the popular dose of thunder and lightning which was the trademark of the group fronted by Dave Coverdale. He stared at the Hitachi and frowned; where had *that* come from? And who was it? He shook his head, walked slowly back to the Chevrolet, and gave the radio one more look before sliding back under the chassis.

Haydn had consigned the incident with the radio to the back of his mind when, on the very next day, he was in Weston's Electricals during his lunch break. He'd decided that his old TV was past its best, and had been looking around for a while. Standing now before a 42" Sanyo HD flat screen he was pondering over the price tag. Suddenly, all the set displays flipped from their individual channels, and played out a grainy black and white image of two young men singing to a couple of guitars. Everyone in the shop stopped what they were doing and gazed around. The voices were the same as in the earlier clip, but these were two different lines of, Haydn assumed, the same song.

The store manager flew out of his office in an instant to fix what was clearly a problem with the shop's receiving equipment. Haydn replaced the price ticket in its place on the shelf and moved away – in that instant all TV sets returned to their original stations. The manager had not noticed his retreat and, making his way to the door, Haydn turned once again and frowned at what had just happened. He had no idea who the two singers were, but now that he had seen them on the screen he was going to find out.

Deciding to ask for the afternoon off, he pleaded the onset of a cold as the reason. Steve gave him one of his famous sideways looks, but since the job on the Chevy had been completed Haydn was allowed to go. He smiled; he wouldn't want the young man to know how highly he thought of him, and good hands were not easy to find right now. The young man headed downtown for one of the old back street music stores – no point in asking any of the new ones about a song as old as this one seemed to be.

The shopkeeper was in his late sixties, Haydn guessed, and frowned in concentration as the younger man tried to describe the song and the singers. He shook his head sadly.

"That could have been any number of folks in the fifties or sixties, son. Got anything else?"

Haydn took a deep breath. He was not a good singer, and restricted all that kind of stuff to the privacy of the shower. Nevertheless, with no other option, and straining to remember words he had only heard once before, he came out with a reasonably close approximation to the song.

"Well, that's the Everlys! Don and Phil. Big shots in the late fifties, and boy, could they sing! The song's 'Ebony Eyes'. You want a copy?"

Haydn nodded and paid for a CD of their greatest hits. Now to find out what it was all about. Once would have been unusual, but twice was definitely more than a coincidence. As if to ram home the point, on the bus back to the apartment a youngster had a radio blaring out the latest Kaiser Chiefs track, much to the annoyance of other travellers. Haydn took the only available seat right behind him, and almost immediately the set crackled and went quiet. A round of sarcastic applause was soon silenced by a fresh burst of sound. This time those same voices as before gave him a complete verse of the strangely haunting song.

This was too much, and as Haydn got up to get off the bus, the offending radio skipped back to the original station, leaving its confused owner and the rest of the passengers staring in amazement.

Back at home, the CD was loaded and the correct track selected. Haydn played it through several times wondering what it all meant. There was no doubt in his mind that he had been the cause of whatever electrical interference had resulted in the song being played. It was not until later that night, when he was talking to Chantel, that he began to get the first inkling of a concern. She had made all the arrangements for the forthcoming trip to Chicago, and was clearly very excited at the prospect of their meeting up again.

She would, she said, be travelling with Stateside Airlines out of Nashville, flight 1203. Haydn froze.

"Haydn, you there...? Haydn?"

"Yeah, I'm here, Chantel. What was that flight number again?"

"Twelve Oh Three. Why? That a problem?"

"Don't know. Look, let me call you back. Just want to check something out."

Selecting the start of the song once more, Haydn listened intently to the lyrics until the middle of verse two. He stopped the CD, reselected the track, and played it again. No doubt about it - there it was: the flight number *'twelve oh three'* came across loud and clear; it had to be a warning of some kind.

He ran the rest of the song. The lyrics told the story of a serviceman sending for his girlfriend so that they could be married. She never made it. The plane crashed killing all passengers. Now Chantel was travelling on a flight with the same number, and he had heard that song three times in very strange circumstances. Haydn had always been cynical about the idea of premonitions, but could not explain what had happened in the past few days. He would have to call Chantel and warn her; but how? How could he do it without sounding crazy on the one hand, or like a heel on the other, if he put her visit off? Anyway, what about all the other passengers? He would have to call the airline to warn them first.

The Stateside Airlines customer services desk told Haydn, firmly but politely, that all their planes underwent regular checks. He kept trying, but realised that he was getting nowhere. He slammed down the phone. Now for Chantel; if he couldn't stop the plane, the least he could do would be to warn her.

"You did *what*? Are you crazy? What did they say?" Chantel did not believe a word. She thought that he was giving her the brush-off.

"Listen to me. You're in danger. That plane is going to go down."

"And you know this because some faulty electrical equipment told you so!"

"Chantel, I'm serious. You have to listen to me… please."

"Forget it, Haydn. All you had to say was that you didn't really want me to come. At least that would have been honest. Guess I'll just go visit my aunt instead, at least *she'll* be pleased to see me!"

She was gone and the line went dead. Haydn cursed; there had to be some way of stopping that flight, but short of taking a trip down to Nashville himself – a journey that would take over seven hours - he didn't know what else to do. Maybe if he made enough fuss in person they'd have to listen to him – he couldn't just let all those people die. That was it, the only solution; he could get there in time for the flight to be delayed, and then everyone would thank him. Chantel would see that he had been right and they'd be happy again.

According to Stateside Airlines' schedule, flight 1203 was due for takeoff at 6.30pm Central Time and Haydn used the excuse of a worsening cold to travel down to Tennessee. He was on the outskirts of the city when his Ford blew a gasket and ground to a halt some five miles short of the airport. A cab was now his only alternative, and it seemed an age before it showed up. Diving into the back, he gave the driver the destination and told him to step on it.

Pre-flight checks for the departure to Chicago O'Hare were well advanced, and passengers had commenced boarding the plane. All would be completed within fifteen minutes and the airliner would commence its approach to the end of the runway. Technical Supervisor Rod Brewer was still scratching his head as the work sheets were handed back to him by the maintenance crew.

"Darnedest thing!" he said to Charlie Mason, the last of the crew. "Anyone get the name of that kid who called this in?"

"Nope." Charlie spat out the taste of the aviation fuel. "Guess they just thought he was some kinda crank."

Brewer overlooked nothing, and the call from Haydn had been so prolonged and intense that the Customer Services Supervisor had mentioned it in passing when their paths crossed during a break. She had treated it as a joke, but he was more cautious. Looking up the logs for the plane in question, he noticed that it was falling due for routine inspection in a couple of days anyway.

He took it out of service and substituted another aircraft. Now flight 1203 would go ahead as planned. The ruptured fuel line had been barely detectible but, when pressure tested, had blown apart in Charlie's face, covering him with the liquid. Had that occurred while the flight was in progress there'd be no way of telling what would have happened.

With all passengers now on board, the plane taxied to its position at the end of the runway to await clearance from the tower. At that precise moment Haydn was approaching the airport in the taxi he had summoned when his own car unexpectedly ground to a halt. The tyre blowout took the speeding cab clear across three lanes of freeway into the path of an oncoming semi. With no room for manoeuvre, the two vehicles collided head on and the taxi was sent spinning off to the right into more traffic. It was a scene of utter carnage. Emergency vehicles cleared two dozen bodies from the scene, including those of Haydn and the cab driver.

The two veteran Nashville cops directing traffic at the scene shook their heads at the devastation as they waved rubber-necking drivers away from the pile up. They had become hardened to the sight, having seen it all many times before, and a certain dark humour sometimes alleviated the gloom.

"Would'ya look at that?"

"What?"

"Cab number. Ain't that the darnedest?"

"Whadd'ya mean Bob? You still taking them pills?"

"No stoopid, look at the cab number. Whaddn't that the number on that old Everlys' song? You know...*Ebony Eyes*?"

There, upside down, and almost obliterated by the force of the collision, was the ID number of the Nashville City Cab – 1203.

Stateside Airlines flight twelve oh three landed later that day at O'Hare on time and in complete safety.

Grapes and Wrath

Linda Bennett stood at the open double doors of the French windows which looked out across the perfectly manicured lawn, and down to the stream which formed the southern border of the ample property. She and Steve had lived at *The Pastures* all their married life, but it had been far from an easy existence. Daddy had bought the place as a wedding gift, and a trust fund set up in her name provided all the income the two of them needed without Steve having to lift a finger... and he didn't. That had been over thirty years ago, and despite being offered a position within the stockbrokerage firm which her father, Martin, had formed, Steve showed no inclination to take responsibility for earning a crust. Not that they needed the money, but it would have been nice for him to have some interest outside the home and those blasted vines of his.

They had been on a trip to France when he had the notion of bringing some back to set up his own vineyard. The Chardonnay grape was his favourite, and the plants were duly purchased and replanted in suitably treated soil on the southern slopes of the grounds. From that point on, all his waking hours were spent in tending and feeding them. Linda wouldn't have minded too much, but it was like trying to compete with a mistress, except that with this one you couldn't slap her around the face and tell her just what you thought. No; all she could do was watch, with increasing frustration, as he cosseted and cajoled the things into growth and output.

"Steve!" she called across the lawn. "Dinner's ready." She knew from experience that it was a forlorn hope.

He turned, shaded his eyes as if to ascertain who had called his name, raised one hand in acknowledgement and shook his head. It was the same every day. Up before her, out in the grounds all day, and up to bed when she was already asleep. She had even begun to doubt her own attractiveness, but standing before the full-length mirror after her bath last night, she could not understand his lack of interest. For a woman in her mid fifties, the reflection looking back could have been that of a woman fifteen years her junior, and more than one set of admiring glances had come her way at the summer fêtes which were the custom in the county. The skin was firm and, but for the tell-tale lines around her neck, she was a perfect specimen... in her own opinion at least.

With one more glance down the garden she snorted in indignation, turned on her heel, and went to the dining room. After an unsatisfying meal, Linda picked up her bag and light summer jacket and headed off for The Paddock, a country pub frequented by the circles of ladies of similar interests to her. Jenny was always good for a moan, and had strong opinions on men like Steve.

"You sure he hasn't got a bit of fluff stashed away somewhere, darling?" She drew lazily on the cigarette in the ivory holder, and blew out a steady stream in the direction of an open window.

"Not a chance! He's too lazy even for that. Perish the thought that he would have to make effort of any kind." They both laughed at the thought. "Anyway, the exercise would probably kill him."

"Shame he couldn't have an accident of some kind," she mused. "Got him insured for enough?"

"Don't need the dosh dear, but an accident sounds promising." She considered it, but then shook her head. "I'd never get away with arranging anything like that, but the thought was nice."

The conversation proceeded in a similar vein throughout two hours, and a steady intake of white wine. When they parted for the day, Linda was left with another evening alone to look forward to. It was a further hour and a half before she made any attempt to discover the whereabouts of her errant husband and, stepping out onto the patio overlooking the grounds, was surprised to find that Steve was nowhere to be seen. It was getting late and time for locking the doors, and despite her annoyance she was not prepared to leave him out there all night. She went down the path towards the vines – he was probably crouched somewhere amongst them; the poor little darlings!

Search as she may there was no Steve to be seen, and it was not until she made her way around the bottom border of the property that she found him. The greenhouses were located some distance from the vineyard, and much of the equipment was kept in an old grain store which stood on a set of broad wooden stilts. Steve was lying at the bottom of a large ladder from which he had clearly fallen whilst she was out. His eyes were open, but lack of movement obviously meant that he had suffered some kind of paralysing injury to his back, or neck, or even both. Instincts took over and she began running back to the house to summon medical help. Stopping halfway through the journey she turned around. What was it that Jenny had said? Shame that he couldn't have an accident? This was manna from heaven; she retraced her steps.

Steve lay where Linda had found him, the look on his face clearly anticipating salvation from his misery. He couldn't speak, and rolled his eyes as if to plead for help. She turned to the open area beneath the grain store and dragged out a small ladder. He looked at her in puzzlement, and then horror as the excruciating pain of movement hit his brain. Clearly not all sense of feeling had been cut off, and she smiled sweetly at him as he came to rest across the rungs. It was now getting quite dark, and with no-one else on the property what she was about to do would go completely unnoticed. Dragging the ladder all the way across to where the vines were growing, she returned to the store for a garden spade. Steve's eyes almost shot out of his head when she moved him into the first space between the rows and started to dig.

For a relatively slight figure (she had always kept herself fit) the loose and well-drained soil presented very little in the way of a problem as she worked her way lower and lower. At around three feet she stopped, climbed out of the hole, and very deliberately rolled him in. The job was completed in just less than two hours; by the time the ground had been compressed and any surplus earth redistributed amongst the rest of the vineyard, there wasn't a trace of any unusual activity at that end of the garden. Now all she had to do was cook up some story to cover his disappearance. His car would have to go in order to make the explanation seem plausible, and taking it down to the local reservoir she released the handbrake and watched as it disappeared beneath the deep, murky waters. Dusting away the tyre tracks with a loose piece of brushwood, she returned on foot to the house to complete the deception.

Having put away all the tools used in the act, she showered and changed, poured herself a stiff whisky, and sat down to write herself a 'farewell' letter. Oh, but it was good! She'd been forging his signature for years, and concocting something like this was child's play. Reading it back at the end, she could not have been more emotional than if he had actually been the author. It explained that he'd left her for a woman up north whom he had met in France. They had kept secretly in touch since their return, and he no longer felt the need to remain with someone whom he had never loved. Sealing the note and reopening it five minutes later, she rang Jenny and explained, through a flood of tears, what Steve had done. Naturally, her friend was round in an instant, if only to bask in the latest gossip which she would be able to circulate around the rest of the girls. Having persuaded Linda that, despite the tears, she was far better off without the unmitigated cad, she took her fill of the free alcohol and went home at an appropriate time.

Linda decided not to report Steve missing, using the letter if anyone asked as to his whereabouts. He had no male friends in the area, so no-one really missed him. She took on a gardener to look after the grounds, a nice young man, tanned and muscular with a twinkle in his eye. They got along famously at first and then, after a suitably discreet time, they got along in a much more intimate way. The talk in the village was how well she was looking now that grumpy old Steve was gone, and the more knowing amongst the sisterhood cast a few sly comments about the company which she was now keeping.

It was on a hot and sultry summer evening in late August, a year after the disappearance of Steve, that Linda was standing by the stream just beyond the vines, admiring the view and feeding a pair of swans which had taken up residence. A rustling sound from behind made her jump as it cut through the perfect stillness of the scene. Anticipating the arms of her gardener she turned, smiling sweetly.

"Oh. What the…?"

Those were the last words that she uttered as the noose looped around her neck and tightened. Grasping at her throat for some relief from the constricting pressure on her windpipe, she was soon on her knees as her head began to throb with pain. With one last pull, the garrotte snapped her neck and she fell, lifeless, to the ground. The rustling sound moved away as the killer retreated and left the immediate area.

Jenny became concerned when repeated phone calls went unanswered, and although Linda's new lover was the talk of the district, it was unusual for her to abandon friends in such a way. She got in her car and drove the short distance over to The Pastures to seek her out. The front door was locked, but with a new gardener that was understandable if they spent all their time around the back of the property. She smiled as she made her way around the gardens, and stood at the top looking down to the stream. At first, she thought that her friend had merely taken a picnic down to the vines and fallen asleep in the sunshine, but as she got closer a more sinister scene revealed itself. The scream sent a shower of rooks out of the oak trees on the other side of the waterway, and she ran to the patio doors at the back of the house. Finding them wide open she rushed inside and called for help.

The police and forensics teams could make no sense of what they found. Clearly, Linda had been strangled but no weapon was to be seen. More gruesomely, her entire body bore the look of a mummy. Her skin was completely without moisture, and the pathologist could find no trace of any blood either inside or outside the corpse. Her face was frozen in one final, terrifying, scream. With the gardener nowhere around, he became the prime suspect but, despite exhaustive enquiries, he was never found. Eventually the case was consigned to the mountain of those labelled as 'open' and gathered dust in the local police files.

New owners moved into The Pastures the following spring and were delighted to discover the now fast-maturing vines at the bottom of the property. Their delight turned to rapture when the first grapes appeared. Tight, boxing glove groups, hanging heavily downwards in large bunches. They were the reddest grapes anyone in the locality had ever seen, and the taste was absolutely sublime.

The vines basked peacefully in the hot sun of that record-breaking year. Feeding from the nutrients of old Steve had given them a colour and sentience beyond their natural chemical make up, and an awareness of the surroundings which had enabled the taking of Linda Bennett. They would, of course, require further sustenance of a similar nature eventually, but by the size of the new family that would not present a problem when the time arose.

Engine Trouble

Or

Custard's Last Stand at the Battle of the Small Brass Trumpet

The problems with the engines had been around for some years, so it didn't really come as anything like a surprise when President University Grant received an urgent telegram from his deputy, Doodley Wilson. Wilson had indicated that the Steams had been gathering force under their new leader, Load-Of-Old-Bull, and were preparing for a showdown. This was a new development, as the engines in general had tended not to co-operate with each other, choosing instead to operate in a hierarchy with the Tractions at the top.

For many years this had worked in Grant's favour, and he had been able to operate a system of divide, multiply, add and subtract which confused the devil out of the engines as they had neither fingers nor toes to count with, and were therefore unable to understand what on earth he was up to. Now that they had formed their own armies he was faced with a serious problem. These armies came equipped with handies, each with four fingies and a thumbie; also, a recent delivery of leggies and feeties (each with five toesies) had caused a considerable shift in the balance of power.

Load-Of-Old-Bull had held a meeting with the elders of the other engineering sheds. There were the Tractions, the Railways, the Pumps, the Beams, and also a number of other smaller groups of equipment. He would have to keep his eye on the unrulier elements among the fraternity, and these were led by the truculent, unpredictable, Clothes-Horse and his brother Buggered-If-I-Care. There had already been one skirmish in the laundry room when Buggered-If-I-Care took exception to a comment made by Trouser-

Press, leader of the Steam Room Plant, and this kind of diversion could not possibly work in the Steams' favour.

There were several options available to University Grant, but all of them carried risks. He could negotiate a peace with the Tractions, as the largest group, and hope to split the opposition down their traditional tribal lines, but this may polarise the other engines into their own shed. He could sit the problem out and defy them all, relying on public opinion to carry him to victory on a wave of 'anti-union valve' feeling. This was a long shot, since the incident at Wounded Ankle when a member of the public was stepped on by Clothes-Horse (he was wearing his steel shoes at the time) escaping from a group of pursuing engineering inspectors sent in by Grant. No, the sensible thing was to send for his best General, Engineer Rhubarb Custard.

Custard had served Grant, and those before him, bravely and loyally since his appointment fifteen years ago. Prior to that time, he had been a Captain, and a Major, in the peanut industry rising to the rank of Kernel, before Grant's head-hunters had located him. He knew that he should have used recruiting agencies, but a trip to South America had sold him on the skills of the natives, and he imported a team of specialists for the work.

Rhubarb Custard, or Ruby to his colleagues, was a known and fearless engine driver. He had driven them all in his time and Load-Of-Old-Bull had crossed swords with him in the past. None of the previous encounters had resulted in success for the engines, and the closest they had come had been a goalless draw which they had lost on penalties after extra time two years earlier. He arrived at Grant's office punctually, carrying with him the design specifications of all the main working parts in Load-Of-Old-Bull's group of Steams.

He also had with him his Scottish nephew, Tart'n Custard, a promising young fitter and son of Rhubarb's brother, C'wardy, who was currently working as chief inspector in the pudding industry. Tart'n was learning the ropes, chains, pulleys, and other lifting equipment under the eagle eye of Rhubarb's assistant, Falcon – a noted bruiser with a penchant for winging it. Grant offered them seats, but Rhubarb declined as he said that he had all the furniture he needed at home. The President asked them to take a turn around the grounds instead, but as Tart'n was allergic to seabirds of any kind they decided to hold their meeting in the library. The chairs here were not of a kind which Mrs Custard had in their lounge, so Rhubarb sat down.

Grant told them that IT was serious, but Rhubarb reassured him that a qualification in computer networking which he gained at the Open University would be all that was needed in the current crisis. The President gave him a worried frown – Rhubarb took it and put it in his pocket for later use (you never knew when one would come in handy). He updated the two of them with the latest news gathered by his deputy "Fingers" Wilson, cousin to Doodley and a noted pianist, who had worked undercover in the Steams' nightclubs. Rhubarb gave him a knowing glance (not as valuable as a worried frown, but the exchange rate did fluctuate on a daily basis). Grant thanked him and said he would smoke it later.

Getting close to the Steams would not be easy. He had tried it once and had gotten his fingers burned, necessitating several days in hospital – still, that nurse in the white starched uniform was nice. Load-Of-Old-Bull was not one to be trifled with, even if you *were* using packet mixes, and some special equipment would be needed to bring him and his army of followers to heel. Incidentally, he thought, why are they called followers? Since Load-Of-Old-Bull never led the way into a fight, how could they possibly follow him? Perhaps this was another one of the old devil's tricks that he needed to watch out for.

Grant smiled a knowing smile – he always did that when he knew something you didn't. Still, it wouldn't be a knowing one if you already knew, and that would make you more knowledgeable, or at least as knowing, as him, and there would be no point to it then. He had, he said, a secret weapon. A weapon so cunning in its secrecy that even Grant himself was not really sure where he had put it and would have to look in his safe for the note he had written telling him the secret location. Now, if he could only remember the combination to the safe. Ah yes, here it was on a piece of paper in the rim of his hat.

The munitions boffins had come up with a revolutionary new gun. It was called the Windcheater Rifle and it was a multi-loading, semi-automatic, with full disaster recovery software as standard. It had a range of at least ten feet and came with a full money-back guarantee. There would be enough of them to fully equip Custard and his team, and all they had to do was sign on the dotted line because all breakages would have to be paid for. Custard cocked his head and Grant ducked for cover not knowing whether it would go off. Getting up off the floor, he instructed Rhubarb and Tart'n to gather the weapons and rid him of this accursed plot.

Collecting his thoughts, Custard proceeded to the armoury. He didn't mind them wandering off on their own, but they refused to take their watches with them, and were always late back. The Quartermaster was out to lunch, so his deputy, the Eighthmaster, issued them with the rifles. Custard then wrote the customary insulting limerick to Load-Of-Old-Bull, telling him and his army to meet them outside at five o'clock for a right old punch up, and went home for a cup of tea.

The Steams turned up right on cue, but the pool players told them to bugger off and find somewhere else to play. Moving off in a huff, they made their way outside – it was a big huff, it had to be as there were so many of them. Custard had set up an ambush and was ready for them when they turned the corner by The Small Brass Trumpet, a pub frequented by distressed musicians. It was annihilation and savagery at its worst. The new rifles had been armed with heat seeking oil pellets, and every one of them found a target. There was nothing the Steams could do – their weapons, crafted for close combat, were utterly useless. They slipped and slid to defeat, and it was all over by half time.

Grant was delighted with the day's events and promoted Custard to Commander of his personal guard. In this role he followed an illustrious list of names including General Disaster and Major Jump. The final conflict against the Steams went down in history as one of the greatest military victories ever recorded. "The Battle of The Small Brass Trumpet" would forever be remembered as the day when Custard truly got his just desserts.

I Am

I am… here, where I have been every night for the past week. Unseen, I maintain my vigil; unmoving, I remain completely invisible to the naked eye. They have no idea as to my location, and the natural foliage provides me with the cover I need for the task at hand. They, on the other hand, are open to my scrutiny at all times, and I see every aspect of their daily routine as it unfolds before me. This will assist in the final stages before I take the action upon which I have decided.

I am… watching. Patience is the key, and just one slip will almost certainly result in the failure of my plan. Patience is something which has always been second nature to me, and victims too many to name would testify to that…. if only they were still alive to do so.

I am… waiting. Waiting for the perfect moment and biding my time until I have them all just where I want them. Nothing precipitate will be allowed; I have taken too much care for everything to be wasted in one moment of utter madness. No, this is not something that must be rushed.

I am… a killer, a cold-hearted assassin, devoid of all emotion save that to please myself. I have always fulfilled my needs in this way, and my skills have been honed to perfection through years of practice. I am the supreme predator; I do not need to kill but do so nonetheless. It has always been so. Nothing is too small to be outside my remit, and the night vision equipment gives me eyes where they cannot see. I find this… amusing.

I am… coming. They do not know when or where I will make my move, but make it I will. It will be slowly as always; care and precision are my watchwords, and the final delivery will be made with a consummate ease and economy of movement. They will be completely unaware of the direction from which I will launch my move.

What was that? Unexpected movement! A figure at the back door – framed dark against the back lighting provided by the fluorescent tubing on the ceiling. He stands looking out into the gloom, but I am too far away for him to detect anything. Now another figure; her this time. Asking, 'anything wrong?' He shakes his head and they both return inside. High powered audio equipment gives me an added edge.

Too close for comfort there, and the slightest movement would have betrayed my position. More waiting and watching. Lights going out across the ground floor signal a likely opportunity, and the chatter of voices from the first storey confirms my thoughts.

I am… moving now. Slowly, carefully, over the fence at the bottom of the garden area and into the perimeter. Stop. Look around and crouch out of sight as the dog from next door comes out for a last-minute visit. Downwind of it I will be undetectable even to its powerful sense of smell. It's gone now, and I am once more alone in the blackness.

An open window. People such as they never learn, and it will just serve to make the entire job so much easier. It's small but perfect for my needs, and I will be inside without making a sound. Now is the time, there will be no better opportunity and I will leave no clue as to my presence. Carefully now… push against the pane… it swings inwards, and pressing with a shoulder has me half way through without a scratch. Just one more twist and I am inside and then… oh no!

The pane bangs shut behind me, and the sound is like a firework going off. Suddenly there is movement upstairs and the sound of feet descending towards my position. I turn… no! The escape route is closed by the non-return catch. I struggle with the mechanism, desperate to escape before… too late.

"George! You naughty boy! Where on earth have you been? Come on, you're wet through. Now, where did I put that old towel?"

I am… Georgius Maximus Decimus Meridius, general of the ninth legion, trusted soldier and close ally to Marcus Aurelius, Caesar of Rome and ruler of the known world.

Actually, no I'm not; I'm just a cat with a big ego. Bugger this for a lark, where's my dinner? Don't you know how cold it is sat there at the bottom of that garden under the hydrangea? You should be prosecuted for letting a poor defenceless thing like me stay out all night in the freezing cold. I'm off to bed now... lights please! Crikey, what does it take to get some peace and quiet around here?

In the Nick of Time

Nick was bored. In fact, Nick was bored and unemployed. Worse than that, he was bored, unemployed, and short of cash. It had been such a long time since he had what might be called a regular job that sitting all day doing nothing had become second nature. He had a vague recollection of a time when he was younger where he had a really cushy number. You know what it's like though - the boss is away and everybody takes liberties but, unfortunately, he went one step too far. The guy came back early and caught him lording it over the rest of the staff, sitting in the big chair, dishing out orders to all and sundry and generally behaving as though he owned the place. It wouldn't have been too bad if that secretary, PA, or whatever she chose to call herself, hadn't chipped in and told the top man what he had been up to for the entire period. What was her name? Angela, Angel, or something or other; although he had used the word 'she', Nick wasn't entirely sure that the terminology was correct – you never quite knew with some people, and he had drawn the line at trying it on.

He had heard on the grapevine that there might be a job working for an old man down by the river. He had a boatyard or something similar, and was looking for someone to help with a rush job for an important client. Nothing ventured, nothing gained: he wandered off down to the place to see for himself. As soon as he got there he could understand why the guy was struggling. There was timber all over the place, and the half-finished hull of a large sailing vessel loomed up at least thirty feet above him. The old man came up as soon as Nick walked into the yard, and apart from three other younger men there was no-one else around.

"You must be John from the agency; so good to see you. Come on in and I'll explain what needs to be done."

The man introduced himself as Mr Adam and pointed out his three sons busily cutting, planning, and fitting sections of timber to the slowly-forming hull.

"No, my name's Nick, and I've just called on the off-chance of some work. Don't know anything about any agency."

"Blast! They've let me down again. That's the last time I use them – come along and I'll tell you what needs to be done and we'll go from there if you're interested."

Well, as he had nothing better to do, Nick reasoned that he might as well give it a go. He could see at a glance that the whole place was in serious need of reorganisation. It wasn't just the timber that was all over the place, but the three sons were constantly getting in each other's way as they searched for materials and tools. He managed to talk Mr Adam into giving him a couple of days to sort out the work routines and material locations, and drew up a quick plan of the yard to illustrate the point. Although initially hesitant due to the tight timescale of the job, which was already two weeks behind schedule, the boss slowly realised that Nick's plan would speed things up considerably. They could be back on schedule with the new routines if only he could get his hands on some reliable help.

Nick assured him that this would not be a problem. Having been around the block a few times, he had got to know a few people and could call in a few favours which were due. He disappeared for the rest of the day leaving the four men to carry out the reorganisation of the yard. When he returned close on tea time, it was to break the news that a dozen men would be there first thing in the morning, ready and willing to help. The other four were, understandably, sceptical of promises made by a newcomer in an area where they had been let down badly in the past, but come the morning they were in for a surprise. Not only were the promised helpers there, but all came ready kitted out with all the necessary clothing and tools. Mr Adam was initially delighted, and even more impressed when it appeared that every one of them had been briefed on their roles and responsibilities. When questioned, Nick merely explained that it seemed the correct thing to do, but that if he had overstepped the mark he was sorry.

The four family members made no comment at the time but had to admit at the end of the first day that real improvements had been made to the work flow, and that the job schedule would be back on time very shortly. Mr Adam was the only one with any reservations, but said that he preferred to wait until the following morning before voicing any final opinion. Suffice it to say that all extra hands turned up the next day, and for each one thereafter until the job was finished. Work continued apace, and Nick was given the responsibility of managing the suppliers and their deliveries to ensure that the yard did not return to the chaotic state of a few weeks earlier. The only thing which niggled away at the back of the boss's mind was the unquestioning obedience of the new hands to every instruction which Nick gave them.

There was no attempt to interfere with whatever was being done by Mr Adam or his three sons, but the extra workers appeared to jump whenever Nick spoke to them. It was something akin to fear but not quite that and, try as he might, the boatyard owner just couldn't seem to put his finger on it. The original job had been ordered by the client with a delivery date of six months, and although initially getting off to a good start, had slipped badly behind schedule by the time Nick arrived. By the end of his third week in charge of the additional labour force, they were three days ahead, and were working from dawn to dusk. Mr Adam asked Nick if he was not pushing the new men too hard, but when the reply came that this was the kind of work which they were accustomed to, he let the matter drop. Anyway, said Nick, the alternative for all of them didn't really bear thinking about, and with that he packed up for the day and left the yard.

By the end of the fifth month, the entire superstructure of the vessel had been completed; the masts and rigging were in place, the steering mechanism had been fitted and tested, and the sails, newly delivered, were being installed. There only remained the matter of making the vessel watertight and seaworthy, and that was scheduled to take place during the coming weekend. If Mr Adam had any reservations about Nick, they had all but disappeared until he witnessed an incident between him and one of the extra hands. He had not been close enough to overhear the conversation, but by the sound of their voices, and the manner in which hands and arms were being waved about, there was a serious dispute in progress. What he saw next shocked him. Without raising so much as a finger, a punch appeared to have been delivered to the side of the head of the man arguing with Nick. He reeled backwards and fell against a bench. Reaching behind him, he picked up a hammer and stepped forward to deliver a blow. The hammer never moved, and the entire length of the man's arm appeared to be frozen in position. At a click of Nick's fingers there was a loud 'crack', and the man fell clutching his right arm, which appeared to have broken in at least one place. Nick picked him up, said something very quietly, and the man left the yard.

It was then that Nick saw the boss and came over to him. Mr Adam's eyesight was not what it once had been, and the new manager convinced him that he had merely witnessed a technical discussion during which one of the workmen had stumbled and broken his arm in the fall. He had been sent to the local hospital for medical attention. Mr Adam was unconvinced, but since there had been no other witnesses, and the work was nearly finished, he reluctantly let the matter go. The job was nearing its final phase when Nick came into the yard to inform the four family members that since they could now finish the job on time, he would be settling up with the extra hands and be on his way. As no amount of pleading could persuade him to change his mind, they shook hands and he departed. The day of the meeting with the client arrived, and Mr Adam welcomed him to the yard for the final inspection of the boat. He was a tall man of indeterminate age, with long white hair and a full beard. He smiled continually, making broad sweeping gestures in the direction of the vessel to illustrate his pleasure that the work had been finished on time. After receiving assurances that the craft was sealed and seaworthy, they retired to the office to finalise the paperwork. Mr Adam presented all the work schedules and technical specifications as requested by the client, who peered intently at the detailed costing reports before stopping abruptly at the entry detailing 'Extra Labour'.

"What is this? I did not authorise the charging of any extra costs for completion on time."

"That is not a cost, sir. If you check the final total you will see that it is exactly as per my original estimate. There are no extras."

"Then how do you explain the completion of the boat now, when I know that you were a long way behind schedule?"

"Nick."

"Who is Nick?"

Mr Adam went on to explain the fortuitous appearance of his temporary yard manager, and his unfathomable authority over the men whom he brought to the place. The client smiled a wry, knowing smile and began to laugh. It was a great, booming laugh which threatened to shake the office to its foundations.

"I wondered how long it would be before he tried to get back into my good books. He must have been watching you, knowing that you were working for me. If all goes to plan he will have his work cut out for him in about forty days."

"You mean sod him, Lord?"

"Yes, and Gomorrah, Noah, my friend. The Devil was in the detail this time and I don't think we've heard the last of him. Don't forget the animals; two of each you know, two of each?"

Last Christmas

Christmas was going to come early this year, and the fact that they were moving only served to increase the excitement for their three children beyond the normal levels. They had been given three weeks by the agent to pack up all their belongings, and there had been an enormous amount of work to do to make the deadline. Ben and Julie Brown had been married for eleven years and had three children; Jason (eight years old and self-appointed leader of the second tier in their family), Polly who was six, and little Elizabeth at four and the apple of her daddy's eye. They had been living in the large five-bedroom house (Elizabeth called it her mansion) since Ben's mother and father moved out just before Polly's birth. The place had become too big for them, and Ben's family needs, coupled with a financial windfall, had given them the opportunity to downsize to a place more in tune with their requirements. It still left the two senior Browns close enough to dote on the three grandchildren, and the extended family had benefits all round for everyone.

This was no more apparent than with the monumental job of packing up their entire store of belongings accumulated over the past decade and more. That was twenty days ago, and as Ben and Julie now sat waiting with their family for the transport, he mused on the efficiency of his wife who had planned the whole thing like some military operation. She had timetabled everything on a day-by-day basis, giving everyone specific tasks to perform, and these had to be accomplished in a set order so that any delay was minimised. Their double garage had become a kind of staging ground for a variety of cases and boxes, all clearly labelled and cross-referenced to her master checklist which detailed their contents. Nothing was going to go astray, and each of the children had been given their own set of containers with packing lists that they had devised for themselves. This was a masterstroke which kept all of them busy whilst maintaining a level of interest in an otherwise traumatic time.

It had been difficult at the start to know where to begin, and when they showed the children the details of their new home as supplied by the agent, they found the excitement infectious. This had cost them a precious day right at the beginning, and any more delays of a similar nature had the potential for serious consequences with the move. Ben's parents stepped in at this point and took the three grandchildren away for a week whilst he and Julie began to organise. All essentials for the new home were packed up first and stored in the garage, leaving them with only the bare necessities for living out their final days. Ben smiled now at the memory of the five of them sitting on one settee in a lounge almost devoid of any other furniture – they had always been a close family, but this was ridiculous.

That first week without the children present had been largely taken up with sorting through an Aladdin's Cave of memorabilia accumulated over the fifteen years they had known each other, and which would have been almost impossible to achieve in the presence of little helping hands. Even then, the time was punctuated by a series of unplanned interruptions as a photograph album or some document grabbed the attention of one of them. Smiles and tears would be shared as some incident came back through the mists of time to remind either, or both, of moments which would never recur.

"Remember the Skegness trip when Polly threw up ten times on the way?" Ben asked, waving the photographic evidence of his then four-year-old daughter in nothing but vest and underpants.

"Yes, good thing it was warm. We ran out of changes of clothing, and I thought three would be enough. Poor baby. Just look at this one of you – what happened to those trousers?"

"You threw them away and there was nothing wrong with them – well, nothing that a patch or two wouldn't have cured."

By the time of the return of their little horde from the clutches of 'Grammy and Grumpy', all the wheat had been separated from the chaff, and the latter safely disposed of out of the prying eyes of potential rescuers. The following, and increasingly shortening, ten or so days were allocated to the children and their exercises in 'keep' and 'let go'. At the end of this difficult period, when the youngsters had made their decisions, a garage sale was held where all surplus toys and games were sold off at knock down prices to neighbourhood friends. The subsequent barbeque was a final gathering to say their goodbyes to the closest ones, and late that evening the family retired to their beds in preparation for their last Christmas celebration in what had been the only home the children had known.

Ben and Julie were left with four days to organise and carry out their usual month-long Yuletide celebration. Jason, Polly, and Elizabeth had been asking about presents for weeks, and since the onset of the move those questions had become more strident and insistent. Evasiveness had never been one of Ben's higher skills, and he had resorted to the 'ask your mother' tactic, completely unaware that Julie had done the same. Eventually, both had to concede to the opening of presents before the move instead of a disappointing session at their destination which would inevitably have been after the holiday was over. Christmas dinner, even in the presence of grandparents, was a subdued and relatively meagre affair as the date of departure loomed ever closer, and the atmosphere in the household took on a decidedly sombre tone.

"Do we have to leave?" Polly asked, brushing away a tear. It was two days prior to deadline day. "I mean, it's so nice here. What about all my friends? Will I ever see them again?"

"Yes, we do," explained Julie. "Daddy's new job is too far away to go there and come back every day. You'll soon make new friends, and there'll be exciting new places to see. You can always write to your old friends at school, and I'm sure they'll not forget you."

Elizabeth was too young to have similar concerns, and Jason simply took it all in his stride as a great new adventure. Ben found him dressed up as a pirate the day before leaving, sailing his bed on some Caribbean quest for buried treasure, and trying his hardest to walk on one leg. For Polly, it was as though a part of her was being torn away and left behind, and she became quieter as the hours ticked away. Julie did her best to comfort the little girl but, in the end, she was sure that her daughter would get over it.

At last, the final evening arrived, and all hand luggage was accumulated in the now empty lounge. The bulk of their belongings had already been collected, and everyone slept downstairs in sleeping bags. Once the children were asleep, Ben opened the bottle of Dom Perignon which he had been saving for that day, and they sat out on the swing in the back garden where the children had spent so many hours at play. Julie leaned her head on to her husband's shoulder and gazed up into the inky blackness of a cloudless night sky.

"Where did you say it was?" she asked, and Ben scanned the sky, pointing to the constellation of Orion.

"Look just to the right of Orion's belt. You can't actually see the star from here, but that's where we're going."

"Funny, isn't it," she went on, "two thousand years ago we set foot on the Moon for the first time, and now we're off half way across the Galaxy to start all over again. What about your mum and dad, do you think they'll be alright?"

"Alright? Dad can't wait – he's been packing from the start, and Mum will be happy as long as he is."

The human race certainly had come a long way since those first faltering steps in 1969. Even in the first half of the 21st century it was taking eleven months for unmanned probes to reach Mars. Now, in 3969, space travel was as common as getting on a land train was then. In the time it would have taken to get from Birmingham to London they would be on board a hyperspace cruiser beyond Uranus and heading for the hyperspatial jump to their destination. Ben turned and smiled as his wife yawned.

"Come on sleepy; busy day tomorrow."

The following morning was a hive of activity as final hand luggage was packed, and all family members gathered to wait for the hover taxi which was to take them to the Birmingham spaceport. Located in the Aston area of the city, it had been the last large development of space travel facilities in the United Kingdom, and although Ben had seen photographs of the place, the sheer size of it as they made their approach took his breath away. The taxi came to a halt outside the entrance to Terminal twenty-four, and the ticket scanner directed them to their check-in desk. They had all heard of the chaos at airports in the twenty-first century, and Julie joked about the time required for document and ticket verification – a mere fifteen minutes; things had certainly improved considerably in the intervening millennia!

Sets of communication badges with unique transmission wavelengths, one for each of their party, ensured that no-one became separated or got lost on the way to the connecting shuttle. This space taxi would transport them to one of the three giant interstellar liners (*Triton, Andromeda,* and *Hercules*) orbiting just outside the Earth's atmosphere. These were scheduled for departure to Thyreia-3, a terraformed planet beyond Orion, where the relentless advance of humanity would continue throughout the Galaxy. As a skilled engineer, Ben would receive preferential treatment on the new planet which was to become their home, and a comfortable life with a well-paid salary awaited them. His parents would be the beneficiaries of a similar package as part of the family group. They were all directed to their accommodation for the two-day journey, the majority of which would be taken up with preparation for, and disengagement from, a hyperspace jump which would take them almost instantaneously across parsecs of space separating them from their final destination.

The children wanted to go to the observation lounge to watch the departure, and as they took their seats, Polly turned to Julie.

"It's beautiful isn't it, Mummy?" She said pointing to the Earth. "Will we ever see it again?"

"Yes, it is, darling. I don't think Mummy or Daddy will, but you might one day."

The large viewing window seemed to tilt as the space liner soundlessly turned on its axis and moved, slowly at first, and then with gathering momentum, away from the planet of their birth. In a matter of moments, the Moon passed by on their starboard side and Mars came into view. Within an hour they had passed Jupiter with its giant red spot, and by what they had commonly regarded as lunchtime, the vessel was clear of the solar system and preparing for the jump into hyperspace. That preparation would take up most of the remaining day and a half, and would involve the detailed calculations necessary to ensure a safe arrival in the vicinity of Thyreia-3. In the meantime, there were a host of entertainment distractions to pass the time, and Ben found himself at the centre of these with the children as his wife shook her head sadly and retired to one of the restaurants with her in-laws. The jump, when it came, was almost undetectable, revealing itself as a slight contraction of the stomach as if a turbo-elevator had come to a stop.

All transport liners arrived within the same hour, coming to rest within a few million metres of each other as their crews went through their standard checking routines. The *Triton* was the last of the three, and on the bridge First Officer Marsh was checking the computer navigation logs against the standard data for this sector of the Galaxy, when a call came through from Collins, the head of engineering.

"Collins to Marsh."

"Go ahead, Chief."

"Commander. We have some unusual readings from the antimatter fuel inlet relays. I may need to shut them down for a while, but essential systems will not be affected."

"Very well, Mr Collins, keep me informed."

The turbolift doors opened, and Captain Hodges stepped out on to the bridge at the start of the arrival procedures.

"Everything okay, Number One?"

"Yes, apart from a slight problem in engineering. The Chief's on to it now, but he doesn't think it will cause us any problems."

"Commander!" It was Collins and he sounded agitated. "We're losing containment on the antimatter relays. We need to…"

The explosion was sudden and enormous. The antimatter relays failed, spewing out fuel into the main engine core. The combination with normal matter tore the ship apart almost immediately, and seconds later it was as if the *Triton* had never existed. A crew of three hundred, together with a passenger manifest of over four thousand, simply ceased to exist.

From the observation deck of the *Andromeda*, Ben stared out into space in stunned silence. The gentle rocking of the transport vessel was the only clue to what had just happened as the shock wave hit the polarised hull and dissipated. Automatic alert systems kicked in, but had now been cancelled, and more passengers were flooding into the room to see... nothing. Julie came running up with the children.

"Ben, what was that?"

"The *Triton* – it's gone. It just flashed and then disappeared. All those people, one minute there, the next gone."

"Wasn't it the *Triton*...?"

"Yes. Our original tickets put us on board, but when Checking-In discovered the overbooking we were transferred here."

"Oh Ben...!"

There was an additional day's delay in disembarkation whilst investigations were carried out into the incident, but with no physical evidence the conclusion was one of complete systems failure due to causes unknown. Both the remaining sister ships were grounded pending engineering overhauls, but all passengers were allowed to leave for the surface of Thyriea-3 and the start of their new lives. Many had friends and relatives on the *Triton*, and stories of the disaster were passed on from generation to generation.

At a family gathering around an old-fashioned log fire, Jason Brown sat in his armchair with a host of grandchildren at his feet. They were not all his, but as he had acquired the reputation of family story-teller, Polly and Elizabeth had donated their families to the gathering around him. Ben and Julie had lived long and healthy lives on their new home world, and the family traditions which Jason and his sisters were now perpetuating had been carefully laid down over the past sixty years. The children never tired of his stories about Earth, the trek across the stars, and that last Christmas on the planet of his birth.

Layers of Innocence

"Emergency, which service do you require please?" The standard reply to a 999 call rang out with a hollow tone in Molly's ear.

"Ambulance! Quickly! I think I may have killed someone!"

With the emergency service vehicle now on its way, and certain to be accompanied by the local police, Molly Green slumped down into the leather chair from which she had risen only a few short moments before. The still form lying just to the right of the glass coffee table showed no signs of life, and a growing pool of blood was spreading out around the head. The fall which had followed the struggle had been swift and precise across the unforgiving corner of the table's 10-millimetre plate glass surface.

Her mother had always said she was too innocent. Like an onion, she had said Molly was. Peel away one layer only to find another identical one just beneath – '*Layers of Innocence*' she called them, and they ran deep.

It had all begun around six months ago, with the discovery of a card amidst the chaos of her shopping trolley. She had been unloading onto the belt at the Tesco supermarket in Nottingham's Victoria Shopping Centre, when she came across an envelope in her trolley. Standing at the checkout with a queue building up behind her, there was no time to investigate further and she dropped it into her pocket until later. Once outside the shop, further examination revealed it to contain a greeting card with a single 'kiss' mark at the bottom of the inside leaf. Molly smiled and shrugged it off at the time, thinking that another shopper had dropped it into her trolley by mistake. There was no chance of returning it now, and she threw it into the first available waste bin.

At 29, and once more single after the death of her husband, Mark, Molly Green lived alone in one of the newly refurbished warehouses in the Lace Market district of Nottingham city centre; on a clear day the view from the balcony of the River Trent some two miles away was stunning. Theirs had been a fairy tale romance after he swept her off her feet, and although still maintaining contact with all their friends, they were very much the archetypal married couple. They had bought the two-bedroom luxury apartment in late 1999 before the price boom which would have taken the property out of their reach. With Mark working as an architect for one of the city's big firms, and her own position as a senior with Brown Golding accountants, they were easily able to afford the high-rise penthouse section of the block.

Mark's untimely death at the hands of a hit-and-run driver in 2006 left her with an insurance policy payout which meant that she would never worry financially again. With no money worries, her life outside of work took on a simple routine of books, music, and all the other entertainment features which the two of them had built into their retreat. Molly had resigned herself, for the short term at least, to a life of comfortable solitude.

The matter of the card had been completely forgotten until the flowers arrived at her desk at work two weeks later. It was a Tuesday morning, and the reception area hushed noticeably as she entered through the main door. She looked around to see who, walking behind her, could have been responsible for such a respectful silence. There was no-one, and as she turned back to the front desk, it was the smiling face of Emily, the receptionist, which gave her the first clue.

"Morning, Molly. Been on the pull?" Emily was not one for mincing her words, and they had both been at the firm for sufficient time that the comment could be treated in jest.

"Pardon?"

"Take a look inside your office. Fancy not letting us in on it." A knowing wink followed.

Molly made her way through the smiling phalanx of staff lining her route like some guard of honour, to an open door where David

Golding, the senior partner, stood awaiting her. He smiled and stood to one side to reveal the biggest bouquet of flowers which she had ever seen. She stopped in her tracks, transfixed by the myriad of blooms which threatened to overwhelm the surface of her desk.

"Go on, open the card," he said. "We're all dying to know what you've been up to."

Molly's recovery following the tragic death of Mark had been considerably eased by the sympathetic responses from all her colleagues, who had formed a kind of protective shell around her. They were almost like family, and she now felt compelled to share the unexpected occasion with them. Putting down her briefcase, she removed the small envelope from the bouquet and pulled out the card. The message was simple and to the point:

'Please don't make me wait too long.'

It was followed, like the card at the supermarket, by a single kiss, and with everyone watching, Molly could feel the colour rising from her throat to cover the whole of her face. Smiling at the assembled crowd, she made some innocuous remark in an attempt to dispel all the attention, and picked up her files for the start of the day's work. The gathering dispersed, and the moment passed without further comment. David Golding, however, remained briefly, still smiling.

"You alright, Molly? You look a little flushed."

"Yes, yes; fine thank you, David."

"Well, if you need anything, anything at all, you know where I am." With that he left, but Molly's entire focus for the day had completely changed.

That evening, back at the apartment, she mulled over the events of the recent past with a glass of Shiraz and the strains of Beniamino Gigli singing the role of Rodolfo in Puccini's *'La Bohême'*. She now regretted her impulsive action in disposing of the earlier card and was certain that the writing was identical to that of today's gift. It was not until more unexpected items began arriving that she started to consider the possibility that she was the victim of a stalker.

With the withering of the beautiful mass of flowers in the bouquet, there came more expressions of someone's interest in her lonely existence. She became wary of unfamiliar faces and began to react nervously to all but the briefest glance in her direction. When the case of wine arrived at her door the following week, she decided to report her suspicions to the police. The bottles, twelve of them, were of her favourite brand of Shiraz, but Steve Rogers, the detective assigned to her case, did not appear to attribute too much of a threat to her situation.

"Have you noticed anyone following you, or hanging around near your apartment?"

"No, I can't say that I have, but then again who checks?"

"Alright. Has anyone at work been paying more than the usual level of attention?"

"Well, yes, quite a few; but my husband died two years ago, so I suppose they're all just being very kind."

"But have any of them been overly attentive, or has their behaviour changed in any way?"

"Possibly. David Golding, the senior partner." She smiled, "He's a real charmer, but he's like that with everyone. There's also Guy Chambers, one of the junior staff, who's normally got his head in some legal book or other, but recently when I've passed his desk he's stopped whatever it was he was doing. Now I think about it, I got a creepy feeling about that."

"That all?"

"I think so. Look, do you think I'm being paranoid? I mean, there must be a rational answer for this."

The young detective frowned as he closed his notebook and picked up his coat. He drained the coffee which Molly had made for him and stood up to leave.

"Mrs Green, there are some quirky people out there. Not all of them are dangerous, but you shouldn't be expected to tolerate any level of stalking. We'll make very discreet enquiries amongst your work colleagues and, in the meantime, I should take a few days off. Keep your door locked and make sure you have a friend with you when you're out – just in case, you know."

Although not entirely reassured, Molly felt much better for having spoken to the police but rang David Golding to inform him of Steve Rogers' advice. The senior partner was very understanding in his usual smooth and charming way, asking her if there was anything that she needed, as he would be only too happy to bring it along personally.

"No, no, David; that's quite alright. I'll be fine; it's just precautionary at the moment, but thank you anyway."

Now convinced that the call had been a mistake, all her earlier feelings of unease began to resurface. Could David have been the mystery stalker all along? He'd certainly been extremely comforting and sympathetic after Mark's death, and more than attentive to all her requirements at work. No, he was a happily married man with a daughter only three years her junior. Shaking her head and smiling at the ridiculous idea, Molly was nevertheless startled by the ringing of the telephone.

"Molly, it's me, Wendy. I just heard about your stalker. You alright?"

Wendy Gilbert was one of Molly's oldest friends, and they had spent many hours together down the years whilst growing up. Three years apart whilst both pursued university studies served only to strengthen the bond between them, and the air of concern in her voice was unmistakable.

"Oh, hi, Wendy. You startled me, that's all. I'll be fine. I'm taking a week off while the whole thing is sorted out, but if you want to come over this evening we'll have a meal and a bottle together while I tell you all about it."

"Okay, Geoff's away on business for a couple of days, and I was at a loose end anyway. Be there in half an hour."

Wendy and Geoff had been together for five years and he was another of life's charmers, but without the charisma of David Golding. At ease in his company, she had made up a foursome on a number of occasions as Wendy attempted to play Cupid to end her, as she saw it, solitary and lovelorn existence. That she had failed so spectacularly thus far was a source of some amusement for all three of them.

That evening in Wendy's company, and subsequent excursions with both her and Geoff, seemed to take the sting out of the entire situation. It was almost as if a recurring dream had ended, and her daily mood lightened considerably. All was back to normal until one evening as she and Wendy finished the dishes after what had become a regular fortnightly dinner for two in Geoff's absence. Leaving her friend to put away the crockery, Molly returned to the lounge with the remains of the bottle of Shiraz and their two glasses.

Placing the drinks on the table, she flopped down into one of leather chairs, leaned back and closed her eyes. Wendy's arrival in the room had her back on her feet and picking up the glasses which she had filled. She was about to turn around, when the touch of hands caressing her shoulders caused her to drop the items, and she whirled around to face her friend.

"What…?"

"Molly, it's alright, I just wanted to…"

"No! You? Get away from me!"

"Molly, calm down. You don't understand…"

"Yes, I do! It was you all along. Let go of me!"

Grabbing both of Wendy's shoulders, Molly pushed as hard as she could to escape her friend's unwanted attentions as a precursor to making for the door. The shove took Wendy spinning sideways and she lost her footing. The impact with the edge of the coffee table was violent and sickening. The blood stain on its corner told Molly a tale which she would never forget. Coming to rest face up, and with glazed eyes staring at the ceiling, Wendy was quite obviously dead.

Steve Rogers, the young detective who handled the initial enquiry, carried out the formal investigation into the incident. With the circumstance of Molly's stalker still fresh in everyone's mind, the death was deemed to be the result of a tragic accident and she was considered to be free from any blame. No formal charges were brought in the case.

One evening, several weeks after the Wendy's funeral, Molly was at home when she heard a knock on her door. Putting down her book and glass of wine, she went and opened it to see Geoff standing there.

"I've brought something to say thanks for all your help in organising the funeral," he said.

"Come in," Molly said. "I was just enjoying a glass of wine; would you like one? I'll get another glass."

Geoff smiled as he followed her into the room, closing the door behind him.

"You know, Molly," he said, moving towards her, "that was a great favour you did me. Now that Wendy's no longer around we can carry on from where we left off."

"Left off? Left off what, Geoff?"

He pulled her firmly towards him.

"We're going to be fine, Molly, just fine. I'll look after you now. Everyone will understand, and you won't have a single thing to worry about ever again."

Mirror, Mirror

1

Joyce Gallagher stood transfixed. The mirror was just what she had been looking for and now, as if by some divine intervention, there it was - ready, available, and apparently ignored by everyone else. She turned the price ticket over in her fingers and let out an almost inaudible gasp of surprise - £75. The stallholder came over to her after serving another customer and asked if she could help.

"No, thank you, I was just looking. It is a nice mirror though."

"Belonged to my grandmother. She died recently and we're clearing out her stuff. These car boot sales really are a godsend."

Joyce nodded and smiled; vendors at sales would tell any story to offload unwanted belongings, and this one certainly seemed to fit the bill. Nevertheless, she hurried off as calmly as possible to find her husband, Dean. The mirror was simply too good a bargain to miss, and the move to their new home needed some finishing touches. She found him rummaging through a pile of books at a nearby stall, and tugged his arm in her excitement, causing a shower of literature onto the grass.

"Joyce! Watch what you're doing." He turned to his wife, and the look on her face transformed his annoyance.

They had been married for over twenty years, and he had never yet been able to maintain any kind of air of irritation with her when she smiled at him in that way. Picking up the paperbacks she had caused him to scatter on the ground, he handed over the money to a grinning old man and followed the lengthening sleeve of his jumper as Joyce marched off with it across the field.

She stopped some way short of the stall and pointed. The mirror was still there, unsold, unwanted, and shining beautifully in the sunlight as it sent a seductive message to them both. Dean had to admit it looked a real beauty and would fit in very well above the marble fireplace in their new home.

"How much?" He asked in as stern a tone as he could manage in the circumstances. It wasn't often that she set her heart on something.

"Seventy-five, and it looks better the nearer you get. You know sometimes how these things seem alright until you get close up? Well this one's the opposite."

"Offer them fifty and see what the reaction is. You can always haggle from that point."

Joyce suddenly looked worried, as if another buyer might turn up at the last minute and steal the thing away in a bidding war.

"Trust me," he continued. "I do this every day at work. You never pay the price on offer, and you have to be prepared to walk away to get people to listen. Go on, I'll back you up."

Grudgingly strolling over to the stall, she smiled again at the face she had spoken to before. Standing before the mirror with her arms crossed and head first on one side and then on the other, Joyce tried to look as disinterested as possible as the woman stood there staring at her. She picked up the ticket again and screwed up her nose at the price. Pursing her lips, she slowly shook her head, half turning to walk away.

"It's worth every penny, missus."

Joyce turned back in the direction of the voice. She hadn't really noticed until now, but the woman's appearance seemed strangely out of place at a car boot sale. She stood around five feet six in a printed fabric dress and a shawl around her shoulders. Her face had that brown, leathered look which seemed at odds with her otherwise youthful figure. The strange thought popped into Joyce's head that this woman could have been offering her lucky white heather, but it was gone almost as soon as it had occurred to her.

"Oh, I don't know; it seems a little pricey for me." She completed the 180 degree turn and started to head off in Dean's direction.

"Make me an offer then." The words stopped Joyce in her tracks and she turned back to the stall. She looked again at the mirror. Was it possible that it seemed more beautiful than before? Dean had said never to pay the full price.

"Forty." She winced as the words came out - where had she got that from?

"Be serious, missus. Sixty-five." Arms now crossed and businesslike.

"Fifty," Joyce replied. "And that's my last offer."

They stood there for what seemed an age, like gunslingers each waiting for the other to make the first move. Then a smile.

"Go on then. Fifty it is, and I'm cutting my own throat into the bargain."

Dean Gallagher came up at that moment, and as the cash changed hands he steeled himself for the task of conveying the item back to the car. It was heavy, and finely decorated with what looked like, but could not possibly be at that price, gold leaf ornamenting the finer points of the carved frame. Covering it up in the back of their Volvo Estate, they returned to the sale ground in search of any other bargains which lay in wait.

Their new house stood in its own grounds just outside of town. With six bedrooms, an extensive lounge, and a smaller sitting room, Joyce felt that it needed other things along the walls to lighten the emptiness of the building. The mirror was the perfect solution for the sitting room. It had a large Adam style fire surround, and the mantelpiece begged for the type of adornment which the new decoration would provide. Dean was given no choice but to mount the mirror on the wall as soon as they arrived home.

It was, of course, a two-man job, and fortunately their son Mark had not been quick enough to see the danger of becoming involved until it was far too late. With heavy duty rawl plugs now in place, the work of art now hung proudly above the fireplace. The three of them stood back to admire the scene; a flood of light reflected back into the room from the French windows which led out onto the back-garden patio. The entire room seemed to have taken on a golden, rosy, glow and it felt as if the mirror had always been there. Dean and Mark left the room, and as Joyce turned around after picking some magazines up off the sofa, something on the periphery of her vision caught her attention. She turned fully to face the mirror from where the movement appeared to have originated, but as she approached the spell was broken when Dean re-entered bearing coffee and biscuits.

"You alright, Joyce?"

"Mmm, why?"

"You look like you've seen a ghost."

"No, it just seemed that… no, it couldn't have been."

"What?"

"Well, I thought I saw something in the mirror, but it must have been a trick of the light. Probably one of the trees in the garden waving about."

Dean put the tray down and went over to the newly acquired piece of décor. Joyce joined him, but all they could see was what they expected. Accurate reproductions of themselves on the other side of a near perfectly constructed mirror. She frowned and shook her head.

"Sorry, could have sworn… never mind."

They had been sitting out in the garden, taking their afternoon refreshments before preparing for the housewarming party which had been arranged weeks ago in anticipation of the move. It was not to be a large affair, just a few friends around for an evening buffet and some drinks prior to a tour of the newly furnished property. Having finished their tea and cake, Dean collected the crockery and took it all back into the kitchen leaving Joyce to catch up once the chairs had been restacked. She came through the patio doors and locked them behind her. The image in the mirror froze the scream in her throat.

2

Joyce was rooted to the spot, mouth open, but silent, as the sounds would not come. Her eyes were out on stalks, wide in fright as the vision looked, yes looked - it was definitely looking at her - out of the corner of the mirror. Not directly forwards as a reflection would normally behave, but at an angle, as if attempting to attract her attention. It moved, as if sensing something outside the room, and then Joyce heard footsteps approaching. The door opened and Mark strode in. The image in the mirror vanished, and Joyce's son picked up his wallet from the coffee table, turned to his mother, smiled a 'farewell' and left. Still she remained where she stood, and the face did not reappear. Slowly, and with much trepidation, Joyce approached the front of the mirror until she stood directly before it. There was nothing out of the ordinary, and the reflection was her own with the empty room in the background.

Mark had noticed nothing untoward as Joyce suppressed her initial shock at the vision, but now that whatever it was had gone she recovered some of her composure and began to wonder if her imagination had been playing tricks on her. She recalled the oddness of the stallholder's appearance at the car boot sale – maybe her subconscious mind had recalled the events and the mirror had merely caused it to resurface. The more Joyce thought about it the more this seemed to be the likely explanation, but it still could not account for the fact that the face looked directly at her and not into the room; it seemed to know where she was standing and was somehow seeking her out. She shivered; for a warm and humid day she suddenly felt a chill - one which went right to the bone. Leaving the sitting room, she closed the door behind her and wondered whether she dared broach the subject to Dean.

He was busy in the kitchen with the preparation of a variety of sandwiches, pork pies, sausage rolls, and all the other bits and pieces which would smooth the evening along. A glass of red wine was in his hand, and he poured an identical one for Joyce as he saw her enter the room. His initial smile turned to a frown as the look on her face reflected some inner concern.

"Another ghost?"

"You'll think I'm crazy, Dean, but come and have a look at the mirror. There's something wrong and I can't quite make out what it is."

"We can't take it back now, love. It was from a car boot sale after all."

"No, I don't mean that. It's in perfect condition, but, well, oh, I don't really know. You'll have to come into the sitting room for me to explain."

Dean smiled. Joyce was well-known amongst their circle of friends for her idiosyncratic ways at times, and he followed as she led the way. They stood before the mirror and marvelled again at its beauty – had it become a little larger since it had been mounted on the wall? The fireplace certainly seemed the correct size, and the two items were in perfect symmetry with each other.

"So, what's the problem? It seems alright to me."

"I saw a face in it, and before you go into one of those comedy routines of yours, no, it wasn't mine. I know what I look like, thank you very much, and it wasn't me."

She had frozen Dean at the start of his reply, and he was disappointed not to get in a pointed comment at a perfect opportunity.

"What kind of face? I mean was it male, female, ugly, pretty, old, young? What? Did it say anything? Did it make any gesture?"

"It was just a face, and it was looking directly at me over there." She pointed to the patio doors, and for the first time Dean seemed to be taking the matter seriously.

"Okay then, so where is it now?"

"It disappeared when Mark came in, and I don't think he saw it."

"So, you think you saw something when we came in from the patio when you were alone, and again before Mark came in. Are you saying that there's only you can see this thing?"

"Sounds stupid, but that's the way it looks. Okay, I think it was a woman, a youngish woman, and she was trying to say something, but that's when Mark came in and…"

"And she vanished. So, if I go out of the room now do you think she'll come back?"

Joyce began to feel uncomfortable, and despite Dean's obvious attempts to be helpful she didn't want to be in the position of upsetting the upcoming party because of some odd event which could, it had to be said, be merely the result of her imagination.

They let the matter drop and pitched back into the organisation of the evening's food and drink.

Guests began arriving a little after seven, and by eight o'clock the evening was in full swing, leaving the matter of the mirror a fading memory for the time being. George Harper, one of Dean's fishing friends, was known to be a bit of an antiques aficionado. Joyce therefore took him into the sitting room to see the new purchase. When she told him about the deal he almost dropped his glass.

"Fifty quid? With that gold leaf decoration alone it's worth over three hundred, and if it has a known manufacturer's name on the back you could very well add a nought on to the end of that."

They took it down and turned it over. There, in the bottom corner where Joyce had never noticed it, was a small, faded, but quite distinct, stamp bearing the maker's name. George could hardly contain himself.

"That's late 18th century, and they were the top Parisian manufacturers of the time. You're sitting on quite a nest egg there, my dear, and you say you bought it at a car boot sale?"

"Yes, it was quite by chance. I wasn't particularly looking for a mirror."

"Well your gain is someone else's loss. I should get it valued and insured as soon as you can."

He wandered off to refill his glass and plate in that order, leaving Joyce alone in the room and standing before the now much enhanced piece of décor. She had begun to turn away towards the door when the face appeared again. Her surprise was considerably less this time than before, and she stood transfixed as the same image looked out at her from a totally unfamiliar room. It was dark, and she couldn't make out with any clarity what was in the background. The woman in the mirror opened and closed her mouth as she attempted to communicate, but Joyce shook her head and pointed to her ears. The image disappeared but this time the background remained; perhaps she had gone in search of something to write on.

It was whilst Joyce was thus distracted that the young man appeared, startling her. Temporarily losing her balance she made an involuntary movement forwards and steadied herself by placing a hand on the face of the mirror. In an instant the young man's hand matched hers in the reflection, and in a flash of light she was on the other side. At first, she lay exhausted on the floor, not realising what had just taken place, but as her strength returned she got to her feet to see the same face in the reflection, except that this time he was in her lounge. She looked around to find herself in strange surroundings. Apart from the reflection she was alone, but that changed when the young man smiled, waved and then disappeared out of the door. The icy feeling that she was somehow trapped behind the mirror gripped Joyce's stomach; she screamed for help.

The woman came running into the room and stood in amazement at the figure of Joyce now on her own side of the mirror. Looking around she guided Dean's near hysterical wife to a chair and kneeled before her.

"My name is Alison Whatmore. What are you doing here?"

Joyce took a while to regain her composure, such that it was, and explained the situation with the young man and his disappearance into her house. Alison's face gaped in shock.

"That was not supposed to happen. We all agreed that none of us would try to escape alone. The boy you saw was William."

"I don't understand. What on earth is happening here, and how do I get back home?"

"That will not be so easy now that you are here on this side with us."

"Us? What do you mean 'us'? How many of you are there?"

"I'd better pull up a chair and explain a few things. You are going to be here for a long time unless we can work out what to do next."

3

The mirror, she explained, had previously belonged to an old woman in the nineteenth century and that it had been confiscated by the local beadle, a kind of parish constable, when she was imprisoned for non-payment of a debt. This woman had been regarded as something of a quack, able to concoct remedies for a variety of ailments, and some referred to her as a witch. She cursed the beadle and the mirror and condemned them to a kind of living hell where it would be his prison. He disappeared, she was accused of his murder, convicted, and hanged at Tilbury in London. They never found him, and the mirror passed on to a sale with the rest of her belongings. Since that date, the thing seemed to have taken on a life of its own, possibly spurred on by the progressive madness of the now insane and wretched public official.

"So, this has been going on for over a hundred and fifty years?"

"It would seem to be that way, but what you must understand is that time stands still on this side. None of us get any older, but our families age in the normal way. Unless we can get you back to your own time very soon it may be too late."

"Is there a way out then? Why not simply smash the thing?"

"We did consider that, but anything thrown at it from this side just bounces back and we do not understand why."

"What about from the other side? Why not try to get someone out there to smash it?"

"That is what I was trying to do when William stepped in and vanished. He will not return, and no-one on the other side can hear us."

"Why don't I try to get my husband to help? He must see me when he comes into the room if I wait at the mirror."

"We tried that too. It would seem that any transfer or communication is limited to one person each time it changes hands."

"Do you mean that we have to wait for Dean to sell the blasted thing before we have a chance to escape?"

"I'm afraid that is exactly what I mean. It must have something to do with the curse, but the Beadle has lost his mind and we cannot get any intelligible information from him now."

Joyce sat with her head in her hands. Alison told her that there were over twenty people trapped inside the mirror, all captured by touching the surface whilst alone, and that the chances of any of them being reunited with their families were reducing with each passing day. There was nothing left for her to do but wait. Wait for Dean to find that she had gone missing and start a search. That, of course, would prove fruitless but he may, in desperation, get rid of the mirror and give them the chance to break free of its clutches.

Dean did indeed notice Joyce's disappearance very quickly, but with George, as the last person to see her, now in a state of some inebriation, it would be some hours before anything useful could be gleaned from him. The police initially suspected that he had somehow killed Joyce and disposed of the body, but when an extensive search revealed no trace of her, the theory collapsed, and he was released. Once sober, he gave Dean all the information he could remember from his conversation with Joyce about the mirror, but that served more to confuse the issue than to clarify it.

Police attention then focussed upon Dean. Guests during the evening could neither confirm nor deny his presence in their midst at the time of the disappearance, and as a result he had no alibi for the time that Joyce vanished. His story relating to her concerns about the mirror was greeted with disdain by the investigating officer but, like George, he was released due to lack of forensic evidence linking him to the matter. That investigation, however, lasted for a period of six months, and Joyce waited each day with increasing concern both for her husband's health and for the chance to break free. George was the last of the guests that fateful evening to suspend his visits to the house, but on his penultimate call he broached the subject of the mirror – a matter which he had taken pains to keep at the forefront of his mind. Knowing its true value, he could make a pretty penny from a resale through his network of antiques friends, and he was certain that Dean had no idea as to its true worth.

"You know Dean, the way you keep looking at that mirror, I'd get rid of it."

"I hate the blasted thing. All this started when we bought it, and Joyce said that there was something odd right from the start. I just never took her seriously."

"Why don't I take it off your hands? I'll give you over and above what you paid for it. Shall we say a hundred?"

"As far as I'm concerned you can have it."

George insisted on paying the sum offered despite Dean's desperation, and it was in the back of his car and away that same day. Within twenty-four hours it was in the hands of an antique dealer, and George was two thousand pounds richer. Joyce watched all of this with increasing alarm. She had thought to attract George's attention once he had bought the mirror, but as it remained under wraps until it reached the dealer's shop, the opportunity was lost. Now all she could do was wait until a private buyer made an offer for it; there would be no point in causing alarm in the sale room.

It seemed like years had passed, and although many admiring glances were cast in its direction, the mirror remained on the wall in the shop. Another fact restricting all their abilities to escape was, according to Alison, that not only could freedom be achieved only once per purchase, but the purchaser alone was the one who could engineer the breaking out. That in itself could only be achieved when they were alone in the room. Now Joyce understood why neither Dean nor Mark could see the other side of the glass.

The man staring into the mirror and combing his hair was in his mid twenties, handsome, and stood about six feet tall. Joyce stepped up to the glass and watched avidly as a silent pantomime played out on the other side. It was clear that some form of negotiation was taking place between the dealer and a customer whom she could not yet see. The man backed away from the mirror and placed his arm on the shoulder of a young woman who was standing in the middle of the room. She had been concealed by the back of the shopkeeper until now, but as he moved to one side Joyce was able to see her entire form. Her face set, and she stood in stunned silence as her brain fought to come to terms with what she now saw.

Melanie, her daughter, had been a little girl of twelve the last time Joyce had set eyes upon her. She had been away at a friend's during the early part of the evening of the housewarming, and presumably Dean had kept her in the background whilst the police investigation had proceeded. Now here she was, some ten years older, and possibly married to the man combing his hair. It was definitely Melanie; Joyce recognised her from the birthmark on her right arm, and although no sounds could be heard, the mannerisms *were* those of her daughter. She was devastated. Ten years had passed since the evening of her disappearance, and she herself had not aged a day. Having remained unsold during a period of changing decorative preferences, the mirror had been consigned to storage, but following a shop refurbishment it was once more on display

Alison came up to stand beside her.

"What is it, Joyce?" They had become close friends and confidants during the time spent in the mirror's trap.

"My daughter. That's my daughter, and she's haggling a price with the dealer, but I don't know what for. What can we do?"

"Nothing until she, or someone else, buys the mirror. We have to wait and see."

"But she's so close. I can almost touch her."

"There is no point in becoming emotional. You must be patient."

The drama on the other side was coming to a conclusion, but it was not the one that Joyce was hoping for. Melanie, for it was indeed her, cocked her head first to one side and then to the other, pursed her lips and slowly shook her head. Where had Joyce seen that before? Turning to the dealer, she said something unintelligible and started to leave the shop. Motherly desperation almost got the better of Joyce as she raised her fists to beat on the glass, but she turned away instead as tears flooded down her face.

"Wait, she's coming back." Alison waved her arm.

Wiping the tears away, she came back to the frame. Melanie was standing once more before the dealer, and a series of hand gestures told the two on the wrong side of the mirror that a serious bargain was being struck. At the end, there was a shaking of hands and an exchange of cash; all that now remained was to see what it was that had been sold. Nothing happened right away as the dealer retired to a back room, returning only when he had obtained an amount of packing materials. The sheets were large in size, and Joyce could hardly contain herself when the object of her imprisonment was taken down from the wall and packed for transit.

4

That Melanie had not recognised the mirror from her home ten years previously was abundantly clear, and Roger, her husband, indulged her every whim much as Dean had tended to do with Joyce. As the covers came off, those imprisoned in the reflection were treated to the sight of a drawing room straight out of Edwardian England; no surprise, then, that the young couple had chosen the mirror to adorn the place. The only question which remained was how to attract the attention of the buyer without causing the same kind of alarm which started the process ten years earlier. Alison and Joyce spent many hours in earnest discussion, but without a foolproof strategy it was left to the mother to confront her daughter directly and hope for the best.

Days passed without an opportunity as people filed in and out of the room on the other side without leaving Melanie on her own. Denied that privacy, the surface of the mirror would not change from reflective to clear, and although all of those trapped could see events unfolding on the far side, those playing their parts were completely unaware that they were being observed. Those days, Joyce realised, were turning into months in the real-time world where Melanie and her husband lived, and she found it increasingly odd that, during the entire period, no trace of Dean had been seen. She consigned those matters to the back of her mind to concentrate on the more important job of breaking free, and one early summer Sunday morning, as the rest of the household slept, Melanie entered the room in her dressing gown and slippers, carrying the first coffee of the day along with the morning papers.

Joyce's heart leapt at the sight of the lone figure but, cautioned by Alison, held back from immediately approaching the front of the frame. Watching first from a distance, and then approaching slowly, she raised one hand in silent greeting to the daughter whose growing up she had completely missed. Melanie was engrossed in the generous folds of the broadsheets spread across the surface of the coffee table, and her attention was limited to their contents and that of her coffee cup. Nevertheless, the size of the pages and their turning necessitated a raising of her head as the current story moved on from one sheet to another. It was then that the movement at the periphery of her vision grabbed her attention. She looked at the mirror out of the corner of her eye and frowned.

Melanie was not, and never had been, one for the dramatic, choosing to believe that all things had a natural and logical explanation. What she now saw defied all logic but, unlike her mother before her, the reaction was totally different. Instead of a near hysterical scream, she calmly placed aside the newspaper, drained her cup, and slowly walked across the room to the mirror. Standing six feet short of the surface, she stared in amazement at the face she had not seen for ten years. The silent voice on the other side mouthed a single word.

"Melly."

At that point the connection was made. From her early years, Melanie had learned to sign as her grandmother was deaf. Both she and Joyce had excelled at the skill, a fact which drove Dean to distraction when they talked together in his presence. Melanie also knew how to lip read, and the one-word reply brought tears to two sets of identically blue eyes.

"Mummy."

Together they approached the mirror, and each extended a hand to the surface. Joyce felt Alison pull her back, and Melanie recoiled in surprise at her mother's sudden movement.

"No, the instant that you touch, you will both exchange places and the curse will continue. I am sorry, Joyce, but we have to find another way."

Melanie was still standing with her hand almost resting on the mirror and had seen what she had believed to be her mother's sudden retreat. She removed it as Joyce approached once more signing that they could not risk contact in that way. Telling Melanie to lock the room to prevent others entering, she explained the story of the mirror and what had to be done to release those trapped. The daughter's initial consternation dissolved with the possibility of their reunion, and she looked around the room for some heavy object to accomplish the breaking of the spell. That act was to be delayed as the rattling of the door indicated family members surfacing for the day. Quickly 'signing' off, she unlocked the door and the vision in the glass vanished. For Joyce this was a minor disappointment, and she set her mind to the following day when she would surely be able to engineer a solution to the problem.

Roger's appearance at the door could not have come at a worse time for Melanie as she fought to regain control of her now turbulent emotions. She and the rest of the family had long given Joyce up for dead, and the circumstances of her disappearance from the midst of a crowd of friends had been the talk of the area for quite some time. Now, and she was struggling to come to terms with what she had just seen, her mother had reappeared, albeit out of reach, with a message on how to free both her and a multitude of other unfortunates from their prison. Roger's knocking at the door was becoming more insistent.

"Sorry, coming. Hold on a minute." Glancing back at the reflection, she unlocked the door.

"What's going on Mel? You alright?"

"Yes, yes, perfectly alright. Sorry love, I must have flicked the catch by mistake and dropped off with the papers. Coffee?"

The rest of the day passed without further incident, and Roger accepted her lame explanation for the locking of the room. He had, however, noticed an edginess in her demeanour as evening approached and she looked for another opportunity to speak to her mother once more. He asked her again if there was anything wrong, and the words she used were to come back to haunt her in subsequent days.

"It must be the mirror - ugly old thing." She laughed nervously. "I've gone right off it. I'll be glad when it's gone."

5

Roger Hartington loved his wife, Melanie, with an old-fashioned fervour straight out of a black and white movie. He hung on her every word, much to her annoyance at times, and would have died rather than see her distressed. If the mirror was causing her unhappiness it would have to go, much as he liked it himself. Whilst she was out the following morning he duly took it down from the wall, packaged it up, and transported it to the very same emporium from which it had been originally purchased. He did not, of course, obtain the price which they had paid for it, but the shortfall was acceptable compared to the relief which his wife would surely feel when she saw that it had gone. Thus buoyed up by an altruistic feeling, he made his way back home to await the grateful thanks which would come his way. Melanie was there when he arrived, and in a state of considerable agitation.

"Roger, we've been burgled! The mirror's gone! I've checked all around, but it appears to be the only thing that's missing. We must call the police immediately."

"Steady on, Mel. There's no robbery. I took it back to the dealer as you were unhappy with it."

"Unhappy? What on earth gave you that idea?"

"Well, you said so yourself yesterday, remember? You were upset about something and called it ugly and old, and said that you'd be glad when it was gone."

The full realisation of what she had done now hit Melanie like a brick wall, and she slumped down on to the sofa with her head in her hands. Roger was all comfort and compassion but could get nothing out of his wife at first. It was only when the floods of tears had subsided that any sense at all came out of her mouth, and even then he could hardly believe the story which she told him.

They would have to go back once more to the dealer and retrieve the mirror in order to stand any chance of Joyce returning to them, she said. Roger, although still not entirely sure of why he was doing it, put on his coat as his wife headed for the door with their car keys clutched firmly in her hand. The drive took them an age through busy traffic, and the shop was closed for lunch by the time they arrived. There was nothing left to do but to sit and wait.

Joyce and the rest of her fellow prisoners had been standing before their side of the mirror in anticipation of freedom for quite some time, when the covers finally came off the parcel which Roger had so carefully packed. The site which greeted them was not the one for which they had prepared. Alison voiced their concerns amid the stunned silence.

"We're back at the sale room. Something is wrong. Where is your daughter?"

"I... I... I've no idea." Joyce was dumbstruck.

"We must convince her to break the glass somehow, or we'll be trapped forever. We are so close."

None of them had seen Roger remove the mirror and transport it back there, and it was only now that the owner was alone that they could see what was happening. As a new purchaser, he would be able to carry out the task if only they could convince him, but with customers in and out of the shop all the time, the chances were few and far between. Eventually he put on his coat, turned the door sign to 'Closed' and left for lunch.

By the time Melanie and Roger returned to the shop after lunch, the mirror which they had both seen hanging on the left-hand wall was no longer there. Enquiries with the owner revealed that it had been sold immediately after his return and just moments before their arrival. The man sympathised with them and took pity at the edited story which they related concerning the mirror and the object which they said was attached to the back lining. He gave them the name and address of the lady who had bought it, and they set off in hot pursuit.

Arriving at the address on the note given to them by the shop owner, their approach up the gravelled path was halted abruptly by a high-pitched scream emanating from inside the house. Roger's uninvited entry via the front door coincided with the flight of a terrified form travelling in the opposite direction. Their collision elicited a renewed cry from the unfortunate woman, now lying on the floor of the hallway and clutching the sides of her face as she fought to regain control of the situation. Shrinking back from Roger's outstretched hand, her head rocked from side to side as if in denial of what she had just seen, and her entire body was shaking like a leaf in an autumn gale. He pulled back, and she pointed with a waving finger in the direction of the door to the right, which he assumed to be the lounge. One glance inside was enough to confirm that the object of their visit was now hanging on the wall just above the fireplace.

Melanie had been standing at the door whilst the drama unfolded, but now crouched at the woman's side with her arm around a shaking pair of shoulders. Eyes goggling in terror looked up into her own, as brain and mouth struggled to reveal anything of meaning to the rescuers. Roger returned to their side.

"In there, is it?" The question from Melanie was more a statement than anything else, and he nodded. She turned to the woman, now sitting with arms pulled around her legs and pressed tightly up against the hallway wall.

"Mrs Colmore?"

Daphne Colmore stopped shaking, surprised that this stranger knew her name. She looked at the couple, smiling faintly and nervously. A stream of incoherence spilled from her lips as Melanie held up one hand to halt the flow.

"Listen to me. We know what you have seen in the mirror. You aren't crazy and it's not going to harm you, but you must believe what I'm about to say. There are a number of people whose fate is in your hands, and you're going to have to be strong."

Daphne looked with puzzlement into the faces of her rescuers. Surely, they were not going to ask her to go back into that room. She started to shake her head; it was a reflex action triggered by something approaching self-preservation and spurred into a gallop by abject fear.

"No! Don't ask me to go back in there. Please... don't do that."

Melanie and Roger outlined the circumstances of the history of the mirror and the people trapped behind its reflective façade. As purchaser in good faith it was she, and she alone, who would have the power to release Joyce and her friends from their incarceration. However, at the end of the narrative, Daphne was adamant at not returning to the room, and Joyce's fate seemed sealed.

6

Ralph Colmore returned home to find his front door wide open and a strange car blocking the entrance to his drive. His day had started badly at work, and the time spent there had not improved its quality by one iota. Now in need of some peace and quiet, he was faced with an invasion of his privacy by goodness knows who. Slamming the door of his Jaguar XJS he stomped up the driveway and into the hallway where his wife was still crouched against the wall. The scene before him was like something out of a Hitchcock movie, and *The Birds* came to mind. The damage had gone unnoticed until now, but the floor was littered with the broken fragments of a few ornaments which had been scattered by Daphne in her flight

Once appraised of the truth of the situation, however, he calmed down, and whilst sceptical about the story told to him, the look on his wife's face and her confirmation of at least part of the tale made him more amenable.

"So, you see," Melanie continued, "the only way to release those trapped is for the buyer to smash the mirror and break the curse."

She winced inwardly at the Dark Ages logic of witches and witchcraft, but with no more plausible explanation there was nothing left to fall back upon. Colmore stepped into the lounge and glared at the object of his wife's fear. Shaking his head, he returned to the hallway.

"There's nothing there that I can see."

"No, there won't be." Melanie reiterated. "You must understand that your wife bought it, and she is the only one who can see what's in there. My mother is stuck behind that thing, and no-one else but the purchaser can release her."

"Why doesn't she just sell the thing to you, then?"

The idea was brilliant in its simplicity, and with Daphne refusing point blank to have anything more to do with it, Ralph's solution was the only one on the table. Roger had his doubts as to the logic of the proposal, but if it made Melanie happy he would have danced an Irish jig at the same time. Agreeing a price, they shook hands on the deal and an amount of money changed hands between Melanie and Daphne. Taking a deep breath, and not knowing what to expect, Joyce's daughter slowly entered the Colmore's lounge.

The mirror was mounted above a large fireplace housing a pile of logs ready for the evening, and at first there seemed to be nothing in the reflection. However, on a little closer inspection the surroundings on either side of the glass were not a match. With heart now thumping loudly, Melanie crept towards the object of her mother's ensnarement. What if someone else on the other side got there first? Would that then prevent Joyce speaking to her through their signing? In the event, and out of the kind of misty background normally reserved for the sort of horror film which Mark, her brother, had used to scare the daylights out of her as a child, the smiling figure of her mother came forward to Melanie, arms outstretched in tearful supplication.

Daphne Colmore's initial shock at the sight of the unfamiliar face in the mirror was matched by the crushing disappointment subsequently felt by Joyce that her daughter may no longer be able to rescue her. Her attempts to communicate with the mirror's new owner had resulted only in the hysteria she herself felt all those years ago in her own home. That the poor woman was going through hell was beyond doubt, but the overbearing problem of how to become free superseded all other feelings. It seemed an age since Daphne had run silently screaming from the room, and without Alison's calming influence she may not have been ready for Melanie's entrance.

"You have to stay by the mirror," she had said. "Whatever happens it is very important that you somehow persuade that woman to help us."

"What if she doesn't come back? Look how terrified she was."

"You came back, did you not?"

"Yes, but..."

"In that case we have to wait. There is no other choice. Look! The door is opening!"

Amidst the collective holding of the breath of more than twenty trapped souls, a female form stood framed in the doorway. Joyce was unable at first to identify the figure, and assumed that the owner had returned much as she herself had all those years ago. It was only when Melanie approached the centre of the room that they realised who it was. Alison pointed excitedly through the mist and shook Joyce by the arm.

"Your daughter, look! She has returned. She can see you. Go to the frame but whatever you do, do not touch the surface. Tell her to break the glass; it is our only hope of escape. I will make sure that everyone is ready."

With both parties to the drama now in place, Joyce signed the instructions to her daughter, and watched as she picked up a heavy ashtray from the coffee table by the window. With both feet planted firmly before the mirror, and not six feet from its silvery surface, she took a few deep breaths and hurled the object towards the face of her mother. Outside in the hallway, Roger and the Colmores heard the splintering crash of the shattered glass, and the cry of alarm from Melanie as her projectile found its target. With legs weighed down like lead, they moved into the lounge and the source of the noise. Within the room, Melanie had fallen backwards onto the sofa covered in a shower of broken fragments. The mirror frame lay on the floor before the fireplace, its wooden back board now bare and forbidding. A dense, slightly musty fog was spreading out across the thick carpet. Melanie coughed, stood up, and brushed the shards of mirror fragments from her clothing. As she stood facing the now broken remnants of the once beautifully ornate framework, disappointment hit her with the force of a demolition ball.

In the midst of the devastation her mother was nowhere to be seen.

7

"Mummy! Mummy! Look at this! Daddy says I can't possibly wear anything so hideous tonight. You said it would be alright, didn't you?"

Melanie came racing down the stairs and into the lounge, her face red with indignation. Joyce stood in complete silence as she came to terms with events of the past few moments. They had all reeled as the heavy glass object crashed into the far side of the mirror, and she had stepped forward as the figure of Melanie disappeared backwards in the foggy air generated by the explosion of fragments into the Colmores' lounge. She reached out automatically, but the hand of Alison prevented any further movement and the entire scene vanished before her eyes.

Now she was standing in the lounge of her own home all those years ago, with her twelve-year-old daughter before her with arms folded and shoulders hunched in an all too familiar pose. Dean took great delight in winding Melanie up at the drop of a hat and, in this instance, it was clearly something to do with the clothes which she proposed to wear after coming back from her friend's house where she had stayed the night.

"Mummy? Mummy, are you alright?"

"What? Oh yes of course, dear, just thinking. Look, tell your father to stop being a fool and get on with whatever he's doing."

"Okay!" Now smiling sweetly at gaining what she regarded as a major victory, the little minx skipped away towards the door. She turned at the last moment. "Oh, excuse my manners. I'm Melanie and she's my mum. 'Bye."

Joyce frowned, curious at her daughter's parting comment to an area just over her own right shoulder. An uneasy feeling crept down her spine and she turned - turned so very slowly that minutes seemed to have passed by the time she came face to face with none other than Alison. A strangled scream died in her throat, and she sat down involuntarily in a chair as the smiling figure approached.

"But... you're... I mean you can't... it's..."

"Please calm down, Joyce. It is me, I'm here, and I'm real."

"But how...? Everyone else...? Where...?"

"Back with their families and in their own times I would imagine. It would seem that, despite what I believed, everything has stood still whilst you and I have been away."

"But you're here. I thought you were from years back."

"Nineteen fifty-nine was the year I disappeared."

"So, what are you doing here? How will you get back to your family?"

"I won't." Alison snorted. "If you could call it a family."

She went on to explain how her husband had mistreated her throughout the entire length of their marriage, and how his family, with whom they lived, had used her as an unpaid servant for the six years that she had been there. The mirror, for her, had come as a knight in shining armour. The last thing she wished for was a return from whence she had come.

"I think I always knew what would happen if someone did break the curse, and when the opportunity came, I simply held on to your arm. If I am trapped now, it is in your time, and believe me it is preferable to mine."

"What will you do? Things have changed an awful lot in the last fifty years."

"If living with my David taught me just one thing, it was the ability to make my way without any help from anyone else. I certainly would not have been given any assistance by his family. They will have to get along without me. I shall be alright."

"Well you certainly can't go out alone until you've become accustomed to how things work now. I insist that you stay with us for the time being. We'll have to replace those clothes of yours though, and you look to be about my size. Come on, before anyone sees you."

Suitably attired, Alison joined the rest of the evening's gathering at the housewarming and was soon the centre of attention as a stranger in their midst. Joyce took some time out to try to assimilate what had happened during her apparently brief spell of absence. The mirror was certainly gone, and its place above the fire was occupied by a print of Constable's *The Haywain*. She had seen her Melanie happily married and twelve years older and wondered about the Colmores. Dean broke the spell with a sudden entrance from the patio.

"Ah, there you are. This acquaintance of yours is causing quite a stir outside. Like bees round a jam pot they are, and one or two of our single friends have their eyes on her. Where did you meet her?"

"Hmmm? Oh, I was in an antique shop and we bumped into each other. Seemed to hit it off right away, and I asked her over on the off chance. You don't mind, do you?"

"Of course not. Look, there's a family not arrived just yet, can you keep a look out for them. Denise and Melvyn Hartington's their name." He looked at his watch. "They said they'd be here by now."

As Dean left the room, Joyce wondered where it was that she had heard of that name before but try as she may it just wouldn't come to her. She shook her head, dismissed the frown from her face, and was making for the kitchen when the front door bell rang. She was halfway down the hall when Melanie beat her to it.

"Hello, I'm Melanie and that's my mum. Have you come to the party?"

Denise Hartington smiled at the greeting and made a play of shaking Melanie's hand. She was followed indoors by her husband Melvyn and their fourteen-year-old son, Roger.

"I'm awfully sorry we're late, it's all my fault. I insisted on buying an old mirror at a car boot sale and made Melvyn hang it before we came. It took longer than we thought, and I was going to cry off, but Roger insisted we come. Strange, he's never done that before."

Dean appeared at that point and, greeting their tardy guests, escorted them out into the back garden to join the rest of the company. Joyce stood in stunned silence. Roger Hartington. No - it couldn't be. What did Denise say? She'd bought a mirror at a car boot sale? Surely not; Joyce had seen it destroyed - in pieces on the floor of the Colmores' lounge just before everything vanished. Her attention was caught by Melanie who had remained at her side when Dean and his guests moved away.

"It's alright now, Mummy."

"What?"

"Nothing." Smiling so sweetly, she turned to Roger. "Come on, Roger, I'll show you around the place. I've got a feeling we're going to be great friends."

Needle in a Haystack

Stephen Davies looked at his watch – 1.35pm and it was just starting to rain. That didn't bother him in the slightest; he had just secured the largest IT installation and support contract since joining Fowkes Barrett, and his quarterly sales target had been blown out of the water. His August salary would contain a substantial bonus, and today's achievement could even put him in line for Salesman of the Year. He had almost two and a half hours until his train back to Manchester was due to leave Birmingham – time enough for some shopping. He and Caroline would be celebrating their fifth wedding anniversary on the 23rd and he wanted to find something special; perfume perhaps, or some jewellery – luxuries which he would be able to afford quite easily after the meeting this morning. He stepped into the Pallasades Shopping Centre, just around the corner from New Street station as the rain came down in a heavy burst. Stopping at the first news kiosk, he picked up a copy of the daily paper, something which he had been unable to do at Manchester in his haste to catch the train.

As he paid the vendor and indulged in a little afternoon chat, he became aware of some commotion a little further along, outside of one of the shops. Someone was calling out a name, and he instinctively turned to face the direction of the voice.

"Dad! Dad! It's Dad! Hey, Dad! Where've you been?"

A teenage girl was running in his general direction and, like other pedestrians in front of him, he turned to see the subject of the question. There was no-one making any obvious move towards her, and he turned back in puzzlement to find the breathless girl standing directly in front of him. Her face was red, her eyes wide open, and the smile betrayed her joyous familiarity with him.

"Dad. It's me, Julia. Where've you been?"

114

"I beg your pardon. Do we know each other?"

"What? But it's me, don't you recognise me? I'm your daughter."

Stephen was dumbfounded. He had no idea who this young girl was, and yet she called him 'Dad'. A crowd of onlookers had now started to gather, and a woman with a younger girl fought her way through them; she also now stood before him. Unlike the teenager, her face bore a look of complete incomprehension bordering upon disbelief.

"Michael?" The question was delivered slowly, quietly, and with some trepidation – you could have heard a pin drop amongst the ordinarily noisy early afternoon crowd.

"Yes, my name is Michael. Actually, it's Stephen, Stephen Michael; but who are you?"

The woman, now clearly in a state of shock, buckled at the knees and her fall was broken by the news vendor who had stepped out of the kiosk. Lowering her gently into a sitting position on the floor, he asked one of the bystanders to call for an ambulance. The man looked up at Davies questioningly, a deep frown cutting furrows across his forehead. Putting down his briefcase, Stephen knelt in front of her.

"Are you alright?" A lame enough question, but the only one he could think of in the circumstances. She regarded him silently for a few tense moments and then smiled.

"You've come back. We've found you."

The girl who had started the whole thing off was now beside him with her hand locked tightly in his, and her head against his shoulder.

"I'm sorry," he said. "I don't understand. You must have me confused with someone else – I haven't a clue who you are."

By this time an ambulance had arrived, along with a police officer alerted by the commotion. Amie Napolis was helped to her feet and into the ambulance, where a brief examination revealed nothing more than a mild case of shock. Clinging to Stephen, the two girls followed their mother with the paramedic, and the crowd of onlookers started to disperse. The policeman, however, sensing that something was not quite right, had remained in attendance and was now removing a notebook from his pocket. Stephen stood at the back of the ambulance before the open doors as the crew packed up their kit and prepared to leave. Amie, now recovered from her fall, stepped down, thanked them for their time, and turned back to Davies. The police officer watched from one side.

"Michael. You *did* say your name is Michael, didn't you?" she asked, looking back at her daughter, Julia.

"Yes, of course."

In a flood of tears, she flung her arms around his neck and sobbed uncontrollably. There was nothing he could do but reciprocate, and with both children now clinging to him, a fresh batch of passers by smiled in appreciation of some family reunion. The policeman stepped in at this point, and after a discreet cough, asked if everything was alright. Before Stephen could open his mouth, Julia was into full stride.

"It's my Dad, he's come home. We lost him six months ago but he's back now, and everything's going to be okay again."

"Whoa, just a minute, what did you say?" Davies was completely taken aback, and clearly had not understood any of what had gone before.

To him, it was a simple case of mistaken identity, but this girl was so sure of her facts that the situation was in danger of getting out of hand. The police officer was now becoming a little more than curious, and asked if he had any form of identification with him. Reaching down for his briefcase, he was horrified to discover that it had been removed without him noticing, and with the policeman now busily writing in his notebook Stephen decided that some convincing action was required. Taking his mobile phone from his pocket, he called home.

"Caroline, it's Stephen. I'm sorry love but I won't be on the early train. My briefcase has been stolen and my wallet was inside it. Can you get on to the credit card company and the bank and cancel all my cards for me? What? No, I'll have to catch the 8.15 train home. Say goodnight to Annie and Mark for me, would you? Okay, see you later."

"Sir?" It was the policeman. He had finished making notes in his book and had been speaking to Amie and her children.

"My wife, officer," he said, holding up the phone. "It looks like my briefcase has been stolen."

"I'm sorry about that sir, but is *this* lady not your wife?"

"No, and I don't know what's going on. I'm sure that she must be mistaken, I don't even live in Birmingham."

Now that he seemed convinced that nothing of a criminal nature had occurred, the officer was becoming keen to return to his normal duties. However, Amie was not to be deterred so easily. Adamantly pointing out that Stephen was her husband, she told the officer that if he had been speaking to his 'wife' at their 'home', he must be a bigamist. This left him with no alternative but to ask Stephen to accompany him, along with Amie and her family, to the local station where enquiries could be continued outside the public gaze. Seeing that the children were becoming agitated and close to tears, Stephen reluctantly agreed, and within half an hour they were all sitting around a table in Interview Room 2 at the Birmingham Central Police Station.

The story of Amie and Michael Napolis was indeed a sad one. Married in 1979, they had set up home in the Sparkbrook area of Birmingham, with Michael working as head of investments at Harrington Firth, a company owned and run by Amie's father. They had two daughters Julia (16) and Clare (11), and on the afternoon of March 14th he had failed to come home. He had left the offices at lunchtime as normal but did not return, and his absence was only noticed at work the following morning when he failed to attend a meeting with some clients. Despite a missing person search and appeals in the local media, it was like looking for a needle in a haystack, and nothing was heard from him. When the news broke concerning the Barings Bank crash, initial fears that he had absconded in a similar fashion to Nick Leeson were proved groundless after an audit of the company books.

Amie pulled a photograph from her handbag and showed it to Stephen. The image before him bore an astonishing resemblance to himself, and he now understood the reactions at New Street station. The detective assigned to the case, Mark Peters, then took up the questioning, and Stephen began to feel that he was being pushed into a very uncomfortable corner. Both he and Michael

Napolis had been born on the same day, June 10th 1955, and apart from their striking likeness, shared similar careers in management. Apart from involving his wife, Caroline, Stephen could not see how he would be able to prove that he had committed no crime. Both his parents were dead, his father in 1988 and his mother two years later. He had married in 1996 and had two children of his own. All of Amie's early good nature had now vanished, as she became more convinced that the man before her was her missing husband.

The police had no firm evidence to justify holding him in custody, so despite Amie's protestations, Stephen was released without any further action being taken. As they left the station, she confronted him again.

"What are you playing at? Can't you see the effect on the children? Have you no heart?"

"Look, Amie, I appreciate how this might seem, but I am *not* Michael Napolis. These children aren't mine, and I have never seen any of you in my life before. I have to go now, I have a wife and children in Manchester, and somehow I have to get home tonight."

As he left her standing there, Stephen Davies began to wonder about the astonishing likeness he bore to her husband, and although he had not told Amie, he knew that he had been adopted by John and Mary Davies shortly after his birth. They had made no secret of that fact, and he had been given all the adoption papers following their deaths. Taking his return train ticket from his top pocket where it had been kept, he boarded the 8.15 Intercity for Manchester and settled back to read his paper.

Caroline had, understandably, waited up for him following a call from the Manchester bound train, and as they sat down to supper the whole tale unfolded before her. Stephen had never lied to her in all the years they had been together, and she had no reason to doubt him now. Still, the uncanny facts of the matter were burning a mark in his brain, and despite the lateness of the hour Stephen opened the family safe and brought out the adoption papers. The facts were clear; he had been born in Salford to a Josephine Patterson, a single mother and alcoholic by the age of eighteen. Social Services had fostered him to a childless couple and had been happy to proceed with an adoption twelve months later. What he had not spotted until now, was the hand-written note at the bottom of the second sheet indicating that he was one of two babies born to the teenager. Now it was becoming clearer – Michael Napolis must be his identical twin brother, Amie's husband, and the father of her children. This was the information he needed to remove the suspicion from his name, and the following afternoon he made a call to Mark Peters at Birmingham CID.

Unbeknown to Davies, the detective had been making his own enquiries into the matter, his curiosity stung by the unusual circumstances. He too had discovered the adoption of the twins, and now also knew that Michael Napolis had been the victim of an abduction and mugging on the day he vanished from the offices of Harrington Firth. He had been beaten, dumped in Leeds with nothing to identify him, and admitted to hospital suffering from concussion and amnesia. Despite medical care over a number of weeks, his memory had not returned, and he was admitted to a long-term medical facility in Armley. Peters had made an appointment for Amie and himself to call the day after next, and Stephen determined to go along with them.

The place was situated in a quiet but slightly run-down area, and although the staff were helpful, they could tell the detective no more than he already knew about Michael. To them he was known as Harry, as names were given out to amnesiacs in alphabetical order, and he was currently tending flowers in the back garden. The manager, Mrs Watson, escorted them through to the rear of the property, and was about to call out when Peters held up his hand and stopped her.

"Let's try something, shall we?" he said with a smile.

Harriet Watson frowned; she didn't like her guests being upset by strangers, but there was something about this one which told her that he didn't really belong here. The detective stepped forward and beckoned Amie and Stephen to follow him. At a distance of around six feet he turned and nodded. Amie came to his side, took a deep breath and spoke, her voice trembling with emotion.

"Michael. Michael. It's me, love. It's Amie." She held her breath.

The man had been steadily hoeing his way around a large flower bed filled with dahlias; he stiffened at the sound of her voice. He remained motionless for what seemed an eternity, and then slowly turned to face them all. For Stephen Davies it was like looking in a mirror – he was wearing almost identical clothes right down to the trainers on his feet. The empty gaze, which moved from Amie to himself and back again, slowly and almost imperceptibly changed into one of recognition. Suddenly the hoe was gone as his arms reached out to her, and tears streamed down his face.

"Amie? Amie. Oh, Amie, where am I? I've been so lost." The rest of his words disappeared into her shoulder as their arms closed on each other for the first time in six long months.

"It's alright, love, you're coming home with me now, and we've missed you so much."

Mark Peters tugged Stephen's arm and they went back into the home's lounge with Harriet Watson. Over tea, they went back through the events of the past week whilst preparations were made for Michael's departure, and a tearful Mrs Watson returned as the reunited couple came back from the garden.

"Amie says we live in Birmingham now, and that you're my brother." He was speaking to Stephen. "Seems we have a lot to catch up on."

Stephen smiled, unsure of what else to do. There was no point in intruding upon a family with six months to find again. There would be time enough for that later, after he had had the chance to explain his new-found family to Caroline and the children. Michael had been one very lucky needle in the haystack.

Rose Cottage

Standing before the little house now brought back floods of memories. They had always called her Aunty Rose, even though there was no family connection. She had been a friend of his mother's, and during the long school summer holidays Keith and Harry Goodrum had spent many happy hours in and around the cottage. In those days it had a whitewashed exterior with dark green window frames and doors, a white picket fence enclosing a small but well-stocked front garden, and a thatched roof surrounding a red brick chimney stack from which emanated a constant thin stream of pale blue smoke. This was always the sure sign that Rose was at home, and usually cooking or baking something tasty. There was a rear garden which formed the working part of the property and supplied Rose's needs for the vegetables which she steadfastly refused to buy from the local shops.

Now the whitewash was discoloured and peeling, and the window frames appeared rotten after years of neglect. The front door still looked solid, but in need of renovation. The picket fence had gone, along with all the garden plants – probably the victims of roaming livestock which now had free access. The chimney stack looked weathered and in need of pointing, and the thatch contained some alarming gaps in its structure. It was a shame to see the place in such a state of disrepair, but what else had he expected to find after his years of absence? He dreaded to think what the inside looked like.

Keith walked up the overgrown path to the front door and tried the handle – locked. Again, he should have expected no less; after all, Rose had been dead for ten years. Her only son, Robert, was living and working in South Africa and he had not been in

England since the funeral, even though the place had become his as her only surviving relative. They had fallen out before he left England, but no-one seemed to know why, and despite a fair amount of speculation the truth had remained within the family.

He recalled from the past that Rose was in the habit of keeping a spare key wrapped in a plastic bag and concealed behind the guttering above the front door. Reaching up, his fingers closed around a small package, and pulling it down from its hiding place he was delighted to see the well-known implement, carefully preserved against the ravages of time and weather. Having excitedly torn away the cover, he inserted the key into the lock and heard the satisfying click as the mortise catch was released, and the door opened at his touch.

He stood on the threshold for a moment as his eyes adjusted to the darkness inside. The cottage had that musty smell of properties not regularly inhabited by people. He remembered his grandmother's front parlour carried a similar, not unpleasant, odour which stemmed from the fact that the room was only used on special occasions. He stepped inside and had to remind himself that Rose had been dead for a decade – there didn't seem to be a thing out of place, and apart from a thin film of dust which covered all the surfaces, it was almost as if she had just popped out for the afternoon. There was even her tea cup on the table, turned upside down on the saucer as she always left it in readiness for a fresh brew when she came back in.

He started to fill up and had to steady himself against the door frame leading to the kitchen whilst he composed himself. He supposed that Robert had no interest in the cottage, and had simply returned to South Africa after the funeral, probably leaving the property in the hands of a local estate agent. It surprised him that no-one had snapped it up as, apart from the obvious cold and damp feeling, the basic structure seemed sound and he always remembered it as a warm and welcoming place to be in. He couldn't leave without having a good look around, and memories of Rose, his mum, and Harry came flooding back in wave after wave of nostalgia.

Moving from room to room, both downstairs and on the upper floor, he could almost see images from the past, and he seemed to be like some alien observer moving around in the time and space occupied by another race of beings. The minutiae of the daily lives of the inhabitants were laid bare for him to see, analyse, and mentally note some of the things which he had forgotten over the years. It was all becoming a little too much for him and, suddenly feeling the need for some fresh air, he descended the stairs, unbolted the back door, and stepped into the rear garden.

Like the front garden, this too was overgrown and neglected. He could still make out all the cold frames at the side of the cottage where Rose grew her lettuces and cucumbers together with summer plants hardening off before being transplanted to the front. There were the remains of the old greenhouse too. Rose had stopped using it when she said she had become 'too old' and had left it to Keith and Harry to use for their own plants. They had spent many hours inside it with pots and compost, lemonade and midday sandwiches, and regarded it as their den. There was a kennel on the other side of the building which was the seasonal retreat of Bob, Rose's dog. She never left him out at night – she was too soft with animals for that, but he used it during the day as his own summer house.

Keith turned once more and went back inside the cottage, bolting the back door after himself. The figure in the middle of the room was cast in shadow. He assumed that a neighbour or passer-by had noticed the open front door and had come in to see who was about. Perhaps this could even be a potential purchaser sent by the estate agent, although he hadn't heard any car pull up outside – he should make his excuses and leave, but the figure seemed to be barring his way to the door.

"Excuse me, can I help you?" he said, as it came forward to meet him.

"No, Keith. I think it's more a case of what I can do to help you."

He froze as the familiar tones of Aunty Rose's voice came from the now recognisable figure as his eyes became accustomed to the darkness. There she stood, exactly as he remembered her, even down to the crocheted shawl she always wore and the pink slippers she invariably had on her feet. The smile on her face brought a warmth to his heart and they met in the middle of the room in an embrace that melted the years away.

Cold reality then gripped him, and he held her away at arms length with a puzzled frown on his face. Aunty Rose was dead, she died ten tears ago – this was just not possible, it must be a dream. As if reading his thoughts, she smiled at him.

"You're not dreaming. I'm really here, Keith, and I've come to help you."

"Help me? How, and with what?"

She smiled again and sadly shook her head – she used to do that when she knew something that you didn't, and it had always been used in the past as part of a game to keep Harry and him guessing. It drove them up the wall.

"You need to come with me now, Keith. It's been a long time and I've been trying to call you, but you weren't listening. You always did that when you didn't want to do something."

"I have to go now, Rose."

"No, Keith, come with me and I'll show you."

She led him out of the front door and down the garden path to the gate. They turned around and the sight of the cottage shook him. The roof was gone, as were the window frames, and the exposed brickwork was black and crumbling. It was a burned-out shell and he looked at her in complete astonishment.

"It was the fire, don't you remember? We all got caught in it and the place went up like an inferno. It was all over very quickly. You're dead, Keith, like Harry and me. I've been trying to reach you for years, but now it's over and you can rest. Come along with me. Harry's waiting… it'll be just like old times."

Sorry

Steve Hackett was going to apologise to his family. Apologise for all the wasted years he had inflicted upon each of them, and somehow beg their forgiveness for the emotional anguish which he had caused. Jennifer, his wife of twenty-two years, had suffered most over the past three of those, and it was to her that he was now hurrying, heart and mind filled to the brim with remorse and self-loathing for the humiliation which he had heaped upon her during that time.

In the early years, their marriage had been a happy one by and large, and had produced two children – Sally (21) and Terry (19). Neither had spoken to him directly for over twelve months now, and the final straw had been the news of his carefully concealed affair with Marcia Cox.

Their paths had crossed some years previously at the annual company Christmas party, to which Jennifer had always been a reluctant guest. This time she had refused point blank to go along, and Steve had been compelled, by protocol, to attend. That he was more than a little worse for wear that night was beyond question; he had consumed more than his usual amount of alcohol due to the company's picking up of the bar tab, and Marcia had dragged him onto the dance floor.

With inhibitions dulled by the free booze, their movements together had become overtly sexual in nature, and it was no surprise to anyone in attendance that evening when they disappeared together at the end of the event. The hotel venue had rooms to spare, and a hurried payment in cash gained access to a first floor double. The act was frantic, highly charged and almost frenzied in its intensity. Marcia stirred feelings in Steve that had lain dormant in his comfortable marriage for many years.

They met at frequent intervals afterwards, and Jennifer seemed to be in total ignorance of his infidelity. Marcia was divorced and made more and more physical demands upon him as their relationship developed. The 'Cold Light of Day' syndrome passed them both by, and ultimately over-confidence in their invulnerability from discovery was to prove Steve's downfall.

Jennifer had called the office. She never did that, but this one time she broke the rule. He was not there, and his secretary was very reticent in her response to questioning. Jennifer was not a naturally suspicious woman and had readily accepted all of Steve's previous explanations for lateness and overnight stays using business reasons as an alibi. This time, however, all her senses went to red alert. She was waiting for him when he came home that evening.

A series of pointed questions had degenerated into a fight which culminated in an ultimatum from Jennifer that divorce proceedings would be instigated if he refused to terminate the affair. He was stunned. He could not afford the open publicity of a breakdown in his marriage, and there was a myriad of reasons, none more than the disintegration of his family, for conceding to her wishes.

He saw Marcia once more, fully intending to simply break the news and walk away, but she was nothing if not enticing. All of her being cried out to him in a way he could not deny; they had one more bout of mutual enjoyment. He awoke with a start in the middle of the night, a night about which he had once more lied to Jennifer. There, at the end of the bed, was the figure of Tom Mason. Long time friends, they had been inseparable in years past. Tom had died in a fire at his home, and now appeared as a kind of advising angel to turn Hackett's life around. Without a spoken word, and by the mere look on his friend's face, Steve knew that his time with Marcia was now truly over; dressing quickly and silently, he left the room and made for his car.

Driving back home that night, his thoughts took flight to each of his children who had also been affected by his years of cheating and lying. In truth, he had not been the most attentive of fathers, treating both in the same way when they reached the point of having minds of their own. Not a week went by without some argument with either or both of them, and usually it centred around their refusal to bend to his will. Their teenage years had been the worst, particularly with Terry who, as he grew bigger and stronger, was more inclined to stand up to the old man.

Sally had left home at nineteen and moved just about as far east as was possible. She was now married and living in Boston to a plumber and Red Sox fan. His name was Carl and they had an eight-week-old son – a grandson which Sally swore he would never see. Father and daughter had finally come to verbal blows over her marriage to the protestant Carl, her own family being staunch Catholics. If her alienation resulting from Steve's affair had not been enough, the final straw of his hypocrisy at their mixed marriage finally, in her eyes at least, put the lid on their own relationship.

Terry, although not overly confrontational on the matter of his father's extramarital activities, had nevertheless firmly taken his mother's side on the issue of Marcia. He was now living and working in LA after leaving the family home in Santa Monica and had stated his unwillingness to return home on a permanent basis. Hackett's son was gay and had attempted on several occasions to talk to his father about his feelings. Steve had reacted badly to the news, and a war of words culminated in the son leaving home to live with his partner. The move to Los Angeles took place soon afterwards.

Hackett looked down at the fuel gauge of his Lexus and mouthed a silent curse – almost empty; he would need to find a gas station pretty soon. As if in answer to some unspoken prayer, the Super Eight appeared a hundred yards up the road and he pulled in to a deserted forecourt. It was eleven-thirty by his watch, and replacing the cap on his thirsty fuel tank, he made his way inside to pay for the gas. The scenario froze him where he stood.

To his right, and standing directly in front of the teller, was a man clad in black and wearing a ski mask. The .45 in his hand pointed straight at the poor man's head, and all three looked at each other for what seemed an eternity. The gunman was the first to move, backing slightly away from the counter and waving Steve closer to bring the two of them into the same arc of fire. The man behind the cash register was shaking visibly with fear, and it was clear that Hackett had stepped into the robbery shortly after the thief had himself entered the premises. The till drawer was still closed.

The gunman now had a problem, and Steve picked up the first signs of nervousness in his behaviour. Beads of perspiration had broken out above his eyebrows and just below the rim of the ski mask. His eyes flitted erratically between the teller and the new intruder. Steve was about ten feet away from the muzzle of the hand gun, and with the robber now in a situation which was rapidly getting out of his control, was working out the odds of disarming the man before anyone got hurt.

All he needed was a slight distraction, something to take the eyes of the robber away from him for the briefest of intervals. He braced his right foot against the shop wall to give any attack the maximum amount of forward momentum. At this point, the gunman could have simply walked away; he was nearer to the door than the other two and would surely have been allowed to make his getaway. Steve could just as easily have raised his hands in surrender and sat upon the floor thus allowing the robbery to run its course.

In one moment, the fate of all concerned was decided. The robber glanced briefly in the direction of the teller and barked at him to empty the cash register. With the distraction complete, Hackett launched himself at the man and carried him backwards into a display shelf. Unfortunately, the gunman held on to the .45 and was first to his feet as Steve scrambled to his knees. Three slugs fired in rapid succession hit Hackett squarely in the chest. He was dead before he hit the floor.

Turning back to the teller, and with the .45 now coming round to the man, the robber was caught by a shotgun blast which took him off his feet and across the entire width of the shop, but not before one lucky round had caught the poor man right between the eyes. It was a bloodbath.

Steve Hackett had very much wanted to apologise to his family. As he stood there looking down at his own crumpled and bloodied corpse, he realised that none of that was now about to happen. Jennifer would not now know of his resurgent commitment to their marriage and his ending of the relationship with Marcia. He would never now hold his grandson and ask his daughter and her husband for forgiveness. His son would never be made to see that he truly did realise all people were not made the same. No, in one moment of madness, in an instant of minding someone else's business, none of them would ever know of the change in his character.

The Damocles Legacy

The first arrival had appeared as a steadily brightening light in the eastern sky and had approached with an increasing intensity over a period of almost two weeks. To the general population it had seemed, at first, nothing more than the usual amount of activity within the solar system caused by space debris which would inevitably burn out in the upper atmosphere as it approached. There would be a brief and spectacular light show and then everyone would go back to whatever it was that they had been doing before its arrival. This time, however, it was different.

The object slowed its rate of approach and came to rest at a distance of about one thousand miles from the surface. It was still too far away for the amateur astronomers amongst the population to make out any details, but all governments' resources had been trained upon it since surveillance satellites orbiting the planet had detected its signature more than a month earlier. At a hastily convened conference, leaders of the major powers met to decide upon the best means of approach to an alien vessel which had clearly come in response to a variety of mechanised probes launched throughout the previous millennium.

Amidst growing concern, and a disturbingly agitated set of demands from the hawks amongst the gathering, a decision was taken to step up global security to level 4, one mark short of a war footing alert. Those members with positions on the Security Council were more cautious in their approach, and a proposal was carried at full meeting to step up communication attempts on all their known channels to the visitor. Initial radio messages had gone unanswered, but experts in universal language techniques had been working night and day to refine all programs in order to widen the range. For the moment, all inter-racial disputes were forgotten, and weaponry of every kind was on the move to positions of maximum effect should they be required. There was no doubt that these manoeuvres would not have gone unnoticed by whatever populated the craft now stationary over the largest continental block on the planet's surface.

As more and more attempts at reaching out were seemingly ignored, a sense of panic began to spread insidiously. Like some airborne viral infection, it afflicted everyone but the fanatically religious within days. Those sects took to the mountains in celebration of the fulfilment of ancient prophesies laid down in all the sacred texts. All differences now forgotten, they proclaimed the return of the messianic being promised to them millennia before.

Secular authorities chose quite a different path. With all armaments now trained in the same direction, and the multiplicity of communication attempts redundant, the first belligerent actions were taken. In response to intercontinental rivalry, satellite laser weapons had been deployed many centuries before. A prolonged stand-off, fuelled by ever increasing expenditure on maintenance and development, had almost brought the entire planet to the brink of Armageddon, and this had only been averted by a strategic arms limitation treaty signed even as weapons were being primed for use. This arsenal was now reconfigured and retargeted in the same direction. All that was needed was a single word of command.

The disappearance of the vessel was sudden and completely unexpected. One moment it was there, exactly where it had been stationed for the past few weeks; the next it was gone. The initial outpouring of general relief amongst the global population was shared by neither those of a religious persuasion, who saw it as nothing more than a delay in the inevitable, nor the government leaders attending the initial conference. Amidst all the general rejoicing there was an ominous calm along the planet-wide corridors of power, and despite repeated media requests for comment, no leader could be persuaded to voice an opinion. All global satellite surveillance equipment remained on full alert and focussed in the same direction as the first approach. They waited.

After the initial media frenzy had died down, a period of something approaching apathy descended across the entire globe.

It was not until the end of the sixth lunar cycle that alarms began to sound around all continental defence databases, now internationally linked in anticipation of further incursions. High powered radio telescopes, situated outside the limits of the atmosphere, had been upgraded to scan even further out into space. Without the distorting effect of atmospherics, their sensor arrays were able to pinpoint the approaching fleet, accurately determine its distance, and provide an ETA for defence installations on the surface.

The fleet consisted of over a hundred vessels of varying size and type. Once again, all attempts at communication were, apparently, ignored. Governments on the surface, now ready for a repeat of the earlier visitation, were less inclined to be patient a second time around. Broadcasting a message on all their available frequencies and in all then known languages, both verbal and electronic, a warning was delivered to the fast approaching flotilla. When it too went apparently unanswered, a general alert was issued, and all nations went to war readiness. The planet had never before witnessed such a united effort, and they now awaited some sign of the invaders' intentions.

The fleet deployed itself outside the atmosphere and at equidistant points around the globe, forming a network driven from a large mother ship some further distance away. Many hours were spent in surveillance on both sides and, as yet, there had been nothing from the visitors to indicate any kind of hostile activity. Once more the population of the planet held its collective breath as their leaders pondered the most effective way to alleviate the threat without involving total annihilation.

Hours turned into days, and days into weeks, as both sides studied each other in some futuristic version of the Battle of the Somme. Then, a call from a mountain top observatory in the southern hemisphere reported a type of scanning beam moving across the entire planet. There did not appear to be any threat contained within what seemed to be a type of sensor sweep, but a volley of missiles left their bunkers from another location and headed for the nearest vessels. They never got there. At a distance of around one thousand metres they disintegrated harmlessly against a protective barrier around each ship. There was no retaliatory action.

The sweep continued for two further days and, as before, the vessels departed the solar system leaving leaders and governments alike in utter bewilderment. Without effective means of defence, they would have been an easy target for a hostile force, and yet this seemingly superior race had simply gone away. This time they did not return, and as all defence systems were given the directive to stand down, an international period of thanksgiving was declared amongst a now unified race.

Analysis of the data from the fleet's central computer system had been started as soon as the command for departure had been given. Admiral Johnson, commander-in-chief, chaired a meeting of senior staff officers aboard the flagship *Damocles* to discuss the findings of both the initial scouting mission and its subsequent follow-up.

"So, what you're saying, Captain Lewis, is that we had no choice in the matter."

"That's right, sir," Victoria Lewis replied. "They are clearly far too dangerous a race for us to even consider as neighbours."

"Pity. We need another site, and the fourth planet would have suited our requirements. Terraforming would have been essential of course, but that would not have taken long, and the effects on the third planet would have been negligible at worst."

Victoria Lewis had known that she was destined to travel in space since her school days in the Welsh town of Abergavenny. Majoring in science and mathematics at college, she was cherry-picked by Space Corps after graduating with first class honours, and finished top of all her classes at the academy. Her early school days had been spent in wonder at the exploits of the legendary Russian cosmonaut Yuri Gagarin; his courage in being the first human to orbit the earth in 1961 inspired her, and Neil Armstrong's 'giant leap for mankind' as he became the first man to set foot on the Moon in 1969 reinforced her beliefs - she had watched those grainy, black and white images over and over again. When the first faster-than-light ship made its inaugural flight on 24th April 2063, she knew exactly what it was that she wanted to do – exploration of deep space was the only thing on her radar, and that achievement had made possible man's colonisation of the galaxy. Now, two hundred years after that seminal event, and with the rank of captain – the youngest person ever to each that rank - all of that seemed to be out there just waiting for her. Victoria had commanded ships of the line before, but this time it was different; the Damocles was the flagship of the fleet, and Thomas Johnson was its supreme commander. She took a deep breath, looked him squarely in the eye, and replied firmly.

"So, there really was no alternative, sir," she said.

"Indeed, it would appear not. Sad as it is, our needs outweigh theirs in the final analysis. We gave them every opportunity after the initial shots had been fired. Are you certain that there were no signals from the surface?"

"Yes, sir. Our computers were monitoring all our known frequencies and languages – there was... nothing. It is just possible that their atmosphere could have been blocking signals, but our science team discounted that eventuality."

"And yet they chose to open fire on us without the slightest provocation."

"Yes, sir. The dispersal ray was the only answer in the end. We could not justify the risk to our own people in either a landing party or a violent conflict. In sixty days their ozone layer will be completely removed, and the ultraviolet effect of their sun will carry out the job for us."

"And how long before the planet is inhabitable again?"

"Left to its own devices, our best estimates are between five and ten years, but we can reverse the effect of the dispersal artificially in around six months. In that time, we can commence the terraforming of the fourth planet. There are traces of primitive plant life, so we should be able to generate a breathable atmosphere within a relatively short time."

"Good. Report back to Earth that we have been able to find a suitable home. They'll be more than pleased; how long until the sun goes supernova?"

"Best case scenario? Ten years, but we need a complete migration well before then, sir."

"Alright, set course for home. We'll come back in two months to complete the job. This will be the Damocles' legacy for the future of mankind."

The Smell of Fear

This was becoming ridiculous, and it was high time that something was done about it. The neighbourhood never used to be like this until George stuck his pug-ugly nose into everyone's business, and boy, was he ugly. A broken leg resulting from a hit and run, a nose spread across his face after a fight in another area, and a fearsome cut diagonally from above the right eye to just below the opposite jaw line, lent him all the attributes of a real bruiser. Mickey would not have liked to bump into whoever dealt *that* one out in a dark alley. He shuddered at the very thought of it.

Nevertheless, George had continued undaunted in his terrorism of the streets, and a system of early warning signals had been set up across the neighbourhood in an attempt to forewarn the unwary of his approach. Today was Mickey's lucky day; Scotty had seen the bully turning the corner of Linden Avenue, and the word spread like wildfire. Pretty soon the streets were empty as doors were shut tight behind the backsides of fleeing escapees. Anxious faces peeped out from behind a multiplicity of curtains as George's swagger took him down the road like some gunslinger out of Dodge City – you could almost hear the theme from Sergio Leone's "The Good, The Bad and The Ugly" ringing out in the background. No prizes for guessing which one the bully wasn't.

He stopped at the corner of Springfield Road and looked back one more time, scanning the bushes and hedgerows for any hidden stragglers who hadn't made it home in time. He snorted his disgust at another day without satisfaction. If things didn't return to normal pretty soon, he'd have to look elsewhere for his entertainment. Yawning long and loud, he finally stomped his way down towards the town's main street and other pickings. Fear has its own particular smell, and the area bore an odour which you could almost taste; it was a taste which George found irresistible.

Slowly, and with much nervous glancing up and down the street, emerging residents breathed a sigh of relief at another successful daily running of the gauntlet. They all knew that it would only be a matter of time until one poor unfortunate would be caught unprepared, and when that day came all of George's frustration would be meted out indiscriminately to the stranded individual. They needed a plan, not just some imported 'anti-bully' who would then set the area up for himself. No, it would need to be one or more of their own number, and for the sake of permanence they would need to stick together, watching each others' backs in case the retaliation failed to remove the perpetrator for good.

George's initial activities had been restricted to basic needs. He stole whatever he could from them and had often lain in wait for his victims at street corners. A simple startling was all that had been needed then, and he would simply pick up whatever it was that had been dropped. However, as his reputation began to grow, and potential victims adopted a more cautious routine, he was compelled to actively seek out his next target. Mickey could cope with running that risk himself, but when the lout picked on Millie it made his blood boil. She was the smallest of the group of friends, and quite unable to defend herself against the unwelcome attentions of Ugly George as they had come to call him. Those attentions had also graduated from merely mugging, to ones of a more amorous nature.

Mickey and Millie had lived next door to each other since forever. Growing up so close provided an opportunity for their relationship to develop, and down the years the rest of the group of friends had come to regard them as an item. There was nothing that Mickey wouldn't do for her. George's intrusion into the neighbourhood, and the relationship with Millie in particular, was the catalyst he needed.

George had a tendency to drool when faced with something particularly tempting, and the thought of him blocking the alleyway where they all usually met, and where Millie had been caught alone, had Mickey in paroxysms of fury. This had definitely been the final straw. That she had been able to escape relatively unharmed was not the point at issue, and it would not take much more reluctance on the part of the rest of them before he committed some far more serious act. A council of war was convened at Robbie's house that night.

George would have to be tackled head on, and one of them would need to be the sacrificial goat. Eight pairs of eyes flitted nervously around the garage where the meeting was held out of the way of prying faces. The silence was deafening and seemed to go on forever. In the end, Mickey knew that it would be down to him as unofficial leader of the group, and he sighed as his volunteering was enthusiastically accepted by the rest of them. The relief of the other seven was overwhelming, but Mickey's stomach was now beginning to churn uncontrollably. The matter would have to be dealt with quickly and soon, before anyone got seriously hurt.

The idea was simple; Mickey would lie in wait for George at the mid point of his favourite route and issue the challenge. He closed his eyes and swallowed deeply at the thought of what might be about to happen to him but summoned up all his courage and smiled at the rest of the group – it was going to be fine, he said. The last thing that a bully wanted was someone standing up to him; in all probability he would simply turn tail and run. 'In your dreams', Mickey thought to himself but kept that one from the rest - now was not the time to crush their fragile bravery - he was going to need their backup when the moment came.

He didn't sleep much that night, tossing and turning, kicking the blanket off his bed, and rising the following morning bathed in a thin film of sweat. Breakfast was not an option, and he was out of the house before anyone else spotted him. It was a Sunday morning and the day for the communal lie-in – for everyone else that is. They were all waiting for him at Robbie's garage, and it became clear that no-one had rested at all since the preceding day.

Mickey laid out the details of the plan which had been buzzing around in his head all night, and each member of the group was assigned a position and a specific role. All clearly understood what it was that they had to do. It would only take one slip up, and George would be off the hook with goodness knows what consequences for the rest of them. As the time ticked inexorably towards midday, Mickey sat with a package on the wall at the end of his yard, waiting in a state of heightened tension for the approach of his nemesis. Right on cue, the stocky form of George emerged from behind the fence at the top of the street. He slowed his walk as he caught sight of the smaller form standing some thirty yards away. An evil leer spread across his battered face and, with his characteristic swagger, he bore down upon the defenceless figure now getting closer and closer. He stopped and glared down at his smaller opponent, puffing out his ample chest.

"Mickey. Well, well, what a surprise. Caught you napping today, have we? Now tell me, what do we have here, then?" He nodded in the direction of the ill-concealed bundle.

Snatching Mickey's lunch, he took a huge bite out of it in his usual coarse manner. The smile disappeared from his face almost immediately as the tell-tale taste of urine, donated generously by everyone in the group, spread throughout the inside of his mouth. Dropping the remainder of the meal, and with eyes now bulging, he coughed and choked his way into the middle of the street, quite unable to make out exactly where he was going. It was the signal for the rest of the action to begin.

From several gateways and concealed hiding places, the remainder of the gang emerged to surround the temporarily incapacitated bully. Mickey moved to the middle of the road to face George as he fought to regain his senses; he grinned at the now pathetic figure as it writhed before him. It was now or never, and if they failed at this point they would suffer for the rest of their lives.

"Now!" Mickey barked out the command, and from every angle teeth and claws descended upon George as he tried in vain to defend himself from the concerted attack.

Mickey had been right in the end. The last thing that a bully expected was someone, much smaller than himself, standing up to his terror tactics. Not only that, George had also badly miscalculated the effects of his regime on a group of close friends. 'Divide and conquer' was all very well with a fragmented opposition, but he had polarised all eight of them into one ferocious and effective unit. He was powerless against the smaller, more nimble and highly motivated squad. Bites and nips were coming in from all angles, and with eight sets of claws to deal with in addition to razor sharp teeth, he took the first opportunity to turn tail and run. Even at the death it was Millie, who had arguably suffered the most unpleasant treatment from George, who got in the final blow.

Latching onto to the middle of his tail, she brought a set of crocodile-like teeth clamping down firmly and with enormous force. The squeal of pain brought several householders running from their gardens to investigate. There was, of course, nothing to see by the time they arrived apart from a celebratory lap of honour around the street. As if in tribute to their successful campaign, an ice cream van turned into the top of the road playing its familiar jingle. The tune, as if it could be any other, was 'The Good The Bad and The Ugly' – Sergio would have been proud of them all. George left one reminder of his presence, and the smell of fear which emanated from the pile he deposited was one which they could put up with for now.

News of the humiliation spread like wildfire throughout the district, and stories came back to the group of a number of similar confrontations, as other groups of former victims extracted similar acts of vengeance on the now bruised and battered labrador.

The Spiders and Johnny Bailes

The greenfly were the first to vanish, and the first clues to their decimation lay in the abundance of roses, sweet peas, and dahlias which were the usual first casualties of their relentless procreation each summer. All the neighbourhood gardens were resplendent in the variety and colour of the flora on display, and the local garden centre reported its worst annual sales of proprietary pest control spray in living memory. Local gardeners then began to notice the complete disappearance of other traditional pests such as red spider mites, woodlice and, surprisingly, ants. Any new predator could feast upon the more vulnerable members of the insect kingdom, but it would take a particularly suicidal or ravenous species to tackle the ant. The gardeners, however, revelled for the moment in the riotous display of nature's bounty whilst failing to notice the absence of the airborne army of pollinators which would guarantee next year's crop. There were no flies, wasps, bees, or butterflies and, curiously, no spider webs either.

Ernest Bailes had been an avid gardener for as long as he could remember and had tried to pass his passion on to his son, Johnny. His success was only partial for, although the lad enjoyed their time in the garden or at the allotment, his interest lay not in the plants and vegetables grown there, but in the wildlife which shared the territory. More particularly, he was a keen arachnophile, and had studied all aspects of the life cycle, habitat and behaviour of the majority of the indigenous members of the British spider family. At the age of thirteen, he already knew more about the subject than any of his teachers, and this had made him a figure of fun for the rest of his class - a matter which caused him increasing annoyance as time passed. Today his attention was drawn quite suddenly to the rhubarb leaf on his right-hand side, where a tubular web spider had appeared, a common enough sight in a garden environment, but what was less than common was the way in which it waved its front legs at him.

Placing his right hand up to the leaf he waited patiently as the arachnid stepped onto his palm as if some instructions were being followed. It was a handsome blue/grey in colour, with a body size of about one inch and legs of around twice that length. Johnny never ceased to be amazed at the reaction which the species engendered amongst humans – what was the saying? *'If you wish to live and thrive, let a spider run alive.'* He knew that there were only two or three British spiders which carried a venom potentially harmful to man, but the general opinion amongst his peers was one of distaste and blind panic at the sight of them. This one now sat in the middle of his hand and once again waved its front legs in the air as if attempting to gain his attention. Johnny raised it slowly to his face for a better look and became aware of a pulsating sensation in his head. He frowned and cocked his head to one side as the gentle throbbing changed slowly but surely into a word. 'Who? Who? Who?'

The spider had stopped waving and now sat quite still as if awaiting a reply.

"Johnny," he said.

The spider remained motionless for a while, and then repeated its performance. 'Who? Who? Who?' The gentle throbbing insisted again, and this time Johnny thought the reply. The arachnid was spurred into action and danced around his palm as if in celebration. More pulsing in Johnny's brain as the spider turned to face Ernest Bailes and the same question with a single word reply, 'Dad', progressed through his subconscious. The boy was astounded – was this spider communicating with him? If so, why? And why him? Too many questions for now, and he needed to keep this arachnid for further study. Seizing a discarded matchbox, he was about to pick up the tubular web when the spider amazed him by walking into the small container of its own accord as if it understood the box's purpose. Putting it into his pocket as his father called to him to help pack away the tools, Johnny had already planned out his evening and couldn't wait to get home.

Dinner was soon over, and both his parents expressed surprise at the unusually clean plate which their son left before excusing himself from the table. Up in his room he took out the matchbox and freed the tubular web spider onto his bedside cabinet. Over the next three hours, a rudimentary system of communication developed, and Johnny wondered if the spider would respond to some commands. He thought a series of basic instructions and was delighted when it performed each one without hesitation. He sat back on his bed and pondered this new-found power as a mischievous smile crept across his face. Ellen Farley; now *there* would be an interesting task for his new friend. The girl next door had made a point of belittling Johnny at every opportunity – maybe this was the time for revenge. No sooner was he aware of his own thoughts than the spider was gone. He hadn't even seen it move and was disappointed that his evening entertainment seemed to be over. How wrong he was.

Downstairs, and a while later as he sat watching television with his parents, the silence was pierced by a spine-chilling scream which seemed to be coming from the house next door. Outside in the street, many neighbours had appeared, alerted by the same noise, and Johnny came out of his front door to see Ellen Farley rolling around on the front lawn in hysterics. Concerned parents were attempting to calm their daughter as she pulled at her hair and thrashed at her clothing in a frenzy of panic.

"Off! Off! Get them off me! Mum! Dad! Help me! Help me!"

It took almost a full hour for Mr and Mrs Farley to persuade Ellen that whatever it was that had scared her had gone. Only then was it clear that a large number of 'enormous' spiders had dropped on to her bed from the ceiling and had run amok in her room. Johnny knew instantaneously that the tubular web was the culprit, but could not, at first, imagine where the others had come from. Only later, when he returned to his own bedroom to find the spider waiting for him, did things begin to fall into place. From behind the curtain another six appeared, all of the same genus, and they lined up behind the blue/grey like some army platoon awaiting inspection. The pulsing sensation returned in Johnny's brain as a single word whispered into his subconscious - 'Friends, friends, friends'.

Later, as Johnny Bailes settled down to sleep, the spider troop left the room and returned to their lair to prepare for the night's hunt. They had no need to waste valuable energy resources in spinning webs any longer, and since they had started to work together there was food for all and some to spare. They knew where their insect prey was, and the hunting pack would flush them out into the waiting horde – it would be a truly memorable feast, an event to which they were becoming accustomed. Soon they would be able to seek out larger prey to satisfy the needs of their demanding ruling elite.

Back at school, the events of the previous week had become general knowledge, and somehow Johnny's name became linked with Ellen's unfortunate encounter with the tubular web spiders. The innocuous teasing gave way to a sinister, and more serious, treatment of his out-of-school hobbies. One or two of the larger boys began following him around school, and it was not unusual for him to return home with a number of unexplained bruises each week. As a result of his last instructions to the arachnid squad, Johnny had refrained from all thoughts of a similar nature in their presence, but with the escalation of treatment meted out to him out of sight of his teachers, he felt that the time was ripe for some payback. Almost as if they sensed his mood, the spiders appeared one evening shortly after the latest beating. Lined up on the table in Johnny's bedroom, they waited motionless for their assignment. He was not aware of any definite command, nor were any names given, but the group vanished into the gathering gloom.

The three boys had arranged a sleepover and were alone in the house during an evening when parents were out. On a windless night, the keen observer would have found it curious that the grass on the back garden moved in a strange manner as if some breeze flitted across its surface. In reality, it was the relentless march of an army of arachnidkind, single-mindedly heading for the upper floor of the house. The same observer would puzzle over the apparent growth before his very eyes of an ivy-like creeper up the back wall towards an open bedroom window. By the time that one of the boys had noticed the invading horde, something upwards of ten thousand spiders had crossed the window sill and were swarming across the floor. Once again, the peace of the neighbourhood was shattered by a series of terrifying screams. This time neighbours were more reluctant to leave the safety of their homes to investigate, and by the time the local police arrived the upper floor of the house was a scene of carnage.

The one boy remaining alive told a story of a sea of spiders attacking from all sides as he and his friends sought to beat them off with anything which came to hand. Bloodstained cricket and baseball bats were discovered at the scene, but not a single arachnid was to be found. Clearly, the boys had beaten at their supposed attackers with a fury which defied belief, but when the investigating officer found a few partly smoked joints in the parents' bedroom, the whole matter took on a different aspect. Despite the boy's vehement denials, the conclusion was one of an evening of drug-induced hysteria which went disastrously wrong. Post mortem results on the two bodies later confirmed a lack of any narcotic substance, but for the present the police were satisfied that there had been nothing suspicious relating to the deaths.

Whispers around school the following week were that Johnny Bailes was at the heart of the incident, and teachers were faced with a boycott of all lessons involving him. An announcement from the headmaster failed to change the mood of the pupils, and the boy was forced into staying at home pending a meeting of school governors. Up to this point there had been no evidence to connect Johnny either to the spiders or the two recent events, but when the remains of Mrs Gerrard's cat were found in the Bailes' garden a few days later, matters began to move quickly forward. The local vet had never seen injuries like them on a domestic animal and called in a specialist friend to advise him. The marks on the corpse, and there were hundreds of them, were all made either by the same creature, or a number of individuals of the same species. In any case, the species was never in doubt – they were arachnid bites, and measurements showed that the spider concerned would be approximately the same size as a human hand.

Police and media interest now took on an intensified role centred upon the Bailes household, but despite meticulous searching of both the property and the surrounding estate, no trace of arachnids of any kind could be found. One by one, the caravans of television and radio equipment left the area, and the police scaled down their efforts to trace the source of the infestation. Quietly, the whole matter became forgotten and life appeared to return to normal in this outwardly peaceful corner of suburbia. The refusal of Johnny's former school friends to attend classes with him forced the family to move away from the district, and there was a communal sigh of relief at their departure. Over the next six years his educational progress found him at university studying entomology, and at the end of his second year he was well on the way to a first-class degree. During the intervening time there had been no repetition of the symbiotic-like relationship with the spiders, and Johnny had consigned the memory to the box marked 'File and Forget'.

All his fears returned, however, one afternoon when rumours circulated the campus of a mysterious discovery at the end of the playing fields which backed on to the main road forming the perimeter of the university grounds. According to a shaken athletics student, he had seen what he believed to be a football left out from the previous day. He went across the pitch to pick it up but was horrified to find not a piece of sports equipment, but a rolled up, and quite clearly dead, spider. Its legs made it appear larger than it really was, but the size scared him so much that he ran back to the changing rooms and reported the find to a caretaker. The body was removed to the Entomology Department where Johnny and two of the staff were waiting. There was a collective gasp of surprise at the size of the spider, and measurements revealed the body to be ten inches across. They were interrupted by the reappearance of the caretaker, who this time carried a black plastic bag.

"You need to see this, Mr Brown. I found it in the hedge bottom in the same field as the spider," he said to the more senior of the two department staff, and emptied the contents on to another table. It was a fox, and a mature male at that.

"Thank you, Mr Holmes. We'll take care of it."

Leaving the spider for the moment, all attention focussed on the second body. It was covered in bites, thousands of them, and had clearly died in some agony. They could only suppose that it had mistaken the arachnid for one of its normal prey during an evening hunt and had come off worst in the encounter. Turning back to the spider, their examination revealed another set of bite marks, far fewer in number and centred on the head and neck. They pegged both bodies out for post mortem examinations and prepared their instruments. Johnny had been watching whilst this was happening and now approached the tables. The spider was *Aaraneus diadematus* the common garden variety, but its size was unbelievable, and it was obviously a mutant strain of the species. The two staff returned and, as he was their star pupil, Johnny was allowed to stay and observe. His attention focussed on the spider, and from the first incision it was clear that something was seriously amiss. Ray Brown, the senior entomologist, stepped back from the table, dropping his scalpel in the process. The noise rang out like an alarm bell in the stillness of the laboratory.

"Butterfingers," Mick Parlour, his colleague, laughed. The silence which greeted this comment puzzled him as there would normally have been some form of riposte. He turned to see an ashen-faced Ray and Johnny standing well back from the examination table, wide-eyed in horror.

"What? What's up then?" He walked across to them and followed their gazes to the table. The spider was spread eagled with its abdomen pinned open, and Parlour could not believe what he saw.

"Ray, Ray... this can't be. Do you realise what this means? The only thing preventing these buggers from being our size is their respiratory system. This thing's got a set of lungs!"

They had often talked about the remarkable abilities and lifestyle of the arachnid, and frequently joked that the day they learned how to breathe would be the beginning of the end for the human race. On the table before them was clear evidence of a major mutation and the question which none of them dared ask was: 'How many more were there out there?'

The isolated and desolate scenery of the North Yorkshire Moors had formed the romantic backdrop for the novels of the Brontë sisters, but in reality, it was the home for the most hardened of farmers and their animals. It was a tough life in an unyielding landscape, but here the sheep farmer eked out a living along with breeds specially developed for the harsh environment. Sid Barks was one such man, and he had farmed this land for forty-five years. He stared down in consternation at the carcasses of a dozen or more of his flock, shaking his head in the resigned manner of all truly Yorkshire farming folk. As if money wasn't tight enough already! This was the last thing he needed, and so close to market day as well.

The hunting pack of seven wolf spiders approached from the western corner of the field, timing their attack to coincide with the setting of the low winter sun. The kill would be easy, and they were looking for a fresh taste from the tough meat of the moorland sheep. Sid Barks would never know what hit him as they made their slow, silent approach, and all the bodies would be removed to feed their growing and increasingly ravenous brood. There would be nothing left to indicate what had happened, but investigations would bring with them a fresh supply of unwary prey.

A Dish Served Cold

Jessie Masoner awoke to find himself in unfamiliar surroundings. He ached in places he never knew existed, and there were wires and tubes going in all directions. A nurse's face came slowly into focus; he was asked if he knew his name and where he was. He replied in the affirmative to the first question and the negative to the second. As his head cleared, he became aware of bandages, lots of them, around his head, his legs, and his chest. He touched his face, and the surface of the skin was not where he expected it to be – it felt much further out, like the feeling your jaw has when you come back from the dentist. At first, he wondered if he had been involved in some kind of accident like a car crash, but then his memory of the night out with his best friend, Ben, started to return, and the horror of what had happened snapped sharply into perspective.

The Saturday night out was a regular thing for them, and would typically involve a meal and a few pints. They had known each other since school, lived only two streets apart, and had even joined the army at the same time. This particular evening had been no different from any other until they left the Rose and Crown on the High Street at around 11.30pm. A group of six young men in their early twenties had followed and started hurling abuse from across the street. Jessie and Ben ignored them as their army training had taught, but this only seemed to inflame the situation; when the group crossed the road, the friends found themselves outnumbered three to one. Despite their unarmed combat training, it had proved to be a futile struggle and they were soon on the ground, being kicked and punched. Instincts for survival told them to roll into a ball and cover their heads. The beatings could not have lasted for more than a few minutes but to Jessie it seemed much longer, and eventually he passed out.

Like any army recruit, his first thought was for his comrade, but the hospital nursing staff would not answer any of his questions on the subject, and it wasn't until detectives arrived that he was able to obtain any more information relating to the events of the night. He answered all their questions and gave detailed descriptions of all six attackers. From an early age Jessie seemed to have an extraordinary memory for faces, and a police artist was able to build up accurate likenesses of the gang. Before the officers left, Jessie asked again about Ben, and one of the constables looked towards the doctor who had just entered the room.

"I'm sorry, Mr Masoner, but your friend died of his injuries shortly after arriving here. The beating he received was so severe that one of the kicks he sustained ruptured his spleen - we were unable to save him. You yourself are extremely fortunate to be alive; there are fractures to your skull, both legs, your right arm, and three ribs. One of your lungs had collapsed and it was touch and go for a while."

This was more information than he could handle at the time and Jessie burst into tears - hot, burning tears that seared down his face like fire and stoked up an anger within him which screamed out for revenge. He could not bring Ben back, but now that the police had his descriptions it would only be a question of time before justice was served on those who attacked them. The case had been all over the TV news and had appeared in all the daily papers for the two weeks since that Saturday evening, but no witnesses had come forward despite the fact that the events had played out in the middle of a busy street at a time when all the local pubs were turning out. He was even more surprised when he was discharged from hospital to discover that no-one matching the descriptions and pictures had even been pulled in for questioning. A visit to the local police station revealed nothing more than the fact that the case was under investigation, but that the police had nothing to go on at present.

Jessie told himself that perhaps he was expecting too much too soon; six months later, when police enquiries seemed to have dried up and he got his recall to unit, he began to lose faith. His injuries had all mended and the army Medical Officer reported him fit to return to duty. He rejoined his company the following week and they shipped out to the Middle East as part of Desert Storm – the allied operation to push Iraqi forces out of Kuwait. It was during his time there that he acquired skills in Special Operations and became a member of an elite team designed to target and remove small, heavily armed, enemy units. Effectively, it was an assassination squad, trained to operate swiftly and in total silence, moving in and out of an area undetected, and leaving it clear for the main forces to proceed.

When Desert Storm was over, Jessie left the army at the end of his term and returned home. Two years down the line, he was dismayed to discover that all enquiries into Ben's death and the attack that night had stalled, and that no further action was being taken. It was at this point that he decided to take matters into his own hands, and the first thing he needed to do was to embark upon a reconnaissance mission to the area he and Ben had visited that night. He couldn't believe his luck when he walked back into the Rose and Crown one evening three weeks later. All six members of the group who attacked them were sitting in the bar, laughing and drinking – there was no mistake; their faces were indelibly etched onto his memory. He walked to the bar and ordered a beer as one of their number approached for another round. As they stood there together it was clear to Jessie that the guy didn't recognise him, but noticing the tattoo which had been added during the operation in the Gulf, he asked Jessie if he was in the services. When the answer came back, there was an amount of back slapping and an invitation to join the group at their table. This was too good a chance to miss.

By the end of the evening, he had all their names and even details as to where some of them lived in addition to a free night out – he didn't pay for a single drink, and the irony of that was not lost on him. It was going to be a deal easier than he had ever hoped, and the only question left was to decide upon the correct methods of execution and the timescale for the operation. Timing was going to be crucial; if he left it too long between individual kills, the other members of the group may be scared off. On the other hand, if he took them all out too quickly police attention may focus in sharply upon him as the most likely suspect. An answer presented itself unexpectedly the following week when Pete, Mark, and Terry decided to spend a weekend away in Manchester following West Ham, and asked him if he wanted to come along. This would enable him to eliminate half the group in one fell swoop and remove all means of identification, thus giving him time to return to London and finish off the job.

The remaining three group members would not be expecting to hear from them before the following Monday, and Jessie decided on Friday night as his best time to strike, but he could not take them all on at once - some diversion to split up the number would be needed. As to method, he had already selected six appropriate means which would maximise his chances of leaving the scene unharmed and untraceable. This had been a long time coming, and he had approached it with a clear head and a passion which ran cold in his blood. They arrived in Manchester shortly after six and found a B&B where they dumped their bags and set out for the evening. Jessie had no fixed plan at this stage for splitting up the group, but fate intervened in the form of a number of local opposition supporters who had latched on to the West Ham colours on Terry's jacket. There were too many to take on, and flight was the only option.

"Split up!" Shouted Jessie. "We'll meet up back at the digs. Pete, you come with me!"

Jessie was too streetwise to be caught by a group of amateurs, and they were soon out of sight and lost to the chasing pack. Pausing in a back street well away from prying eyes, Pete was struggling to get back his breath when Jessie pulled the home-made garrotte out of his coat. The loop was formed and over Pete's head as he rose from his crouching position. The look of surprise, and then horror, on his face was replaced by sheer terror as he struggled in vain to claw the slowly tightening noose from around his neck.

"Take a good look scumbag! Remember me now? This is the last face you'll ever see!"

At the last moment Jessie spun him around as the wire cut through flesh, windpipe, artery, and finally his spinal column, releasing a gush of crimson. Pete's lifeless body crumpled to the ground in silence. One final pull on the garrotte ensured no mistakes had been made - Jessie wiped the wire on Pete's jacket and walked away from the scene without a speck on blood on him. Now for the other two.

He returned to the spot where they had split up to find the Manchester locals still hunting down Terry and Mark. He joined in the search and became one of the anonymous mob. It didn't take long to track them down in the unfamiliar streets of an 'away' city, and they were soon cornered in a blind alley. Jessie stood back in the shadows as the same treatment was meted out which he and Ben had received a lifetime ago. The two of them were still writhing in agony when the pack moved on in search of other entertainment. This was his opportunity; putting on his gloves and approaching Mark from behind, a sharp twist on the head snapped his neck and he fell, lifeless, back to the ground. Terry had pulled himself to his knees, but by the time he realised what was happening Jessie had him by the throat in the kind of death grip only taught to those in Special Forces. Too weak to fight off the attack, his life ebbed away under the relentless pressure of Jessie's fingers. All three deaths would be attributed to a football-related attack, and there would be no means of identification left on any of the bodies. A brief call back at the digs for his belongings saw Jessie on the late train to London in plenty of time to carry out the remainder of the operation.

He returned to the capital just after midnight and, after calling in briefly at home, made his way quietly back to the Rose and Crown. He was out of luck but remembered that one of the remaining three had suggested a night in with a video. Making his way to the address, he saw Martin leaving the house, presumably on his way home. He trailed victim number four through the back alleys of the council estate where they all lived, keeping to the shadows and looking for the opportunity to intercept. That came when the thug stopped to argue loudly with another man, giving Jessie time take up a position some fifty yards further on in the shadow of a row of garages. Here he waited until he saw his target approaching and, allowing Martin to step just beyond him, he pulled back on the mop of hair exposing the whole expanse of his throat to the sweep of a razor-sharp hunting knife. The incision cut off all possibility of a scream and whilst the hapless thug was struggling for his last breaths Jessie reminded him of Ben's fate. Martin's eyes glazed over, and he was gone.

Dragging the body to the rear of the garages, Jessie concealed it behind a stack of rubbish bins. It wasn't a perfect hiding place, but it would suffice for the time being. He retraced his steps carefully back to the house, taking care to avoid passers-by and making as little noise as possible so as to avoid attracting attention. It never ceased to amaze him how criminals invariably vacated the scene of their wrongdoings at top speed and with maximum noise. The place was in darkness, and it was obvious that he had missed his chance to complete his revenge that night. Perhaps this was no bad thing, as it would give the remaining two something to think about, and who could they go to? To be taken seriously, they would both have to admit to having participated in the beating which cost Ben his life, and that would land them a serious amount of time in jail. No, this was a time for cooling off, taking stock, and planning the final act.

Jessie had left no evidence at any of the scenes - his army training had taught him that - and there was no-one who could reliably place him in Manchester apart from the remaining two. He was safe for the moment, and when the news broke of the four deaths neither the media nor the police linked them immediately. By the time the dead men were associated with each other, he had destroyed all the clothing which he had worn during that weekend, and all the tools he had used were now at the bottom of the Thames in a weighted bag. The police had interviewed him simply because he had provided graphic descriptions of his and Ben's attackers which now miraculously seemed to match those of the four corpses. Those interviews were superficial purely, Jessie believed, because no-one in the force wanted to be caught holding a hot potato.

Two years further on, the thirst for revenge was as strong and raw as ever, and he had kept track of the remaining two members of the gang. Their initial fear of retribution had made them ultra cautious in their movements, but with the passage of time came complacency, and this was just what he had been waiting for. Joe had moved away from London to the South West, and Dave had taken a job lorry driving for a local haulage firm. Jessie fancied a holiday, and Cornwall was a place he had always wanted to see. The fact that he knew Joe was living in Penzance could have been a pure coincidence.

A week would be plenty of time to find his target, select a location, and time the act for maximum effect and minimum risk. As he walked along the sea front at Penzance, he felt a sudden tinge of regret that he would not be staying longer. He had been given an address in the town and waited for two days before catching sight of the fifth member of the gang as he returned one night with a woman. Jessie had to be certain that there was no-one permanent who could provide a description to police, and an hour later she left the building followed shortly afterwards by Joe – this had clearly been one of the local ladies of negotiable virtue.

He tracked his quarry, at a respectable distance, to a location just outside the town centre where a transaction for a small package took place prior to Joe's return journey to his digs. Obviously, alcohol was not the only thing which he craved nowadays. Jessie had noticed one or two likely places where he could lie in wait and quickly made his way to the first of them. It seemed to be an age before he heard footsteps approaching down one of the back alleys, and by the irregular rhythm he assumed that Joe had already had his fix. Stepping out into the path of the pedestrian, Jessie took the thug by surprise and a single blow with the cosh which he produced from his coat pocket had him reeling backwards. In the shadows, Jessie's identity was safe but this was no longer sufficient, and he dragged Joe's semi-conscious form into the half-light of a street lamp.

"Look at me!" He shook his victim by the shoulders. There was no resistance, and Joe stared into the twisted face inches away from his own. Sudden realisation of the identity of the man holding him dawned, and his eyes widened in terror.

"You? We thought you was…"

"Dead? You should be so lucky. Not so brave now are you, you piece of garbage!"

There was no time for a reply, as a swift follow-up blow to the right side of his head caused a massive fracture and haemorrhage. Joe slumped sideways, but Jessie cushioned the fall to minimise any noise. Once more, a place was found amongst some rubbish bins for the body – quite apt when he came to think about it. The usual cleaning up of the site followed, and he made his way quietly but swiftly back to his lodgings and checked out the following morning for another pressing appointment back in London.

Potentially, this would be the trickiest job of the six. Jessie would somehow have to discover Dave's schedule and routes before he could plan what was, after all, an execution. It had been a week since his return from Cornwall when he hit upon the idea of simply following the rig from the depot to whatever destination was on the worksheet for the day. Dave was a reassuringly predictable driver, always pulling in at the same motorway service area on a regular run up to Leeds and back, and always taking an overnight bag with him. Jessie tracked him for a fortnight before working out the details of his plan and, in the end, it was simplicity itself. One of the less publicised trades he had picked up in the army was that of gaining entry into locked vehicles. All he had to do was wait until the rig had been secured and was alone, break into it, and lie in wait for Dave's return.

His regularity even extended to the length of time he remained at the service area, never more than forty-five minutes and ample time for concealment in the cab. Jessie was positioned behind the driver's seat when his target returned, ready with a hatchet which he had purchased for cash from a local DIY superstore three months previously. No-one was going to remember having sold one that long ago, let alone who they sold it to. Having let the driver settle into his seat, and with nobody in the lorry park to witness what was about to happen, Jessie brought the weapon down onto Dave's skull and killed him with a single blow. It was a messy job, and there was blood all over the inside of the driving area and spatter on the clothing Jessie was wearing. Jumping down from the cab, and looking around to ensure that he had not been seen, Jessie removed the hooded overalls and gloves which he had been wearing. Rolling them up, he shoved them into a rubbish bag, quickly cleaned his face and hands, and added the disposal wipes to its contents. The kill had been silent, and the lorry park was still deserted.

Jessie went back to his own car and put on a second set of overalls brought along to prevent any transfer of forensic evidence to the vehicle. Once back home, he would burn all the incriminating evidence and wait for the inevitable media attention on two apparently unconnected and random killings three hundred miles apart. No doubt some enthusiastic young detective would eventually pick up on the six murders of the same gang which attacked Ben and himself, but all evidence would be circumstantial at best and the same witnesses who remained silent at the time would probably sleep easier in their beds with half a dozen local thugs out of circulation permanently. As the saying goes, revenge is a dish best served cold, and this one had been in the freezer for quite a while.

The News at 1066

In our age of high-speed satellite communication, news gathering is almost instantaneous, but for those reporting events in earlier times, weeks or even months may have passed before any details emerged. The circumstances surrounding the Norman invasion of England, if related using modern technology, may have sounded something like this...

Good evening. I am Tim McDougall here in the newsroom, and today is Wednesday the 25th of September 1066. In our main story tonight - victory for the English forces at Stamford Bridge as the combined armies of the Norwegians under Harald Hardrada and Tostig, the brother of Harold Godwinson, are routed after a forced march northward by the English army to head them off. Over to our political correspondent on the spot, Richard Major.

Yes, hello, Tim. It's all over here and the English are understandably jubilant at their victory. Hardrada's Norwegians had been in the country for about a week and had disposed of Morcar and Edwin just outside York, but Godwinson's army were simply too strong, too many, and tactically too good for them. They're looking a pretty sorry lot now, and I can see in the distance wagons being loaded for the long journey home. We understand from our sources inside the English camp that Harold Godwinson has a signed document pledging no further incursions on English soil by the Scandinavians. Back to you in the studio.

Thank you, Richard, and we'll keep up to date with the after-battle celebrations as the army heads back home in the coming days. Now some breaking news from our foreign team in France. Over to David Sleet in Normandy.

Good evening, Tim. We have a considerable build up of forces around the coastal area as William, Duke of Normandy, and his military staff carry out a series of manoeuvres which they say are in preparation for defence against a possible cross-channel attack. No-one here is taking that idea too seriously though, and it looks to me more like the organisation of an invading force the other way. This situation has been building up since the death of Edward the Confessor and Harold Godwinson's usurping of what William still regards as his right to the English throne. I am sure that there will be more to report as the days progress, but for now it's back to you in the studio.

Thanks, David. Now, for a brief summary of other news, it's over to Dominic Soul.

Good evening. Tim McDougall in the newsroom on Friday the 27th of September 1066. In an extraordinary development across the Channel, we understand that there has been movement of the French forces. Over to David Sleet in Normandy.

Yes, hello, Tim. I'm standing on the deck of the Norman flagship as final preparations are being made to put an invasion force to sea across the English Channel. I've lost count of the number of vessels but if the weather holds fair, Harold Godwinson's going to have a real fight on his hands. The Normans are keeping their cards very close to their chests right now, and I have no idea where they are going to land. Back to you in the studio.

Thanks for that, David. Now, Richard Major is still with Godwinson's forces as they make their way back south after success at Stamford Bridge. Richard, do we know if Harold has received any information concerning the Normans?

Hello, Tim. Yes, word reached us just hours ago about the impending departure of the French, and Harold Godwinson is furious. Although they've just seen off the Norwegians, there's a physically demanding march before them to try to intercept any invasion, and he'll have to recruit replacements for lost forces on the way. This might not be as easy for him as one may think, because a lot of people I've been speaking to off the record regard him as something of a tyrant after the reign of Edward the Confessor, but we'll have to wait and see. Back to you in the studio.

Okay, Richard. Well, I am sure that we'll be hearing more from both camps in the coming days. Now for details of a startling new medical development we go to our science correspondent, Fergus Welch.

Good afternoon. This is Tim McDougall in the newsroom with a newsflash. We have reports coming in that French forces have landed at Pevensey. Over to our reporter on the spot, David Sleet.

Yes, Tim, we're here in England on the beaches at Pevensey in Sussex, and the landing has gone completely unopposed. I gather that Harold Godwinson's forces are still some way north of our position at the moment, and the Normans are setting up camp having established their beachhead. There are French soldiers as far as the eye can see, and they are all fresh from extensive training. You worry quite seriously at the ability of the English to carry this off after their exploits in Yorkshire and the forced march back down south. For the moment, back to the studio.

Thank you, David, and for an update on the English forces it's over to Richard Major with the Godwinson army. Richard?

Hello, Tim. Well, we're a long way short of London at the moment, and it has to be said that recruitment has been difficult. Harold's army is nowhere near the strength it was before the battle against Hardrada, and there's an ominous rumbling of discontent amongst the troops. We're making best possible speed, but I feel it's going to be a long hard journey, and early indications are that we don't expect to be in Sussex until at least October 12th. Back to the studio.

Thanks, Richard, and we return you now to your normal programmes.

Good evening. Tim McDougall in the newsroom on Thursday 10th of October 1066, and with no more ado it's over to our reporter David Sleet with the French forces in Sussex. David.

Yes, good evening, Tim. Here in the Norman camp we're just about ready for the arrival of the English forces, and final training sessions have been going on throughout the day. It's noticeable that confidence here is sky high at present with all troops fresh and rested. William has been holding meetings with his senior staff and although we're not allowed access to them, several unofficial sources are predicting a resounding victory within the next few days. Back to you in the studio.

Thanks, David. Now for an update on Harold's situation we go over to Richard Major who, I gather, is approaching London. Richard?

Yes, we are, Tim, but it's been a weary journey and I reckon these men will need a good rest before flying into a fight with what we gather are completely fresh French forces. We believe that arrival in the capital will be around ten o'clock tomorrow evening, and plans are already well advanced for a recruitment drive amongst the residents. Back to the studio.

Okay, thanks, Richard. It looks like we are going to be in for a remarkable few days and the fate of the entire country now hangs in the balance. Now, it's over to the weather desk and Mick Pike.

Good evening. It's Saturday the 12th of October 1066, and I'm Tim McDougall in the newsroom. With dramatic events unfolding, the French and English armies prepare for a showdown in Sussex. Over to our reporter Richard Major with Harold Godwinson's Saxon forces.

Hello, Tim, we arrived in London as planned yesterday evening, and recruitment began almost immediately to replenish the English ranks in readiness for what we now believe will be a battle some time on Monday. It leaves very little time for a march down to Sussex where the French have dug in and are preparing their forces for a classic pitched battle. In their favour, the English have that victory in Yorkshire under their belts, and the knowledge that they, at least, are battle-hardened troops against a largely inexperienced, albeit well-trained, Norman outfit. It's going to be interesting. Back to you, Tim.

Okay, Richard. Now over to Sussex and David Sleet.

Good evening, Tim. Well, the Normans are ready, and we think that the site selected will be just outside Hastings. This gives William all of tomorrow to move his forces into place and means that he should have the pick of the battlefield positions. All the indicators are in his favour, and frankly the English are going to have to pull something pretty spectacular out of the hat. Back to you Tim.

Thanks, Richard, and we'll be staying with this story over the next forty-eight hours, but for now over to the sports desk and Paddy McGinty.

Good morning. This is Tim McDougall in the newsroom on Monday the 14ᵗʰ of October 1066 as dramatic events unfold in Sussex outside the town of Hastings. Over to our correspondents David Sleet with the French, and Richard Major with Harold's Saxon army. David, how's it going?

Not well, Tim, good morning. William appears to have made a serious tactical blunder. With numbers on each side of around seven to eight thousand, field position was absolutely vital in ensuring a victory, but he seems to have allowed the English to occupy the high ground leaving him an uphill attack as the only option. At this point all the advantages seem to be in Harold's favour.

Okay thanks, David. Richard, what's your view on this?

Hello, Tim; yes, I agree it's a serious error. We are behind the main English force, and looking down on the French from a seemingly unassailable position. It seems to me that all Harold has to do is fend off a series of attacks from what is bound to become a tiring force, and then simply mop up the battlefield. It looks to be all over before it's even started. We think the initial movements will be taking place very shortly. Back to you.

Thanks, guys. We'll be staying live with that story as the day unfolds, and we'll bring you all the latest news as it happens.

This is Tim McDougall in the newsroom with dramatic news of the battle at Hastings in Sussex. Over to our two reporters at the scene, Richard Major and David Sleet. Firstly David – what has happened?

Well, Tim, as we said, the Normans had an uphill struggle before them, and initially their archers had little impact on Harold's shield wall because of two factors. Firstly, the arrows that were on target simply hit

English shields, and secondly, many flew straight over the top of the Saxon lines through sheer inaccuracy. The next thing I saw was a shower of rocks coming down the hill from the English lines right into the midst of the Norman ranks. William then sent in his cavalry far too soon, and they struggled to get up the hill. It just fizzled out. We then had the amazing sight of the Breton and Flemish lines retreating down the hill in apparent disarray.

Okay, David. Richard, what happened next?

Tim, this was unbelievable. The Saxons broke ranks and pursued the fleeing Normans down the hill, but as soon as they got on level ground the fitter and fresher French outmanoeuvred them, and in the ensuing melee Harold's troops lost the advantage. William then regrouped his archers and changed the point of their attack to land arrows over the remaining Saxon shield wall. Reports are coming in that one of these arrows struck Harold Godwinson and that he may already be dead. Certainly, the English forces now seem to be in full disarray, and the Normans appear to have snatched victory from the jaws of defeat.

Thanks, Richard. Well, that's truly amazing, and we'll bring you more up-to-date information as soon as we receive it. Until then, we return you to our normal schedule.

Hello. This is Tim McDougall at the news desk with the latest from Hastings. Harold Godwinson, King of England, is dead. He was struck in the eye by an arrow during the battle against Norman forces today and succumbed to his injuries. After a resounding victory against all the odds, William of Normandy has proclaimed himself King and is, as we speak, on his way to London for his coronation. We will bring you more news on events as they unfold, but for now we return you to today's match at the National Archery Centre.

Jumping to Conclusions

"Well, thank you, Mr Richmond. I think that's all we need for now. We appreciate you coming along again, and we'll be in touch in the next few days."

Gerald Richmond shook hands with his two interviewers, smiled a forced smile, and left the office. He'd got to the last three for the position of divisional accountant and now had to wait for the inevitable polite, but firm, rejection letter. Six months before, life had seemed so good; now it lay in ruins.

"If you don't spend more time around here with me and the kids instead of at that electronics firm, you're gonna come home one day and find that there's no family to spend time with!"

His wife, Joyce, had been forthright in her warning, and it was something that she had been saying on and off for quite a while now. He'd been at Simeca Electronics as their Chief Financial Officer for just over ten years, and in that time they'd married, had two children and moved upmarket on the property ladder. They'd even taken advantage of a new type of mortgage to afford their six-bedroom house with double garage. 'Sub Prime' the broker had called it, and with his financial background and a rising property market, Gerald had seen nothing wrong at the time. When the bubble burst, his mortgage lender threatened to foreclose.

"Bastards!" he cursed out loud. Okay, he'd missed three payments, but they'd been in like lightning. Joyce had hit the roof.

Standing in the elevator in the fifth-floor lobby, he mused over the interview he'd just been through. His finger hovered over the ground floor button as the doors closed, but he changed his mind. Punching the top floor one instead, he decided to head for the roof. After all, what was there left? Joyce had gone, he was out of work at forty-nine years of age, and the guys across the lobby were probably already writing his 'No Thanks' letter.

The air was cool up here at the top of the building. Cooler than the hot, steamy streets down below, and he would spend the last moments of his life in contemplation of what might have been. He pulled the pack of Marlboros from his pocket and smiled grimly. The last cigarette in the pack. The last cigarette that he would ever smoke, and it would be here, on the roof of the headquarters of the company which was confirming his consignment to the business scrapheap – ironic really. He lit up and took a long, deep, satisfying drag on the final nail in his coffin. 'Coffin Nails' – that was what Forsyth called them in '*The Dogs of War*'. Well, he wouldn't be needing any more of them after today.

Yes, Joyce had left him. Taking the kids and the car, she'd headed off for her parents' home in Phoenix. Her final warning came back to haunt him in stark relief. He loved them all, always had, and the ten years at Simeca had been the backbone of their financial stability. Trouble was, he had spent far too much time there patching up an old IT system because they were too mean to re-kit, staying late into the night catching up on work for the CEO, and generally coming home too tired and too late to minister to the needs of those who should have been precious to him.

Then, out of the blue, he was finished. Had it been only six months ago that Bradshaw had called him into the office?

"Hey, Gerald, c'mon in. Take a seat; got something I need to talk to you about. Oh, close the door behind ya, yeah?"

'Close the door' – that should have set the alarm bells ringing. Bradshaw never closed his door. His face then set into a block of stone as he sat down the other side of his oak office desk.

"See, we've been goin' through a tough spell." He suppressed an embarrassed laugh. "S'pose you know that already, though. Well, this is kinda rough on me too, but I'm afraid that we're gonna have to let you go."

The words tore the heart out of Gerald, and he sat there transfixed at what he had heard. In the blink of an eye, Bradshaw had cast his career onto the rocks. The rest of the placatory speech was lost on him as he headed for the door, cleared out his office, and was escorted out of the building. Four weeks later his family was gone too. Now with no job, no family and, potentially, no house, he was desperate. The job at United Investments had held out a lifeline, and the recruitment agency said he had all the qualities that the company was looking for.

All his hopes had been pinned on this second round of interviews. He knew that there were three candidates; three slimmed down from a list of twenty, and his initial expectations had been sky high. That was until the final round of questions, much deeper than the rest, and he had struggled to keep a lid on a rising sense of anger at the interrogation.

He took another pull on the Marboro – halfway down now, and not long to go before the act that he had come up here to carry out. He stepped to the edge of the roof and looked down. Twenty-four floors and he could probably wave to his interrogators as he flew past the window; maybe he would see them sealing his envelope. Stepping back and sitting down in the afternoon sunshine, his mind continued its meandering through the last few months.

He'd called Joyce and begged her to come back but she had been adamant in her refusal. They were finished, and all he would have to look forward to would be the occasional visit from the kids. Missing out on their growing up was something that he couldn't bear to contemplate; just one more reason for ending it all.

"Okay, Mr. Richmond, I think we can both see how well qualified you are, but what prompted the departure from Simeca? From what I see they're well-placed to move up the market ladder."

The question had stumped him briefly and he stuttered through his response. Rising costs, poor budgeting, window dressing, off balance sheet financing, and a curious letter from the SEC, had all been matters which the CEO had refused to discuss with him.

"So, you just let it go?"

"No. I pushed matters as far as I felt I could without compromising either my position or that of the company, but Mr Bradshaw just wouldn't talk. In the end I think he fired me just to get me out of the way."

"You didn't fight your corner then?"

"I fought. I redrafted the whole budget, reforecast the cash flows for all divisions, and produced a strategic plan that would have seen us out of the woods inside twelve months."

"So… what then? You just backed off?"

The questioning went on like this for a further fifteen minutes and the effect on Gerald had been draining. When he left the office, it was with an immense feeling of relief. He now knew what it was that he needed to do.

The view from the top of the building was quite spectacular; all the way across the Chicago skyline to Lake Michigan in the distance, and a clear blue sky to frame the entire picture. He'd certainly chosen a beautiful day to make the jump. A sudden fluttering caught his attention, and he shielded his eyes against the glare as a white dove descended onto the rooftop and settled ten feet away from him. It cocked its head on one side, maybe curious of his intentions in a domain not of his own. It hopped around the area picking up pieces of bread clearly left by previous visitors – visitors who didn't have the same appointment with destiny that he did.

"Hey, buddy, how much better off are you?" The question, ordinarily, would have been incongruous, but now seemed quite apt in the circumstances. The dove stopped, almost as if it understood, and turned to face him.

Like an Exocet missile, a hawk descended at breakneck speed, plucked the dove from the roof and was gone in an instant, leaving only a shower of feathers as evidence of its predatory act. The incident stunned Gerald Richmond, and he stood open-mouthed, the Marlboro hanging from his bottom lip.

His words to the dove now came back in stark contrast to the changed circumstances. He was still alive, the dove almost certainly dinner for a growing brood. Casting the smouldering cigarette to the ground, he crushed it beneath his heel and headed back towards the roof door. Moments later he was out on the sidewalk and breathing a life that he had believed to be ending. Back inside, a conversation was taking place which would seal his destiny.

"So, we got three to choose from. You think Gerald Richmond fits the bill? You gave him a pretty tough time with that last round of questions."

Martin Kelley was VP Finance for the group and had pretty much taken a back seat in the proceedings of all three interviews. Gerald was his favoured candidate, but the reply from Duane Pearson, the CEO, was not what he expected.

"No, I don't. Michaelson is much better suited to the role."

"Pity, I kinda liked the guy. Plus, he handled you and your grillin' well."

"That's why I did it to him. With what I have in mind, he'll need all the backbone he can muster. Shelbourne retires next year and we're gonna need a replacement with enough punch to keep that western division on track."

"You're giving him the entire western seaboard?"

"Too right! With the package I got in mind he'd be crazy to turn us down. What's his cell number?"

Gerald had turned left and was deep in thought as he walked along the street. The raucous sound from his pocket shook him from his musings. The number displayed stopped him in his tracks.

By the end of the call he was too stunned to continue but was brought back to reality by the screaming of a woman on the other side of the street. He had not travelled half a block when the body hit the sidewalk. He'd never heard the sound of a jumper hitting the ground before, and the 'splat' was a sickening reminder of what had awaited him only a short time before.

Suddenly, there was concentrated action from all quarters. Some people running away, some running towards the prone and now bloody figure of a middle-aged man. He too was wearing a suit, and Gerald wondered at the guy's fate. A sudden icy chill enveloped him as he realised that the jumper had landed at the exact spot where he would have been had the call to his cell not interrupted him.

Behind Closed Doors

Corridors stretching out as far as the eye could see. Sandra Devine squinted as she peered into the gloom, trying to make out anything which would tell her where it was that she stood. Stood – there; in nightdress, dressing gown, and pink fluffy slippers, at the crossroads of a labyrinth of corridors in a hotel whose name she did not know.

Each corridor was flanked by rows of doors heading away into the distance. She looked around uneasily for what must have been the umpteenth time, and a shiver ran down her spine – the air seemed suddenly much colder. Hesitantly, she approached the first one; it was on her right and the light appeared to brighten as she stood before it. It was nondescript - a typical hotel bedroom door, bland in colour and with nothing to differentiate it from the myriad others which she could see.

The number, the room number, 295, was emblazoned in strangely bright golden figures two thirds of the way up its surface. Sandra turned around and looked at the opposite door. She shuddered; 295, exactly the same number. The next door also bore the same number in the same style, and the one after that; in fact, every door that she could see on either side of the corridor was identical. She was in no doubt that *all* of the doors in *all* of the corridors would bear the same three digits in the same order.

A small, almost indiscernible, feeling of panic started to rise from the pit of her stomach as she slowly reached out for the doorknob of the one she was now facing. It turned with a firm 'click' which echoed into the distance, and she stopped with the opening a mere crack on her left. Her mouth was dry, and she swallowed hard to suppress a sense of foreboding. The door began to open of its own accord and she stepped back, releasing the knob.

Behind the opening, and to Sandra's astonishment, was another door, but there the similarity ended. This one was white; no, not just white. It was the brightest, purest, blinding white she had ever seen, and there at the top of its central panel, in numbers as black and shiny as highly polished jet – 102.

"What?" She spoke out loud, though there was no-one else there to hear. There was, of course, no answer, and yet she looked around, as if expecting to see John standing behind her.

"John!" she called. She cursed in exasperation! Never there when she wanted him. She turned back to the door and reached out for the handle. The blinding flash of light had her reeling backwards and falling to the floor.

She awoke with a start, bathed in perspiration and wrapped tightly in the bedclothes. Home - she was back at home, in her own bed, in her own room. The noises from the kitchen downstairs told her that John, her husband of almost thirty years, was busily preparing breakfast, a task which he carried out with unerring regularity every Saturday morning. Her appearance at the kitchen door elicited the kind of humour which had attracted her to him all those years ago.

"Good grief, missus, which cat dragged *you* in?" A change of voice and he was Groucho Marx personified. "Come on, spill the beans an' me an' the boys'll go get him!"

This time, however, she was not amused, and one look across the room told him that a career in comedy would never have earned him the kind of living he enjoyed as a teacher.

"What's up?"

"Odd dream, and it's happened three times now. Didn't bother to tell you the first couple, but now it's getting a bit worrying."

Over breakfast, she explained the strange scenario of the doors and the flash of light before she had the chance to see what was behind the second one. Whilst concerned at his wife's sense of unease, John nevertheless tried to lighten the mood by pointing out the cheese supper that had been consumed the night before. She was, he said, a martyr to late night meals and the restlessness which inevitably followed. The upcoming two-week holiday in The States would take her mind off it and banish all thoughts of doors and suchlike. She frowned – he was always so sensible about things like this, and all her misgivings were starting to fade away.

The next two weeks positively flew past, and in no time at all they were circling New York in the clear blue sky of a June morning. The excitement had been building to a crescendo for the past few days, and with Hayley and Dave waiting for them in the Arrivals area at JFK, Sandra and John hurriedly collected their baggage, eased their way through immigration, and into the welcoming arms of their old school friends who had moved to the Big Apple years before.

"C'mon; we have lots to do." The twang in Dave's voice was pronounced with their living in America for so long, and he shepherded them to his waiting Buick. "Let's get you guys to the hotel, and we can go eat."

"Money." John Devine held up his hand as if addressing a classroom full of 'A' Level Geography students. One finger was raised in admonishment to his old friend. "We're not sponging off you two just because you live here. We need some Dollars. Nearest bank, please."

"Okay, but you gotta get rid of your bags first." Hayley laughed, and they made their way to the Crowne Plaza on Times Square.

The hotel wasn't cheap, but when in New York John was not about to scrimp. They dropped off their cases and headed out towards Broadway and the first available bank. Everything here was drawn on a much bigger scale than at home. Tall buildings grew like oversized Lego pieces on either side of the streets and shafts of bright sunlight rained down at the intersection of each block. He shook his head and smiled – it was like something out of the movies. Sandra shook him from his reverie with a sharp tug on his sleeve.

"Come on, we haven't got all day. I'm hungry."

"Alright, alright, keep your hair on, woman. Just taking in the atmosphere."

Across the street of the Upper West Side stood the impressive premises of Citibank at 2350 Broadway, and this was their destination in the quest for usable currency. The canopied entrance off the sidewalk opened out on the inside to a grand foyer from which came the sounds of daily business being transacted. They had never seen the like of such an establishment before. A uniformed figure approached from the right.

"Morning. Can I help you folks?" The face was broad, the smile seemed broader, and the salute crisp.

"We're here on holi... vacation, and I'm afraid all we have is Sterling." John was almost apologetic in his admission of forgetting to exchange it before leaving Heathrow.

"That's no problem, sir. Just take a ticket from the machine way over there and go to the teller when your number comes up." He smiled again and returned to his station. Sandra became suddenly very uneasy.

"What's the matter?" John frowned at his wife's sudden change in demeanour.

"Hmm? Oh, I don't know. Something's not right. Did you see his number?"

"Number? What number?"

"The number on the epaulette of his uniform. 295. That's his number – he's the security guard."

"Yes, I know that, but what does it matt... oh, the dream. Look, it was just a dream that's all. The number's just coincidence. Come on, let's get in line."

He took the next ticket from the dispensing machine and they moved towards the row of tellers. The queue was long but moved along quite quickly. 99 flashed up on a screen above the counter and John looked down at his ticket. 100 came up and a frown began to form on the smooth surface of his forehead. He looked up at Sandra and she took the ticket from him. 101 – her eyes widened in astonishment, their ticket was number 102.

102 - the number on the white hotel door, the one which she could not open, the one where the blinding flash of light snapped her out of the dream. 295 had been the number on the first door which she got past. 295 was the security guard's number, and they had just passed him.

102 was now flashing up on the sign which called out 'Next Customer Please'. She stood rooted to the spot. Impatient voices

began to stir from behind her as busy New Yorkers queued for service.

"C'mon, lady, move along. We got places to be."

Sandra turned to her husband and shook her head with increasing speed as she fought to control the rising sense of panic which was slowly paralysing her. She snapped into action.

"Out! We have to get out of here! Now, John, move! Now!"

"Yeah, now, youse two, move it. Let somebody else in!" An anonymous figure pushed past as the number sign changed – 103.

John retreated on the end of the arm of his now running wife as the first shots were fired. They had made it to the door and were almost out in the bright sunshine when everything kicked off inside the bank. He turned at the last minute to see the body lying in a pool of blood. The body of the anonymous customer who had pushed past them just moments before. The body which occupied the very place which should have been taken by one of them. One more tug on his sleeve and they were both outside in the relative safety of the New York street.

Sirens split the city air as more shots came from inside the bank, and the NYPD cavalry arrived to take on the bank robbers who were presumably by now amassing hostages from amongst the ranks of customers inside. Ranks which could so easily have included both of them.

The Sins of Charlotte Swinscoe

Charlotte Swinscoe had never considered herself to be a bad person. She had, it was true, been involved in some dubious matters in her youth, but at the age of thirty-six that was now well behind her.

"Morning, dear." The cheery voice of Raymond, her partner, preceded him into the dining room like a warm summer breeze.

She smiled over the top of her newspaper in reply and went back to her coffee while he prepared his breakfast. Raymond Martin was, on paper, a millionaire, and had made his money in the boom years of the Thatcher government's economic revolution in the 1980s. From relatively humble beginnings with a string of northern market stalls, he had expanded operations on the back of some shrewd wheeler-dealing. He bought his first high street shop in 1986, and by the end of that decade had a further six.

"You're in the news again." She laid the daily paper across the table and tapped a section of the financial press. "Looks like the new trainee management initiative's going down well."

Martin had taken a calculated gamble six months earlier by placing an advert in one of the Sunday broadsheets. The company was offering a five-year apprenticeship to university graduates holding a business qualification, with a guarantee of full-time employment at the end of the term. It had been a resounding success, and had gained him and the firm widespread approval with a slot on prime-time television as the scheme achieved national publicity. Sales, of course, moved sharply upwards as a result.

"Yes." He smiled. "It was a rather a good idea after the weeding out process had ended, wasn't it? Good job I employ you."

The idea had been Charlotte's, but there was no conflict between them over the success or failure of the gamble. As a team, they had been working in this way for a number of years, and the future was looking very bright.

"We'll have to float the company to generate the cash for the extra shops you're going to need for your team of managers." She drained her cup and poured another.

"Already taken care of, sweetheart." He sat down opposite with his tea and toast. "I'm seeing Miles Underwood this afternoon. Barkers will underwrite the issue, and should make a killing for their trouble. We'll have all the funds we need, and more."

Charlotte had begun to think that life was passing her by, and the relationship with Raymond, though satisfactory, occasionally left her with a feeling of unfulfillment. He was fifteen years her senior, attentive to her needs, but never satisfied her physically in the way that she thought she deserved. A few younger men had crossed her path, but loyalty to her partner and the company which they ran had always held her back from anything more than social flirting. That had been before the arrival of Daniel – a twenty something who had seriously turned her head.

Daniel Thorpe was a university graduate who had successfully applied for one of the aforementioned positions. He was clever, handsome, and carried himself with an air of supreme confidence. From what Charlotte could make out, there were no girlfriends in the picture, and he had responded to her flirting in more than merely a social way. From his standpoint, there would be no harm in playing along with her as long as things did not get out of hand – he needed the job, and Raymond Martin was not a man who would take kindly to his private life being invaded. The young man had come to London on a quest of sorts, and any major distraction caused by Charlotte could not be allowed to divert him from that path. They had met socially on a few occasions at events organised by the firm, and on one other at a private location when Raymond had been out of town.

Thorpe's relocation to London had been an emotional wrench from his native county. He had lived in Derbyshire for as long as he could remember, and the Dales town of Bakewell, with its markets and busy retail sector, had been everything that he wished for. Once out of school, however, finding a job had become problematic and he had gone away to university more as a means of delaying the inevitable until economic conditions improved than with any clear idea of where his future was to lie. A postgraduate course at the Manchester School of Business had given him a firm grounding in the cut and thrust world of the British economy, and it had been with this qualification that he had been able to find his way down south and into the company run by Raymond Martin.

This, however, had not been his true quest, but was more a way of sustaining himself whilst the mission continued. He had left his parents' house with a heavy heart at the end of his education, but remained focussed upon the true reasons for his journey to the capital – it was here, he had been informed, that the end of his quest would materialise.

"Penny for them." The voice of Charlotte Swinscoe stirred him from his concentration on the project on which his day was focussed.

"What?" he replied. "Oh, nothing; just a few thoughts on this." He pointed at his computer screen, where the current files were on display.

"It's not good to work as hard as you do all the time." She smiled. "Raymond'll start to think you're after the company." She paused. "He's away this weekend, if you have the time."

The suggestion was clear, and after their first encounter some weeks earlier, Daniel had recovered from his earlier reservations about becoming involved with a woman much older than himself. Charlotte had been quite a catch in more ways than one, and stirred feelings within him that girls of his own age simply could not match.

"Need to be discreet," he frowned in mock concern.

"Oh, yes," she pursed her lips. "As discreet as you were last time, I suppose. There's no going back now, young man. I need you."

Raymond Martin's trust in his partner was not entirely justified, and he knew that. Nevertheless, despite what she had told him of her past during the years which they had spent together, he had believed that their relationship was on solid ground. He retained an open mind on most things, but where Charlotte was concerned he was not a man to compromise. He had seen the looks which passed across Daniel's face each time she was in the general office, but never for one moment believed that any feelings which he had would have been reciprocated by her. To that extent, Charlotte believed herself to be free from his scrutiny as long as she and Daniel kept their assignations out of the London area; they were travelling back from the latest of their trysts when all their careful planning came to nothing.

They were driving north on the M20 near to West Kingsdown on a dark and rainy Sunday evening, and visibility was down to less than fifty yards.

Dariusz Banaszewski was tired; he had made the trip from his home town of Wroclaw, picking up a load in Munich, and had turned his rig around immediately after making delivery in the West Midlands. One brief stop during his southwards journey on the M40 at Cherwell Valley was all that he allowed himself in order to make his ferry crossing at Felixstowe on time. He was squinting hard through his windscreen, trying to filter out the pounding rain and the hypnotic sweep of his wipers. It was becoming harder and harder to remain awake, and he shook his head to refocus his tired eyes.

The atmosphere in Charlotte's Audi A7 could not have been more different. Allowing Daniel to drive whilst she caught up with some work on her laptop, she was completely unaware of the worsening weather and the speed at which her younger companion was driving. On a clear day, and in good conditions, his control of the car would not have been compromised. However, youth, overconfidence, and a powerful engine lulled him into a false sense of security as they sped north and back to the capital. The distance between them and the rapidly tiring Polish truck driver was diminishing by the minute.

Banaszewski tried everything to revive his flagging concentration. He switched stations on his radio, desperately seeking something which would keep him from falling asleep at the wheel. His command of the English language was very limited, being restricted to the vocabulary required to make a return trip after dropping off a load in a foreign town. Nothing on the airwaves made much sense to him, and he switched the radio off.

A blaring car horn alerted him temporarily to the fact that he had begun to stray across two lanes of motorway, and he pulled the wheel over to the left to avoid a collision. He cursed loudly and shook his head once more. There was no time for another break in the trip – he would barely make the ferry as it was, and Folkestone seemed a long way away.

Charlotte looked up from her laptop and cast a glance at the Audi's speedometer. "Slow down," she said. "What's the rush? He's not back until the morning; you'll get us both killed at this speed."

"Chill out," Daniel replied. "I can handle this car."

The reproof and reply were given in good humour, and she returned to her files. Neither of them saw the oncoming artic on their side of the motorway. In his confused and tired state, Dariusz Banaszewski had fallen asleep. He had crossed all three of the south bound lanes, knocking out a line of rubber cones marking a temporary gap in the barrier, and was now barrelling down the northbound overtaking lane. Daniel Thorpe had a matter of seconds to take evasive action, but with vehicles in both of the lanes to his left he had nowhere to go.

"Oh, no. Please... no!" he whispered, and Charlotte had time only to look up and see the rig heading directly for them.

The impact took both vehicles, and several others, crashing across the hard shoulder. Most of the others involved ended up in the relative safety of the grass banking. The Audi, however, taking the full force of the Polish driver's truck head-on, was rammed backwards, and steamrollered into the reinforced concrete support of a flyover. Charlotte's last memory was of excruciating pain as the car concertinaed around the two of them like a metal coffin.

"How bad is she?" Raymond Martin had hurried to the trauma unit at London's Kings College Hospital.

"Critical," came the reply from Luke Bradbury, emergency medicine consultant. "There was a lot of internal bleeding, and she may not even survive the night."

"When can I see her?" His voice was trembling, and he was fighting to retain control.

"Not for a while. We need to stabilise her, and she's been sent for a complete body scan. Once we've seen that, we'll know more. There's nothing you can do right now."

Martin was not to be put off, and took a seat in the reception area to await developments. Daniel Thorpe, in a separate ambulance, and about half an hour later than Charlotte, had been taken to a different part of the Accident & Emergency department. She had, somehow, been thrown clear of the car as her side of the vehicle exploded outwards as it came to its final resting position. Thorpe, trapped behind the steering column, had to be cut free by the Fire Service. Raymond was completely unaware of his presence at the hospital.

He was awoken from a fitful slumber by Luke Bradbury at the end of his shift. The consultant told him that Charlotte was stable but not yet out of danger.

"She's asleep at the moment, and I'd leave her like that if I were you. We've done all we can, but with a bit of luck and a lot of recuperation, I think she'll make it. She was very lucky, though. Shame the same couldn't be said for the young man in the car with her."

"Young man?" Martin suddenly snapped back to full attention. "What young man? I thought she was alone in the car."

"Sorry, have to go." Bradbury was already on his to the main door. "The day staff will fill you in."

It was whilst this conversation was taking place that Charlotte stirred from her recuperating sleep. As her surroundings came slowly into focus, the memories of the journey northwards and the ensuing accident began to return. An attending nurse spotted the movement on the bed and summoned the on-duty resident, Paula Summers.

"Back with us, then?" Her smile was genuine, her voice reassuring.

"Yes... where am I?"

"Kings, in London," Summers replied. "You had us very worried for a while there."

"All these tubes..."

"Have been keeping you alive, but we'll soon have them off now that you've regained consciousness. You lost a lot of blood – rare type, too," Summers said.

"AB negative. Both my parents were the same," she replied automatically. "Only one percent of the population share it. Look...what happened to...?"

"The young man?" The resident's face turned suddenly grave. "There's no easy way to tell you this – I'm afraid his injuries were far too serious. We did all that we could, but we just couldn't save him."

"Oh, no." Charlotte buried her face in her hands.

"He wouldn't have suffered," she continued. "He never came round, but the two of you exhausted our supplies of blood and more had to be flown in. We didn't realise that you were even related until then."

"Related?" Charlotte stiffened, all thoughts of the crash momentarily forgotten. "What do you mean? That's not possible."

Summers pulled up a chair and sat at the side of the bed. She was puzzled at the reply, and went on to explain how unusual it was for two people in the same accident to be unrelated when they shared the same rare blood grouping.

"We naturally assumed that he was your son. That must make it doubly hard for you."

Charlotte needed some time alone to assemble her confused thoughts, and was relieved when the doctor smiled once again and left the room. Daniel Thorpe...her son? She shook her head; how was that possible? Suddenly a number of facts fell into place. He was on a quest, he had said, but did not elaborate. Could it be that he had come to London in search of his real mother? That single thought sent a shock wave through her, and dim memories of a time from twenty-two years earlier resurfaced.

Her pregnancy, as a schoolgirl of fourteen, was the talk of the village in her native Devon. Her parents, though initially supportive, had bowed to family pressure and persuaded her to give the child up for adoption and carry on with her education. At the time she had not developed any feelings for the baby, and acquiesced to their wishes with little resistance. They were never told of either the baby's destination or its adoptive parents. It had been a boy.

A sudden wave of shame hit her with all the force of a demolition ball. She had flirted with this young man, had courted his attention... and had ended up in his bed. She felt nauseous, but dared not call out for help. Swallowing deeply and struggling to hold on to any sense of reality, her feelings were interrupted by the opening of the door. Raymond was standing there, his face ashen and devoid of any clue as to the thoughts inside his head. What was she to believe? Did he know? Had someone on the medical staff told him the very same facts which had only recently been revealed to her?

Charlotte Swinscoe had never considered herself to be bad; not until this very moment had she believed herself to be a sinner. Now she knew that she was. From the first sin of giving away her baby, to the final chapter in that person's life when she committed one of life's cardinal sins. In her own mind she was now irredeemable, and any explanation offered to the man now standing before her was never going to be enough.

Neal James

Wishful Thinking

1

John Gurnhill was always one for a laugh, and nothing gave him the same kick as dressing up at parties and the like. It enabled him to act out another character which couldn't exist in his day-to-day life. Accountants are dull, boring people who are not given to flights of fancy or acts of impulse. It had been just like that at the office since he started at the mill in 1988, and the chairman was one of the old school who just didn't understand the need for a little levity to brighten up the day. He could have come straight out of Dickens' *'A Christmas Carol'* except that he wasn't really a Scrooge. In fact, he was quite a nice old guy, and the day he died was completely taken up with a general outpouring of grief, and pretty much nothing was done during the entire day.

With his passing, however, came a new dawn when the other two younger company directors took it upon themselves to modernise the firm from top to bottom. John's job changed in its scope to include the new IT system and future development. It made him a very popular and sought-after guy; everyone wanted new programs writing, and with the new skill acquired from courses with ICL his life changed dramatically. Gone were the dusty old accounting books and in came spreadsheets, flow charts and the like. The firm's Christmas party took on a whole new look, and the general mood around the place was that of a long-awaited spring after a cold, drawn-out winter.

The day before the Christmas break became a designated 'dress-down' day, and John and his closer friends decided to make a real go of it by coming to work in fancy dress. Mike came as a conductor, dressed immaculately in a black three-piece suit and wielding a baton ready for the orchestra. What gave him away was the ticket machine around his neck and the constant cries of 'Any more fares please?'

Steve was the schoolboy, replete with short trousers, woolly jumper, school cap, catapult and a pair of glasses from which eyeballs would fall, each one on a spring. Kirsty turned up as a nurse, constantly advising staff to 'take it easy' and sitting them down with a thermometer in their mouths. For John, this was the opportunity he had been waiting for – the chance to strut his stuff in quite outstanding fashion. He knew what costumes each of the others had chosen, but had been very guarded about his own. He resisted all attempts to prise the information out of him and in the end they had given up, resigned to the fact that they would just have to wait it out.

He had known all along what it was to be, and accumulated the necessary kit to assemble his disguise over a period of weeks. The night before the event however, a dry run was needed to ensure that the final effect was exactly what he wanted. Out came the midnight blue suit (still a good fit despite years without being worn), highly polished black shoes, black socks and a white shirt complete with frills at the cuffs. A good look in the mirror was enough to confirm that this foundation was not going to spoil the show. Now for the finishing touches, and Linda stepped in at this point.

"You'll never get it right unless I show you how it's done." Bless her. She could always be relied upon to come to the rescue.

Over the next half hour his hair was slicked back and the orbits of his eyes were darkened with eye-liner. Blood red lipstick took care of enhancing the mouth, and a trickle in the left corner was enough to simulate the last time he had 'drank'. When all else was done, a fine dusting of talcum powder reduced his pallor to deathly grey, the black St John Ambulance cape with its blood red lining was donned, and the transformation was complete. Turning off the main light, and now standing in the semi-darkness, a chill ran right through him. Dracula was in business. It had seemed such a shame to take it all off again, but he had to know that it would work. Now for tomorrow.

Travelling to work in the darkness of a cold December morning at 6.30am gave John all the cover from prying eyes that he would need, but he knew that he'd be unable to resist the temptation of a scare on the way to the mill. Pulling up at the traffic island at the bottom of Croft Lane just outside town, he wound down the car window and stared at the sleepy-eyed motorist in the next lane. The guy turned a tired face to look at him just as John opened his mouth, exposing a near perfect set of plastic fangs. The car stalled as the motorist jumped in his seat. John could only imagine the conversation that the poor man would have with his boss at work. This was not enough – he was now on a roll, and pulling up in the deserted company car park he made his way to the office, and past the security system. Leaving his briefcase at the side of his desk John returned to the yard at the side of the canteen and stood in the shadows to await his first 'victim'. He was not to be disappointed.

The weavers were accustomed to call in early at the mash-house for an early morning cup of tea and some toast. Three voices could be heard making their collective way up the street from the car park at the corner. Turning into the small entrance to the front of the factory, they stubbed out their cigarettes before entering the cotton mill and walked the 20 yards to the small canteen. They never got there. At the last moment John stepped out of the shadows, cape up to his nose and suddenly whipped it away to reveal a face made up perfectly to take advantage of the gloomy buildings. A final 'hiss' was enough to scare the living daylights out of all of them. It was Hazel who recovered first.

"John Gurnhill! You idiot! You scared the life out of me!"

It was the best part of his day, and the women soon saw the funny side of it; he got away fairly lightly with the promise of a repeat performance half an hour later when Beryl, the shift supervisor, came in.

The end of the day was marked by a general unrobing when all the day's participants assumed their normal office dress, but Terry Poulson, one of John's co-conspirators suggested they both go along to a fancy-dress party taking place across town that evening. John knew that Linda wouldn't go, it wasn't her kind of thing, but with his wife's blessing and the promise of a ride home at the end if he weren't too late, he went along.

By the time he and Terry got there, the party was in full swing and a trip to the bar was followed swiftly by John being dragged unceremoniously on to the dance floor by the Christmas Tree Fairy (her name was Stephanie Hughes she said, but he could call her Steph). They danced, they had a drink, they danced some more, and then they sat down. They talked about this and that and it was generally a very pleasant evening. Terry had, by this time, paired off with a very fetching version of Morticia Addams, and they had vanished into who knows where. Consequently, when Stephanie latched on to him for the rest of the party, John thought it only polite to remind his partner for the evening that he was a very happily married man, and although extremely flattered by her attentions, he considered that it was time to be leaving.

"Is there nothing that you would wish for?" She pouted in that look made iconic by Marilyn Monroe.

"Not really." He answered nervously, suddenly thinking that all was not as it appeared to be.

"Nothing I can *do* for you at all?" she cooed, seductively.

"No, I er...better be off now."

"Not even one wish?"

"Well, I suppose...if I could live forever, now that would be quite something." It was said more as a means of escape than anything else, but she dragged him back down into his seat and waved her baco-foil wrapped wand over his head.

"Tane iri tes." The words were spoken almost in a whisper, and were accompanied by the sprinkling of what John supposed to be some kind of white powder.

He didn't hang around too long to find out, and beat a hasty retreat towards the door in search of Terry as she sat there with a curious smile upon her angelic features. One look backwards from the safety of the hallway was enough to convince him that a swift telephone call would have his wife there to collect him pretty quickly. Terry, in fact, was nowhere to be found, and with his surreptitious departure with the Morticia 'thing', John now doubted whether he would see his friend again this side of the weekend.

Half an hour later, and still in full make up, John was relieved to see the Sierra containing his wife, Linda, turn the corner at the top of the street. Taking one last drag from his cigarette, he crushed it beneath his shoe and got in beside her.

"Early finish? Wasn't expecting you for a while yet." She smiled and pulled away.

"No, it wasn't really as good as Terry said, and he's disappeared somewhere with some woman. No point in hanging around any longer."

"Better take your fangs out then, we don't want any frightened motorists careering off the road."

"What?"

"Those plastic fangs we got from the joke shop. You don't want to keep them in too long; they'll make your mouth sore."

"I haven't got them in, see?" He pulled the crude plastic teeth from his inside pocket. "They were chafing a bit so I took them out when I left the house."

"You're pulling my leg. I can see them still in your mouth."

John pulled down the sun visor and looked in the vanity mirror. Sure enough, a perfect pair of fangs was protruding from his upper jaw just where the plastic ones had been not half an hour before. In fact, exactly at the time when the fairy had waved her magic wand and muttered the strange words as she doused him with the powder. He was silent for the rest of the trip home, and had a better look in the bathroom mirror once they got there. No mistake this time, and in the full light of the overhead bulb he made a careful examination of his new teeth, if that's what they could be called.

He shook his head in disbelief and started to wash off the make up so carefully applied by Linda earlier that evening. The hair gel used to slick down his crowning glory came out with no trouble at all and after vigorous towelling his hair was back to normal. Not so the rest of his face, however. Where previously there had been a white dusting to give his skin a death-like pallor, he now found a grey, almost waxy surface. His eyes were sunken and hollow with pin prick irises of pure black set in blood-shot surrounds. Lips that once had been vivid red were now no more than thin, pallid slits in a face which resembled more a death mask than his own. A banging on the bathroom door shook him from his examination.

"What are you doing in there, making your will?" Linda, clearly wanting her evening soak in the bath, was becoming impatient.

"Ok, I'm coming." There was nothing for it but to open the door and let her see.

Taking a deep breath, John unlocked the catch in readiness for a hysterical scream. He was barged out of the way by his wife desperate for the use of the bathroom facilities prior to the soak, and as she sailed past him he managed to escape undetected. Turning back to the now fastened door he sighed in relief.

"Just going out for some more cigarettes; be back in a while," he called out as he made his way down the stairs, not waiting to hear any response. He was outside in the darkness moments later and, pulling on a coat, made his way across the local park to sit down and think.

2

Maude Collins ambled across Greenfield Park with her Pekingese, Charlie, in tow. He was a dog of habit, and the late-night excursion into the green area just down the road from Maude's flat was one of his real pleasures in life. Beyond the usual personal needs at the end of each day, it gave him the opportunity for a good sniff around when the bigger dogs were long gone. Tonight was no exception, and he trotted in and out of the shrubberies like some four-legged metal detector in search of anything which might take his fancy. He had been snuffling in and around one of the bougainvillea bushes when he caught the first hint of something very unusual. His teeth bared automatically and the hackles at the back of his neck came to full alert; a deep, guttural, almost primeval growl began way down in his throat, gaining intensity and volume as it made its way up through his windpipe and out of his now frothing mouth.

"What's the matter, Charlie? Silly boy, there's nothing there."

Maude's eyesight was not what it had been of late, and her new spectacles had yet to arrive at the opticians. Consequently, anything remotely distant was a mere blur, and with there being no apparent threat from any quarter her attention focussed on the Peke and his sudden, out of character, behaviour. Charlie had started to back away and was now straining at the leash in an attempt to flee the scene of what he perceived to be the gravest danger. Maude hung on to her end of the tether and tried to restrain the dog. Charlie, however, was having none of it, and slipping his head sideways was out of the collar and away into the darkness as fast as his little legs could carry him. Maude was left standing alone in a pool of light shed by one of the park's numerous street lamps, and would have turned and made her own way home if a sudden movement had not caught her failing vision.

The figure on the park bench had remained invisible to her up to that point, but a slight shift in its posture revealed a white shirt beneath the dark coat which it had been wearing clutched around itself. It was this flash of brightness which arrested her attention and, squinting through the gloom, she could just make out a hunched figure sitting on one of the benches provided by the council for weary ratepayers to rest their feet. She looked all around her, but the two of them seemed to be the only ones in attendance. Greenfield Park was noted for being a relatively safe place to walk at any time of the day, being one of the areas unfrequented by the groups of troublemakers who normally gathered in such places – it was too far out of town for them to make the effort. With this feeling of self-assuredness, Maude made her cautious way towards the figure, and was about ten feet away when she made her enquiry.

"Are you all right, young man?"

The figure was that of a male, casually dressed, and wearing a jacket. Maude frowned; as with most elderly residents she felt the cold, but understood that this did not necessarily apply to those of a younger generation. Nevertheless, it was chilly and he had made no attempt to refasten the coat which had fallen open. He was sitting hunched forwards with his face in his hands, and his shoulders were shaking almost imperceptibly. She moved closer, concerned at his lack of response and wondering whether to summon medical help.

"I said are you alright, young man?"

Close enough now, she reached out her hand, placing it on his left shoulder and giving him a gentle shake. Slowly and with an almost dramatic movement, a face emerged from the shadows created by the hands. John Gurnhill had seen her from the moment she entered the park gates but, choosing to ignore her in the hope of remaining undetected, had shrunk back into the shadows at the far end of the bench. Charlie's reaction had startled him and forced the movement which Maude had picked up – now there was no chance of remaining concealed, and the shaking of his shoulder forced an automatic response. The face which emerged to greet the old woman had her reeling backwards in abject terror.

John stood up, now revealed completely for the first time to the pensioner, and stepped forwards. Maude's mind reeled at what she could not believe she was seeing; her head shook violently from side to side in futile denial of what her eyes told her had to be the truth. She had seen her share of the classic vampire horror movies, but shrugged them off as products of Bram Stoker's over-active imagination. The thing before her was no Christopher Lee or Bela Lugosi, but bore an uncanny, spine chilling resemblance to the Nosferatu played by Max Schreck in the 1920s. All this assaulted her senses as she tried desperately to mobilise her ancient legs into flight. With heart rate now racing out of control, she staggered back against a streetlamp, transfixed by the approaching spectre with its hands outstretched in some macabre gesture of hate.

John had risen from his seated position, anxious to prevent the woman from raising any kind of alarm. How he intended to achieve that aim whilst appearing as he did was not something which he had considered to any great degree. That the situation was now rapidly spiralling out of his control was quite evident, and it became abundantly clear that he would have to make a concerted effort to calm her down. His outstretched hands had been more a gesture of supplication than threat, but with the target initially backing away and now trapped against the lamp, any approach was doomed to failure.

Maude sank to her knees as the hideous vision bore down upon her. The scream which could have brought any passer-by running to her aid died in her throat as she fought for breath against the vice-like pain which now gripped her chest. She hardly noticed the tingling sensation running along her left arm; the darkness enveloped her, but the rattle of the old woman's final breath told John that it would have been an academic exercise – she was dead.

She was dead, and he had caused it. He had scared the life out of her – had actually frightened the poor old lady to death. He was a murderer, and looking as he did there would be no way out of the situation were he to be caught. He glanced around; the park was a place of total silence and completely devoid of any living thing. He laughed at that thought – he couldn't include himself; after all vampires were the undead, weren't they? Standing up, he looked back down at the body on the ground. He had to get out of the park quickly before some late-night drunk stumbled across her and raised the alarm. There was only one place to go, and that was home. He had run out to prevent Linda seeing him, but now she was the only one who would believe the story which he was about to tell.

Standing with his back to the inside of the front door, he gathered himself for the worst moment of his married life. Linda would have to help him find Stephanie Hughes. It had to have been she who caused this with the strange words she muttered after he gave her the brush-off, and the consequences of failure to track her down just didn't bear thinking about. The soft footfall at the top of the stairs told John that his wife had emerged from her soaking in the bath, and was now making her way downstairs for a drink. She had been towelling her hair but stopped, wound the towel around the back of her head and threw the trailing ends back over the top. Bringing her eyes back down to face him she stood frozen in horror at the sight which greeted her.

3

The telephone ringing at the corner of his desk shook Dennis Marks out of the daydream into which he had strayed. The voice on the other end was familiar, business-like and to the point.

"Dennis, it's George Groves. You'd better get down to the lab right away. We've got a really strange one just come in off the streets."

'A really strange one' was George Groves' euphemism for a body that defied all of his abilities to determine a cause of death, and Marks had learned long ago to trust the man's judgement in all matters relating to forensic science. He closed the file on Solomon Goldblum which he had been reading, and slid it back into his top drawer – he would return it to Records later. The last thing he needed right now was 'a really strange one'; they couldn't come any stranger than the old man who had leapt through the office window to his death six floors below in the car park. With a huge sigh, he finished his lukewarm coffee and headed off for the mortuary. Groves was standing over one of the tables when he arrived, hands planted firmly along one of the sides and shaking his head slowly in puzzlement. He looked up as the detective entered the room.

"You're going to love this one after the Goldblum saga." Groves certainly knew how to cheer him up.

"So, what is it that's so urgent and 'strange'?" Dennis Marks had been shaken by the events leading up to the suicide of Solomon Goldblum, and his manner was testy to say the least.

It had taken three months of regular treatment before the nightmares stopped. Three months of uncertainty, three months of mind-numbing analysis, before he was deemed fit to resume his duties. The entire episode had projected him to the very brink of a nervous breakdown, and although he had managed, somehow, to conceal the worst of the situation from the police psychiatrist, Marks' wife, June, was quite another matter. She had tried her hardest to persuade him to take the retirement package which had been tentatively suggested by the top brass, but he was having none of it. Now, here was another oddball case to test his mettle.

Groves whipped back the covering sheet to reveal the body of Maude Collins, and Marks' involuntary sharp intake of breath showed that the man was still not back to his best. The frail corpse before him was that of an eighty-year-old woman who had been found lying in Greenfield Park by an early morning newspaper delivery boy. Groves pointed out that she had been dead for somewhere in the region of eight to nine hours, and that there were no apparent signs of any injury which could have resulted in her death.

"Well, what killed her then?" Marks was not enjoying this latest test of his ability to return to normality.

"Heart failure. More specifically, a massive cardiac arrest. Look here." He handed the DI a set of stills taken by the Scene of Crime Team earlier that day.

"Her face, it's…"

"Yes, creepy, isn't it? A look like that on anyone and you start to think that she was scared to death."

"Anything else? I mean, you surely can't be serious on the basis of just one photograph."

"Well, when your men made enquiries around the area, it seems that the old woman was out with her dog on his nightly walk."

"So, what?" Marks was not following the line of logic at all, and Groves heaved a sigh of frustration. This was hard work with a man normally so in tune with events.

"The dog was nowhere to be seen, and it wasn't until a door-to-door exercise was carried out that we found him. He was crouched under a bush in a neighbour's garden."

Charlie, the Pekingese, had returned home after breaking free from the leash which attached him to Maude, and took refuge in the front garden of the neighbour. When officers found him, he was still shaking and wide-eyed with fear. Attempts to persuade him out of hiding had resulted in a visit to casualty for one of the PCs after a vicious bite pierced the young woman's hand. The dog itself was now under sedation at the surgery of a local vet who had expressed considerable surprise at the damage inflicted by one of his more mild-mannered patients.

"So, we've got a dog that wouldn't say boo to a goose suddenly putting one of our officers out of action, and an old woman with a Halloween mask for a face. That it?"

"For the moment, until I carry out a detailed examination, although you might be interested in this."

He picked up a plastic evidence bag from a table behind him. It contained a cigarette butt which had been found underneath a nearby park bench. The sheet of paper which accompanied it had come back from DNA profiling, and even to Marks in his current state it seemed unusual.

"These markers..."

"Are not what they should be." Groves finished the sentence. "What we have here is the trace of fresh saliva which could have come from a person who was in the vicinity around the time the old woman collapsed. The fact that this person chose not to report the matter is suspicious, but then, you are the policeman, not me."

Marks grinned – the first time for a while, and Groves picked up on the change in his demeanour, pressing on with his analysis.

"The DNA is not entirely human..." He left the statement hanging, looking for a reaction in the DI's face. It was not long in coming.

"Wait a minute. Let me get this straight. The fag was smoked by someone who wasn't 'entirely human'. Isn't that as daft as being 'slightly pregnant' or 'a bit dead'?"

"Dennis, what I'm saying is that this profile cannot lie. The markers are 80% human in type, but the rest of them? Well, your guess is as good as mine for the moment. I'll let you know more when I've carried out the autopsy."

Marks returned to his office with more than he bargained for after his return to work. The psychiatrist provided for him by the department after the case of Solomon Goldblum had signed him off as fit to resume his duties, but Marks had never revealed the true details of the old Jew's final interview and the events leading up to his flight from the small office where it had been carried out. Had those facts been revealed, it was by no means certain that he would ever have been allowed back on the premises.

With Peter Spencer on leave somewhere in the Caribbean, he would be on his own with this new case and it had all the hallmarks of being a tricky one to solve. He was shaken abruptly from his thoughts by the uniformed desk sergeant's call.

"Sir, Hollis on the front desk here. We've got a report come in from neighbours of a young woman just off Greenfield Park.

Seems she's in a bit of state and says that something broke into her house last night."

"Something? You mean someone."

"No sir, 'something'. She was quite specific when neighbours managed to calm her down. Oh, and she says it happened while her husband was out."

"Do we know where he is?"

"No, sir, he's not been seen since."

Marks put the phone down and stared out of the window. Days like this you just didn't want too often. Suddenly he wished he and his wife, June, were on the same beach in the Caribbean as Spencer and his wife. He picked up his coat, drained another lukewarm cup of something, and headed for the door.

4

John had moved forwards from the front door, but now stopped in his tracks as Linda backed away before coming to an abrupt halt as she met the surface of the bedroom wall. The whole scene was frozen as they stood there, each apparently waiting for the other to make the next move. That his wife did not recognise him despite his familiar clothing was abundantly clear from the terror-stricken look on her face. He had no option but to attempt an approach.

"Linda. Linda love, it's me, John. You have to help me. I don't know what's happened, and I think I've killed someone."

There was no response. Linda had not heard a single word. Her mind was unable to cope with the apparition which she now saw before her, and its movement towards the stairs served only to increase the sense of horror which had overtaken her only moments before. Though made of sterner stuff than Maude Collins, she had been initially paralysed with fear by the thing which had somehow broken into their home. Now, however, survival instincts took over, and the ear-splitting screams which might have saved the old woman tore the silence asunder, and had John clutching the sides of his head in agony. They increased in volume and intensity as he retreated down the stairs and towards the front door. Linda paused only long enough to gather breath for a further tirade, and John sensed his chance. Grabbing a scarf from the coat rack, he was out of the house and running down the street as fast as his legs would carry him.

That flight took him clear across town and away from the park where the old woman still lay. He had covered a distance of some three miles before he stopped amongst the terraced houses which formed the area of town allocated by the local authority to immigrants and the poorer members of the indigenous population. The breathlessness which he had anticipated simply was not there, and a feeling of supreme fitness ran through his entire being; it was as if he had been given a whole new lease on whatever life had taken him over. He wrapped the scarf around the lower portion of his new face; it was a cold night and it would attract less attention to his features. Strange, and he had noticed it in Greenfield Park - he had no sensation of the biting temperature which was fast approaching sub-zero. It was now clear that his body was changing – changing into that of the abomination which stirred abject terror in the minds of all normal people.

A sudden sound shook him from his trance-like state. A voice – no, voices; two, or maybe three - yes three - and approaching quickly from behind him. More voices, this time from the opposite direction. His sight, another fast-improving sense, had yet to pick out anything visual, but the bat-like radar quality of his hearing alerted him to several young males homing in on his location. He stepped back into the shadow of an alleyway between two of the houses, for the moment perfectly concealed.

The voices grew louder from each direction, and it became clear to John that this was an episode in one of the turf wars which spasmodically infected the more run-down areas of the city. He remained perfectly still – even the holding of his breath was no longer a problem. It was the cat which gave him away. Loping down the street it tried to turn into an escape route down the alleyway where he stood hidden. It stopped dead; fur bristled, ears lay flattened to its skull and with an arching back the ginger tom let out an almost primordial screech, the quality of which John had never heard before. It turned tail and vanished across the street.

The incident was enough to halt the progress of both groups, now numbering a dozen or more, as the fleeing cat alerted them to John's position. With two more individuals now approaching down the alleyway itself, there was only one way out of the situation, and he stepped out of the shadows into the pale light of one of the, as yet unbroken, streetlamps. He was trapped between at least two gangs of young men hell-bent on violence. They all stopped some ten feet from John's position, and one approached from either direction. A shove from behind propelled him further into the street as the two in the alley now joined in the fun. What he supposed were the two leaders stepped forwards.

"Hey Barnesy, what we got 'ere then? Little boy lost, is it? Does your mummy know you're out on yer own then?" This from a tattooed skin-head, now leering as he came closer.

"Could be, Bomber, could be. Looks a little sweetheart to me. What say we have a bit of fun tonight and save the scrap for another time?"

Barnesy, the opposing leader, wore a blade slash like some badge of honour from the hairline above his right ear, across the bridge of his nose and down to the left-hand side of his mouth. The scar was from a previous encounter. He had come out on top with the perpetrator suffering a fatal stiletto wound to the stomach. These were not the kind of people John would have hoped to meet under any normal circumstances. These circumstances, however, were far from normal.

With the two of them now only a matter of inches away, John's demeanour changed. Something within the new him had taken over, and primeval instincts kicked in. He saw the fist, normally a blur from the practiced arm of 'Bomber' Toonan, as a slowly arcing blow aimed at his head. Turning quickly to one side he grabbed at the wrist as it whistled past his nose. With one sharp twist downwards, a loud 'crack' told all present that it was broken. What it did not reveal was a complete severing of the hand from the rest of the arm. Toonan screamed in agony as he looked down at the wreckage where the hand had once been. Barnes made his move.

A red mist descended before John's eyes as his new persona took over. In minutes the entire group had been reduced to a crumpled mass of writhing, screaming forms, the rest of the two gangs now in full retreat from whence they had come. He stood alone in the middle of the street, totally unaware of how he had inflicted the carnage before him. There was blood on his hands, blood which was not his. An almost magnetic attraction compelled him to lick his fingers; it tasted good, so good – but only briefly as yet. A feeling of intense nausea permeated his whole body and he vomited. The injured had dragged themselves back to their feet, and were now seeing for the first time the horrific thing which had taken them on. John's scarf lay on the pavement, and they fled in sheer terror.

Lights were coming on in some of the adjoining properties, and in the distance the wail of police sirens split the cold night air like some banshee cries. John shook himself and ran. He had to find someone who could help – someone who knew him and who would not be phased by his physical appearance. Terry – Terry was the one who had suggested the party. Terry was the one who had introduced him to the fairy, Stephanie Hughes, and Terry was his best friend. It was four miles across town to the bachelor flat where he lived, but for the new John that journey, even through an approaching police presence, would be over in a matter of moments.

Standing at the entrance to the block, John pressed the intercom button at the side of his friend's name. Hoping against hope that Terry would be there, he was relieved when a sleepy voice crackled through the speaker and asked who it was at that time of night.

"It's John. You have to let me in; I'm in trouble and there's nowhere else I can go."

"John? Come on, man, do you know what time it is? Trouble? What kind of trouble?"

"Just let me in and I'll explain! Quick! There's cops all over the place looking for me!"

The door clicked and John was inside a dimly lit atrium area with a staircase and lift at its centre. He took the lift – no point in scaring the pants off anyone unlucky enough to be around if he passed on the stairs. Terry was at the door of his apartment when he arrived at that floor. The scarf was back around John's face.

Inside the flat, Terry rubbed the sleep out of his eyes and turned back from the door; the sight which greeted him sent a shiver the length of his spine, but unlike Linda he recognised the thing which now stood before him.

"John? What happened to you?"

Explanations over the next hour or so had the fugitive hiding away from prying eyes in Terry's spare room. Stephanie was the relative of a friend, and would be fairly easy to find. What would be more difficult was bringing her back to put right what she had done. Until then John would be confined to the apartment, out of the way of those now looking for him. The only fly in the ointment would be Linda. She knew where Terry lived and would reveal that to anyone asking about John's whereabouts. That call was to come much earlier than either of them anticipated.

5

John's wife, Linda, had regained something of her composure by the time Dennis Marks arrived at their home, and with neighbours now ushered politely but firmly back to their own properties, he and the WPC who had accompanied him set about the task of interviewing her. John, she said, had left the house at around 11pm for the short walk to the corner shop across the park. The entire trip would have taken no more than ten to fifteen minutes even allowing for queues at the place, and the intruder broke in during the intervening period.

"Can you remember what he looked like?" Marks glanced up from his notebook.

"Hideous!" She spat out the words and buried her face in her hands, shaking her head as if trying to rid herself of the image. "His eyes…they were almost all white with pinpricks at the centre, and the skin was grey and waxy."

Linda stopped abruptly at this point. Clothing – why had she not seen it before? He was wearing John's clothes, the ones he had changed into when they'd got back from that party! No, it couldn't be; what had he said in the car? He'd already taken the teeth out, but she was sure that she'd seen them as they pulled away from the house. An uneasy feeling crept through her as she realised that the apparition she had seen, and which had tried to say something to her, was John. He'd run off into the night and could be anywhere now. No, not anywhere, there was only one place where he would go from here, and she had to get rid of this detective before he found out too much.

"Clothes. What was he wearing? Can you remember that?"

"Yes." She cleared her throat. "A dark blue top, black trousers – trousers not jeans, and white trainers."

That should be enough to put them off the scent for a while, and with no-one else as a witness Linda would be able to call Terry and get to John before anything else happened. He said he thought that he'd killed someone; she shook her head and Marks closed his notebook, interpreting that as an end to the interview.

"Alright Mrs..."

"Gurnhill."

"Okay, Mrs Gurnhill, that will be all for now, but if you remember anything else please call me on this number." He handed her his card and made his way back to the car. Looking back at the house from the kerbside, he drummed his fingers on the roof.

"Rogers, notice anything odd about Linda Gurnhill?"

"Sir?"

"Well, she stopped rather suddenly in the middle of her description, I thought."

"Perhaps it was too much for her. We got a list of his clothing."

"Hmm, I think she's hiding something. Loose ends..." he shook his head, "...I hate the buggers."

They got in the car and drove away, unaware that Linda had been watching from behind the net curtains, and was now on the phone to Terry. The phone rang out for what seemed an eternity until a strained voice answered at the other end. It was an 'old' voice and the words had a cracked and almost ancient quality to them. It was interrupted quite abruptly by the slamming of a door and another voice – one which she recognised immediately.

"What are you doing? I told you not to touch that thing while I was out!" The reprimand was hissed behind a palm which partially covered the receiver, but Linda heard every word. "Terry Poulson, who's calling?"

"It's Linda. Is John there with you?"

"Linda, what's happened? He says he's killed someone."

"The police have been here. I thought John was…well, not John, and I screamed. He ran and neighbours dialled 999. They've gone now – I'm coming over."

"No, wait. Are you sure that they've gone? I mean, there's no chance that they'll follow you is there?"

"I watched them drive away."

"I'll come and get you. Leave by the back door and I'll pick you up on the corner of Marshall Street – twenty minutes, alright?"

Back at Terry's flat some forty-five minutes later, the two of them stood outside his door, and he turned to Linda before opening it. She nodded in answer to the question he never asked. She was ready to face whatever lay within, and took a deep breath before stepping over the threshold. John was sitting at the kitchen table and Linda started at his appearance. If he appeared horrific before, there had been more changes in the intervening period. His hair had started to thin with alarming speed, his eyes were sunken, and he bore the haunted look of Nosferatu in the old black and white films. She stepped forward cautiously and sat down.

The full realisation of what had happened dawned upon her as John related the events of the past few hours since the party. That he had been responsible for the death of the old woman was, Linda said, tenuous and not provable unless he actually laid a hand upon her. John said he had not. Terry stepped in at this point.

"You have to stay here with him while I go and find this fairy. She might be the only one who can help. John said she muttered some words as he left, and threw some sort of dust over him. I know where she may be and I'll try to bring her back. Do you think you'll be alright?"

Linda smiled for the first time and assured Terry that she would be quite safe. She pulled out the silver crucifix which John had bought for her last birthday. Her husband shrank back involuntarily and held his chest. Terry nodded.

"I'll try not to be too long, but if things get hairy you're going to have to make a run for it."

He left the flat taking with him John's last hope for a return to normality, and secretly wondered at his own confidence in tracking down the catalyst of the current situation. The target for his attentions was, unknown to him, weaving her magic at another party across town at that very moment. His arrival at the home of her grandmother could not have come at a more opportune time. The old woman who answered the door bore an uncanny resemblance to the witch in Snow White, and Terry was momentarily taken aback by her appearance. Nevertheless, she gave him the address of the party to which Stephanie had made her way, and at the stroke of one o'clock he was standing in the front room of a large well-proportioned detached house.

Stephanie, he spotted her immediately from her grandmother's description, was sitting to one side with an older man who was clearly flattered by her attentions. Time to act, and striding purposely over he let rip with indignation.

"So! This is what you get up to when my back's turned. Away on a business trip for five minutes and you're already touting yourself around. What's she told you then?" He looked at the confused and clearly embarrassed man. "Single girl? All alone? No-one to take her home? All the usual stuff. Come on you - home, before the children wake up!"

Terry frog-marched Stephanie out of the room and the house, before spinning her around at the bottom of the yard where he had left the car. The old guy would never know how close he had come to disaster.

"Who do you think you are? What's with that pack of lies in there? I was just warming to him."

"Same way as you warmed to my friend and turned him into a vampire?"

"Oh him." She smiled sweetly. "He was cute. I liked him - we could have been good together. Where is he?"

"At my place, with his life hanging around him in tatters and it's all down to you. You...whatever you are, are going to put things right."

He shoved her into the car, clicked the central locking and drove away.

6

Marks found the note on his desk as soon as he walked in the following morning. It had been timed at around midnight of the preceding day, and was from the duty sergeant. A call from the Accident and Emergency department of the local hospital reported an odd admission. A young offender known to local constabulary had been brought in and dumped by what appeared to be a group of friends all bearing scars from minor injuries. The lad in question, one Marcus 'Bomber' Toonan, had suffered a horrifically crude amputation to his right wrist, and the injury had been wrapped in a rudimentary bandage consisting of his right sock tied at the wrist with a shoelace. The friends had then beat a hasty retreat, anticipating the inevitable call to the local police.

Marks' arrival at the hospital coincided with that of George Groves, who had picked up on the same report and was carrying a plastic bag stained on the inside by what appeared to be blood.

"Got anything of interest to me there, George?" Marks homed in on the package, which seemed to contain a hand.

"Could be, Dennis." He raised the bag. "This was found on Carrington Road; just down the road from your lad's turf. Shall we see him together?"

The casualty doctor showed them to the cubicle where Toonan was lying sedated. The wrist was heavily bandaged, but photographs taken of the arm at the time of admission showed the wound to be a match to the ragged edges of the amputated hand.

"Only questions now are how he lost the thing and why it turned up half a mile from where neighbours reported a scuffle at the time." Marks looked to Groves for answers, but the pathologist merely shrugged.

"You're the detective, Dennis; I just state the facts as I see them. The hand fits – end of story. Why he was there and what happened are really no concern of mine."

Toonan stirred, and Marks whirled around from Groves' apparent unhelpfulness. The young man's eyes opened wide, and there was a look of abject terror as he glanced around the room as if in search of who, or what, had caused the injury.

'Bomber' Toonan was well known to CID, and his exploits had caused them significant problems in the past. Toonan's gaze fixed on the detective.

"Mr Marks! You gotta get 'im. He's evil – look what he's gone an' done!" Hysteria had gripped the thug, and he was on the verge of tears. His favoured right hook was now a thing of the past, and his status within the gang hierarchy now severely compromised.

"Get who, Bomber? Lose a fight and come running to me, is it? What's the matter, bottle out?"

Toonan's statement was disturbing. Whilst not revealing the name of any others involved in the confrontation, it was apparent that a number of gang members had cornered some hapless individual who had strayed onto their stomping ground. Similar occurrences had come to light before, but this time the worm seemed to have turned. Bomber painted a picture of some sort of martial arts fighter, but his description matched nothing that Marks had come across before. The man had a scarf across his face at the time, but the face that was revealed once it fell away had them all frozen in their tracks. Toonan's injury had been by far the worst, but others had suffered cuts and bruises as the 'demon' went to work.

Bomber's choice of words to describe his attacker had Marks poised with pen in mid-air as he made a series of notes. He closed the book and turned to the doctor.

"I want him in a private room right away. No-one in or out of there without my permission, and I'm leaving a couple of uniforms outside to make sure. Clear? George, you and I need to get back to your lab for another look at those DNA profile results."

Terry had arrived back at the flat with Stephanie Hughes to find John huddled in a corner of the kitchen. Linda was seated at the table with the silver crucifix held firmly before her and pointed in her husband's direction.

"You been alright with him?" He nodded in John's direction.

"Yes, but I'm glad you're back. The changes are coming thick and fast now, and it's getting to the point where I don't think he'll be able to recognise me soon. This came in handy though." She waved the chain at John and he shrank back further into the corner. "He's responding less and less to it now."

Stephanie Hughes, the fairy, took one look into the corner of the kitchen and stifled a scream with the fist of her left hand. Apart from a few wisps of hair around the nape of his neck, John was completely bald. His eyes were now sunken bloodshot orbs hidden in deep shadow and a constant stream of saliva ran from a set of hideous fangs which seemed to have grown and rotted since the party. Clothes hung on his frame like those of a Belsen survivor.

"This is all your fault." Terry shoved her in the general direction of John's corner and she squealed in terror. "We need you to change him back. How are you going to do that?"

"It was only meant to be a joke. He snubbed me and I don't like that. Not many get offered the kind of thing I put on a plate for him. He made me cross."

"Did it never occur to you that he might be happily married and that you had nothing to offer? He's my best friend and I want him back."

"Alright, alright, keep your hair on. Just need to wave the wand."

"What about the 'fairy' dust?"

"Fairy dust?" She laughed. "That was only for effect, the real power's in the wand and the words."

"Get on with it then."

"Not so fast, he's got to make a wish first. No wish, no change. That's how it happened last time. He wished to live forever and 'bang'! What you see is what you get. Make him wish for something."

Terry turned carefully to John, whose demeanour was changing by the minute. Soon it would be too late, and the wild look in his eyes told him that they were running out of time.

"John! John! Look at me." John's expression changed back to something approaching normality as the familiar voice commanded his attention. "You have to wish yourself out of this. Tell her to change things back."

John looked from Terry to Stephanie. The sight of the woman who had caused his misfortune had him out of the corner and reaching for her neck. Only Linda's timely intervention with the crucifix prevented a disaster, and he recoiled in pain. Once more calm, and struggling with a garbled almost inhuman order, he yelled at Stephanie to reverse the spell. She approached cautiously using Terry as a screen.

"*Tane iri tes.*" The words had a dramatic effect and John was on his knees, gripping the pit of his stomach, writhing on the floor in agony. Stephanie stepped back and smiled.

"How long?" Terry glared at her insensitivity, and snatched the wand from her fingers as she waved it around in mock salute to her efforts.

"I'm not sure, but the book says it works eventually."

"Book? You did this from the pages of some bloody book?" Linda stepped into the conversation. "My husband's been turned into some monster, and you learned how to do it from some bloody book?"

"Of course. How else are trainees supposed to learn? Anyway, I've done. Must fly now."

"Too right you must!" Terry waved the wand over her head *"Tane iri tes."*

The last look on Stephanie's face was one of stunned amazement as she disappeared in a flash of light, reappearing in the form of a canary. Terry had her in his hand immediately.

"Wait." John was struggling to his feet, the power of speech returning to him. "Linda, find a box. We've got an old birdcage in our box room. She's too dangerous to let free again." The fate of the fairy was sealed.

7

Dennis Marks and George Groves looked down at the report from London Zoo. Groves had contacts there, and had called in a few favours to get the information quickly. There was no longer any doubt about it – they had identified the unknown portion of the DNA found on the cigarette butt at the scene of Maude Collins' death. Although, as Groves had put it at the time, the sample was 80% human, the remaining component had remained a mystery until now. That 20% was now positively identified as that of *Desmodus rotundus* – the common vampire bat. Small wonder, if Marks was correct, that 'Bomber' Toonan had been scared half out of his mind at the sight of the thing which had removed the hand from his right wrist. It was Groves who broke the silence.

"Dennis, you can't be serious. A vampire? Here, in twenty-first century Britain? What next, the Wolfman?"

"After what I went through with Solomon Goldblum I'm quite prepared to believe anything at present. What about that look on Maude Collins' face? Tell me that wasn't the look of someone who had been literally scared to death."

"I can't explain that, it's true, any more than I can give a logical reason for the injuries to Toonan's arm. There must be another reason."

"What about that piece of cloth we got from the hospital? They said Toonan had it in his other hand when they brought him in. Where is it?"

George Groves produced the small plastic evidence bag which contained a dark brown section of cloth approximately one inch square. It was frayed at the edges as if it had been torn from an item of clothing – maybe a coat, the coat of his attacker.

"Time I paid another call on Linda Gurnhill. She was very nervous the last time we spoke, and I'm certain that she's holding something back. I'd love to know what the something was that broke into their house that night, and I'm sure that it's connected to her husband's disappearance."

Terry Poulson was on the point of leaving when Dennis Marks arrived at the Gurnhill home, but remained at the request of the DI whilst he spoke to Linda again. They were the only two in the room as all three sat down in the lounge. Linda Gurnhill seemed to have recovered completely from the shock she had suffered, and that fact alone seemed curious to Marks.

"Mrs Gurnhill, the last time we spoke your husband had vanished and you encountered an intruder in your hall. The description you gave," he looked down at his notes, "was that of a particularly unpleasant looking individual wearing some nondescript clothing."

"Yes, that's right. I was very upset but I feel much better now."

"And your husband, John, isn't it?"

"Yes, he's..."

"Here, inspector." John Gurnhill, now completely restored to his former self, chose that moment to make his appearance. In truth, neither Linda nor Terry had been prepared for the speed of his recovery from the spell cast by Stephanie Hughes, and he had been listening at the door. Dennis Marks was, for the moment, caught completely off guard. He had put one and one together, convinced that two had been the answer, and was ready to put John Gurnhill into a tight corner.

"Mr Gurnhill, I am pleased to see you've returned. Tell me, please, is that your coat in the hall? The dark brown one?"

Before either Terry or Linda had the chance to step in, John had confirmed that it was his, and the DI looked back up from the notes he had been making with a wry smile on his face.

"In that case, I must ask you to come along with us to the station. We will be taking the coat along with us for comparison to some other evidence which could place you at the scene of a recent assault. Your wife may accompany you of course, but that is all."

The story which John related to Marks over the course of the next two hours was incredible in the extreme, and included details of the events of the past few days. Marks thought that he had seen and heard everything after the case of Solomon Goldblum, but this story sent him into a completely different dimension.

Vampires, werewolves, and the bogeyman were all creatures of fantasy and horror utilised by a legion of fiction writers down the years, yet here was an intelligent, articulate executive telling a story which came right out of Medieval Transylvania.

Marks sat back in his chair. If he took this man into an official interview room, the testimony was going to sound very interesting should the matter come to court. Here, there would be a detective recently returned to work after a near nervous collapse at the end of his last case, a man confessing to recovery from a vampiric state, and two virtually unprovable crimes. He looked down at his notes and shook his head. He could not definitely tie John Gurnhill to the scene of Maude Collins' death. His presence at 'Bomber' Toonan's amputation could only be confirmed by one or more members of the local thuggery, and these would not willingly expose themselves to the forces of the law.

Marks laughed to himself and closed the file of notes which he had been writing. In a matter of a day or so, a serious young criminal had been removed from the streets, and his gang members would probably disown him from now on. That could make him a valuable source of information for future use. Maude Collins was a frail old lady who was not likely to have lived much longer anyway, and Marks himself would have much to lose in the form of credibility if he took the case to the Crown Prosecution Service. John Gurnhill was off the hook and released without charge. Maude Collins' autopsy report showed the cause of death to have been due to massive cardiac arrest due to causes unknown, and 'Bomber' Toonan was allowed to check himself out of hospital without any further action being taken. He would be easy to identify now anyway.

Linda and John heaved a huge sigh of relief and left the police station for their home. It was much later that night that they sat down to talk about the events which had turned their lives almost upside down since the party, and a full week before all of the effects of the magic spell finally wore off. The trainee fairy was no longer able to help them out this time as changes began to take a hold on them both. The wild night of passion which they had enjoyed was to prove as much an undoing for Linda as a new way of life for the both of them. She had always believed that a bite on the neck was the only way to be drawn into the fellowship of the undead: this was a whole new experience for her.

A Cut Above the Rest

The body, or what remained of it, had been found by a dog walker out for an early morning stroll. He had parked his car close to Mapperley Reservoir in Derbyshire's Shipley Country Park, and let his Jack Russell terrier out of the back of the vehicle, watching her disappear on one of her customary forages around Shipley Lane. Having seen the dog stop abruptly, sniffing the air, ears erect, he was surprised when she vanished into the trees to the right instead of following their customary course left and up to the wooded area encompassing the remains of what had been the Miller-Mundy estate.

"Where is it?" DS Meade crushed the stub of the cigarette beneath his shoe after the disapproving look from one of the park rangers.

"Over here." Stan Powell, the ranger, led the way into the trees. "The chap who found her is still in the ambulance back there." He jabbed a thumb over his shoulder in the direction of the car park. "He's pretty shaken up, as you'll soon understand."

Meade's progress halted abruptly, ten yards into the undergrowth, as he came upon the scene.

"Oh my… " His hand went quickly to his mouth in an attempt to stifle the rising taste of bile, and he turned briefly away. As a serving officer with over twenty years' experience he had come across some sights in that time, but nothing to match the one which confronted him now. The ranger had returned to the roadside and Meade stood, briefly, alone with the carnage. A voice from behind came as a welcome relief.

"Morning, Chris. Not a pretty sight, is she?" Harry Radford was the county pathologist attached to the Derbyshire Constabulary, and his matter-of-fact manner provided Meade with the respite that he needed.

"Over to you, Doc." Meade shook his head. "Who does this kind of thing?"

The body of the young woman lay, quite exposed, on a bed of ferns just out of sight of the road. She had been butchered, Radford's words, and no attempt had been made to hide her remains. The lower portion of the body, detached with surgical precision, was nowhere to be seen, and a crimson shower had covered much of the undergrowth.

"Not my area of expertise, I'm afraid." The pathologist sighed as he donned the customary white protective one-piece suit. "Single knife thrust through the heart would have killed her outright, though. The rest of the injuries would have been post mortem."

Meade shook his head, turned, and made his way back to the road, the relative normality of the country lane standing in stark contrast to the horror which he had just witnessed.

The woods to the north of the Breadsall golf course provided thick cover for the hooded figure waiting patiently beneath the trees. Moor Lane was a favoured place for couples indulging in late night illicit activities which their spouses knew nothing about. He was careful, very careful. Not for him the tell-tale cigarette or chocolate bar wrapper; there would be nothing left at the scene to tie him to what was about to take place.

The headlights were not too long in making their way towards his position from the main road in the west, and he smiled at his fortune as it pulled up just beyond his spot amongst the bushes. An evil grin expanded across his features as a figure emerged from the car and strode into the trees.

"Where you goin'?" A hissed question split the dead silence of the area. "We 'aven't got all bleedin' night!"

"Shut up! I'm goin' for a leak. Don't want that all over you, do you?" the man cursed quietly in response. "I'll be back in a minute; just stay where you are."

The hooded figure crouched and waited for the approach, invisible amongst the thick cover. Passing only feet from his killer's position, the unfortunate victim never saw the attack. A hand clamped firmly across his mouth, and the butcher's knife slid smoothly though his back and pierced his heart. He was dead before he reached the ground.

Working quickly, and with practised skill, both legs were removed with a surgical saw, and wrapped in polythene to eliminate the blood trail which would have certainly indicated his exit route. The rest of the cutting would be carried out later, as before. The sound of approaching feet froze him to the spot, preventing the quick change of clothing which would have hidden any stray evidence.

"George? Where are you? It's getting cold. Are you coming, or what? My Barry'll be wondering where I am. George? C'mon, George, stop playing silly buggers."

A bonus! Two in the same night. He crouched once more, invisible again to the woman now nearing the scene of her lover's slaughter. He smiled; he would let her see the body, relish in her horror at the sight of what remained of her George. Then, only then, would he take her as well. Lost in the euphoria of the moment, his approach was less than meticulous, and the snapping sound of the twig beneath his foot had her spinning around to face him.

"What?!" Her exclamation was followed by a scream of banshee proportions as he struggled to bring the knife back out of its sheath. Instinct took over for the victim; she grabbed automatically for his hood, and sent it flying into the bushes.

"You?!" The look of surprise temporarily halted her panic. "I buy my..."

The words died in her throat, as the now unsheathed knife plunged underneath her ribcage and upwards into the heart. He stood there, momentarily panting as the realisation of his carelessness sank in. She had recognised him and, but for the swift despatch, may well have returned to the car and made good her escape.

Working now with feverish efficiency, he picked up the parts he had come for, collected the stray hood, and made his way around the edge of the golf course and back to his van, parked off Morley Lane to the south.

DS Meade and Harry Radford stood at the scene of the carnage wrought once again by the individual which the local media were now calling The Shipley Slasher. It had been a week since the discovery of the first corpse, and with no viable forensic evidence to go on, the Detective Sergeant was coming under increasing pressure, as national TV networks had set up bases outside the Butterley headquarters of 'C' Division of the Derbyshire Constabulary.

"Is there nothing more you can tell me?" Meade's voice bore a distinctly desperate edge. The country park had suffered its fair share of miscreants in the past, but this was completely out of that league.

"Afraid not, Chris. It's the same killer, though. I'm sure of that. The cuts are precise, and in the same direction. Could be a surgeon, a vet, a butcher... any of those."

He shrugged and continued with the preliminary examination, before having the bodies removed to the mortuary.

Heanor was a town in decline, and The Tastee Joint had set up in some vacant premises on the High Street. Joe Marriott had been running the hot meat café since its inception six months earlier. A Derby man, he had two shops in that city, along with several others around the Amber Valley area. He smiled as Chris Meade walked through the door.

"Good morning, Detective Sergeant. The usual?"

"Yes, and better make it quick. We've a right carry on with this Shipley Slasher business. Give me two, I've a hungry DC in the car around the corner."

"Coming right up." Two hot meat pies, filled to overflowing with prime chunks of meat, were wrapped and handed over with calm efficiency. "Cheers." Meade smiled ruefully as he turned to the door. "Nice meat, Joe. New supplier?"

"Home grown, mate, home grown."

Marriott smiled again at the retreating form of the policeman and returned to the back of the shop where he removed another joint from his cold store. Times were tough in the recession, and you just had to take the meat when and where you could. Business had certainly been booming during the past six months.

Books by Neal James

A Ticket To Tewkesbury

Julie Martin is the most unlikely of heroines in a struggle for supremacy which reaches to the very pinnacles of power within modern Britain. The letter, found amongst her recently deceased aunt's belongings, sets in motion a chain of events which had their roots in the death throes of Nazi Germany in 1945.

Roger Fretwell and Madeline Colson, two young lovers at the end of hostilities, are in possession of a set of files which fleeing survivors of the Third Reich would rather had lain buried. Now exposed once more, the secrets which they hold put their very lives in peril, and set in motion a chain of events from which there could only be one winner.

Set against the idyllic backdrop of the West Country, Roger and Madeline's love story weaves its way into the dark and troubled waters of espionage, as competing forces will stop at nothing to gain control of a situation so vital for the future of democracy in modern Britain. The breathless pace of the storyline is unrelenting, as the chase over the length and breadth of the country comes to a shattering climax on the platform of Nottingham's Midland Station. The final solution to the drama leaves a surprise ending for the reader to ponder.

Short Stories Volume One

How would you write to God for clarification on matters of the utmost urgency? Find out how Moses might have done it.

Dry your eyes after a heart-rending tale of Aunty Rose, and the tragic story of Liz when she finds the father she never knew. Shake your head at Mike's naiveté in dealing with a stranger in black, and share with Dave his hidden guilt when Tommy Watkinson returns to talk to his son, Paul.

Fly into the realms of fantasy with James Taylor as he gets lost in a place that he knows only too well, and try to sympathise with Ray when the old couple ask him to save humanity.

Follow Dennis Marks in a trilogy which brings the book to its close as he searches for the truth about his grandfather. This collection of little gems will expose every emotion on the rollercoaster which you are about to ride.

Two Little Dicky Birds

On Saturday 8th April 1975, in a fit of rage, Paul Townley took the life of his father, Harold. The significance of that single event was to affect the rest of his life, as he resolved to make it his mission to rid society of the kind of person that the man had become.

The first killing took place six months later, and over the following fifteen years seventeen more were to follow, as the trail of devastation left by a serial killer covered the length and breadth of England.

Detective Chief Inspector Colin Barnes looked down at the letter which lay on the desk before him. An icy hand gripped his heart as he read once more the details of the eighteen murders. Murders which had come back to haunt him from his past as he realised that he would, once more, be faced with the serial killer who had called himself... Petey.

Follow the chase for Petey, two and a half decades after his first appearance, as its climax takes you across the Atlantic to New York's JFK airport and into the arms of Detective Tom Casey of the 113th Precinct, in a plot so intricate it will leave you breathless.

Threads of Deceit

George Carter is a man with problems – big ones, and of the financial kind. Accustomed to getting his own way, he rules his roost at Brodsworth Textiles with an iron fist.

James Poynter is a young man out for revenge. Set up for a crime which he did not commit, and by someone whom he believed he could trust implicitly, his sole focus becomes one of retribution against his former boss and the firm which he is defrauding.

His future at Brodsworth Textiles disintegrates one Friday evening prior to his wedding, when conscientiousness overtakes him and he returns to the factory after work to rectify an administrative error.

What he learns in that moment sets off a chain of events which sends him spiralling downwards, and out of a job which had promised to propel him to senior managerial level.

Murder, deception, drug trafficking and embezzlement combine to derail the futures of everyone connected to the company, and set off a Europe-wide chase for the man at the centre of a plot so intricate that the forces of law and order in several countries are thwarted at every turn leading to a stunning climax at Bristol Airport.

Full Marks

Dennis Marks thought he had seen it all. That was before Solomon Goldblum crossed his path – after that, things were never the same again. The trauma which the old Jew had inflicted upon him had brought about a near psychological collapse. That the DCI had been able to conceal the fragility of his mental state from the shrink whom the Met had forced him to see had been down to his sheer determination.

Now, all of that effort was about to be challenged by one of the most daunting figures at New Scotland Yard – Superintendent Eric Staines. The Independent Police Complaints Commission were about to take Marks' life apart, professionally and personally, and Staines, as one of its fiercest inquisitors, was not a man inclined to show mercy.

A month was all that the DCI had to prove his innocence of a range of charges dating back to his days as a detective sergeant. A career spent putting away the dregs of London's criminal world was to hang in the balance, and he was, he believed, for the first time...alone.

The Rings of Darelius

Darelius – a planet in crisis with its civilisation facing the threat of extinction from a virus to which it has no natural defence.

The Darelian people had not been at war for many generations, but now faced not one, but two threats, as a warlike neighbour lay in the wings, awaiting its opportunity.

The only hope of salvation lay in a cure derived from the flora of a primitive planet in the Orion System – eighty light years distant.

It all began on Balan – a planet at war, and also facing its own apocalypse – hundreds of years in Darelius' past...

Twelve Days

It has nothing to do with Christmas – Christmas is a time of good cheer, and there's nothing like that in any of the chapters which you are about to read.

It is nothing to do with the Christmas song. There are no gifts being handed around – only tragedy, heartbreak, and disappointment feature within the lives of a number of players in the dramas which unfold before your eyes.

Set in the industrial areas of Amber Valley, Derby and Nottingham, 'Twelve Days' peers into the secrets of some of its inhabitants, taking you on a journey through their lives and sharing with you all of the emotions which they face as the stories progress.

Not for the faint-hearted, be ready for murder, witchcraft, embezzlement and a touch of the paranormal as the book takes you into the murky world of crime.

Three Little Maids

Billy Robertson is out for revenge and the target in his sights is Dennis Marks. Holding the DCI responsible for the death of his younger brother, Jack, Robertson seizes on the opportunity given to him by Harold Shaw - another violent criminal falling foul of the skill of one of the Met's finest detectives - from the confines of his cell at HMP Wandsworth.

Fresh from his run-in with the IPCC, Marks is plunged into a murder case involving the death of a teacher at Lainsford Grammar School in Edmonton. Without the services of Home Office pathologist, George Groves, and with the prospect of his own team breaking up, Marks' abilities are tested to the limit as he follows a trail of false leads, lies, and a wall of silence.

About Neal James

Neal James has been writing since 2008 when his first novel. 'A Ticket to Tewkesbury', was released. Since that time eight more books have followed, and 'Short Stories Volume Two' is his tenth work to be published in as many years.

He has appeared in both the national and local press, and has also been a regular at branches of Waterstones and local reading groups and libraries in his home counties of Derbyshire and Nottinghamshire.

An accountant for over 40 years, that training has given him an insight into much of the background required in the production of his writing so far. He lives in Derbyshire with his wife and family.

Find out more about Neal James and all his writing on his website: www.nealjames.webs.com

Find Neal James here:

https://www.facebook.com/neal.james.125

https://www.goodreads.com/author/show/3104298.Neal_James

https://www.linkedin.com/in/neal-james-14700533?trk=hp-identity-name

https://twitter.com/philneale1952

Contact: georgius4444@hotmail.co.uk

CPSIA information can be obtained
at www.ICGtesting.com
Printed in the USA
LVHW090018131118
596932LV00001B/13/P